T0156535

ECHOES OF MEMORIES PAST

The Price

MARK DOUGLAS HOLBORN

ECHOES OF MEMORIES PAST
THE PRICE

Front cover artwork done by Desiree Kern

iUniverse books may be ordered through booksellers or by contacting:

iUniverse
1663 Liberty Drive
Bloomington, IN 47403
www.iuniverse.com
1-800-Authors (1-800-288-4677)

ISBN: 978-1-4917-4294-5 (sc)
ISBN: 978-1-4917-4295-2 (hc)
ISBN: 978-1-4917-4296-9 (e)

Library of Congress Control Number: 2014913591

Printed in the United States of America.

iUniverse rev. date: 08/06/2014

CONTENTS

This is dedicated to Mom, Dad, Eryn, Adam, Damien, Cathee, Wendy, Kurt, Meaghan, Jonathan, Lisa, Candice, and Nicole. A special thanks to Alison who suggested I write the sequel, to Marion & Maggie for all your hard work.

In loving memory of Georgina O'Neill.

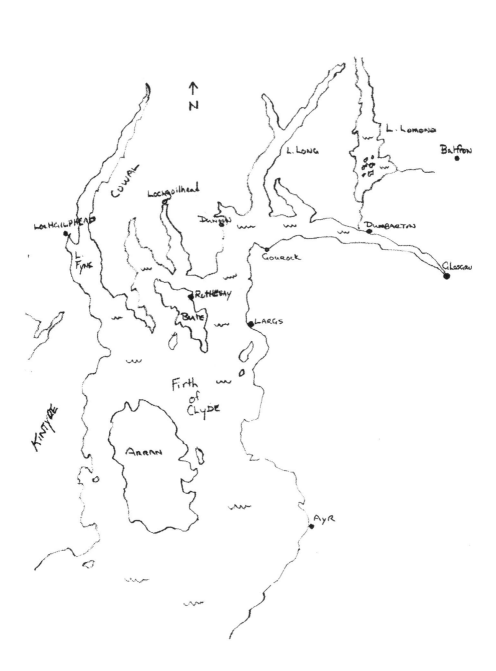

N

L. Lomond

Balffron

L. Long

Lochgoilhead

COWAL

Dunoon

Dumbartn

Lochgilphead

Gourock

Glasgow

L. Fyne

Rothesay

Bute

Largs

Firth
of
Clyde

Kintyre

Arran

Ayr

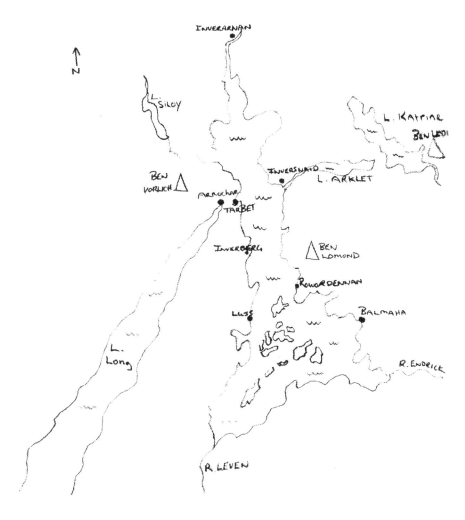

Loch Lomond

N

L. Torridon   • Torridon

Achnasheen

Applecross   Achnashellach   L. Monar

Raasay   Torrapress   Loch Strathcarron

Inner   Loch   Achintee
Sound   Lochcarron
    Attadale
Kishorn   Carron
Plockton   Ardnaff

Scalpa

Kyle of   Eilean
Lochalsh   Donan   Kintail.

SKye

Sound of
Sleat

The Present

CAMERON TURNED AWAY, leaving everything behind him. The woman had her revenge—killing him would have been better than this existence. The pain he felt inside was more than he could truly bear. He had lost everything, all that he was had been taken from him. He was alone in a world in which he did not exist. Cameron walked away, turning into an alley that he had ventured into only a few days ago. He stopped, his mind reeled in confusion and despair, falling to his knees; his tears clouded his vision.

There was a noise behind him and he heard footsteps approach. The rank odor hit him before his vision cleared; he looked upwards to see the towering figure of Crazy Ted standing before him. The derelict's steel-gray eyes seemed somehow warm and caring. "You have lost what you once were." Cameron shook his head in confusion. He remembered it was in this very alley that Ted had warned him, *"all gifts will carry a price that only time can reveal"* Cameron looked hard at the man and noticed the odor had disappeared. The soiled rotting rags changed to rich silks and satins, his eyes changed from gray to amber, his face lost the scraggy beard and the hair turned almost silver.

"Tamlyn?" Cameron could not believe his eyes—the Elf Lord stood tall before him. "How . . . how? What has happened to me?"

"I have searched for you a long time, my old friend. Your soul came into this world last night and I stretched forth my mind to summon you to meet me here," Tamlyn said empathically.

"How?" Cameron asked. He felt hope; the Elf could help where no one else could.

"Centuries ago when I first met you, you were so different from anyone else on your world. Two souls existed, both the same yet different, overlapping. Our 'mind-meld' allowed me to see into your soul and I saw your future self and the lives that you had not yet lived. I saw the recognition in your face at the sight of the Goddess on that dark world. I sensed her power in this. When I saw you still trapped on the other side of that portal, I knew then what was wrong. So in your world I stayed; I waited and I watched for you. Your souls are unique to each and every one of you, like a radio frequency; you just have to know how to tune it in. All these years I have been waiting for you, knowing something like this was going to happen. I owe you a debt Cameron for all that you have lost and for all those who know nothing of what you have done for your world and so many others."

"Can you get me back, back to my own time line?"

"I cannot, I do not know how. I am truly sorry. Through all these years I sought for a way to help. I sent you that warning from your old world; although that world, that dimension is fading, it is still visible to those who can see it: a world just like this one but slightly out of faze. This is the true time-line in your world now; Cameron MacLean does not exist," Tamlyn said. His eyes reflected the sorrow within.

Cameron knew then what he had done. "She egged me on, pushing me to get to Kerry faster. I was meant to save her from the Norseman, to save her life, but not before the rape. When I killed that man, I knew somehow it was wrong from the moment I did it."

Tamlyn laid a comforting hand upon his shoulder. "No, you did all that you were supposed to do. It was your arrival that was altered—originally you could have taken the long road, a different path. How could you know? You were meant to save her but the child of that rape seems to be the progenitor of your family line. You married Kerry quickly after, perhaps as much out of love as to protect her honor," the Elf's words made sense to his troubled soul.

Cameron nodded dumbly. "Did you stay with them, and were they happy?"

Tamlyn smiled thoughtfully. "Cailean and Kerry were very happy, with many children. Cailean knew nothing of you or the time you shared."

Cameron smiled, wishing so much to be back there. "So what is to become of me now?" he asked, holding out his hands. Yet as he did so he noticed that his flesh was fading—he could almost see completely through it.

"It is as I feared, your world of Cameron MacLean is fading out of existence, it takes you along with it. The life and world you knew only yesterday fades, as this the true world replaces it. I can feel that your world is almost gone now. But know you this; I followed your soul in this new time line. It lives on in this world, and I can tell you with all my heart that it is truly happy and it is where it should be, with Marina."

Tamlyn watched the fading face of Cameron smile with peaceful content, knowing that in this existence he and Marina had found each other again, the life he felt that was so out of sync was aligned as it should be. As Cameron Maclean faded completely out of existence, Tamlyn wept for the loss of his friend, for the sacrifice this man had made and for the price he had paid. Cameron had been induced to believe that he could live an entire year in the past with his soul-mate for a single night in the present. Tamlyn went over in his mind the mission he took up since the separating of Cailean and Cameron through the portal on that dying world over 750 years ago. He owed this man his life several times over and he spent all these centuries following the life and rebirth of this man's soul. The friendships they shared through the ages with him, the past lives of joy and sadness, of fortune and misfortune. Tamlyn had always been his friend who never knew the connection to the Elf, only recognizing that Tamlyn was one he could deeply trust. He had indeed sought for some way to save Cameron, knowing that perhaps this day would come, his re-emergence into the world and the repercussions.

The Sharing of his mind in the distant past enabled Tamlyn to warn Cameron before he made his choice to go back in time through the derelict Ted. His message had to be cryptic, to seed enough doubt for Cameron to question and to resist; it was all Tamlyn could manage through the different dimensions between Cameron's time line and this new emerging one. The lavender eyed Goddess by then had fully engulfed his mind, creating the madness within, clouding his mind and his judgment. Had Tamlyn been any more forthcoming in his warning, there was no telling how the Goddess could have reacted and thus destroyed whatever advantage Tamlyn had in knowing her true intentions. With everything he had done or tried to do he knew in his heart he failed his friend and that had weighed heavily upon his soul.

He scanned the full length of the darkened alleyway. This world had moved on as it should, as it was meant too, humankind its dominant species and not the Azael and its dark brethren. Tamlyn took a deep breath and sat down, crossing his legs as he pulled out a red ruby like stone the size of a thumb. A traveling stone. He started to sing, casting his power to open a portal to his home in a far distant quadrant of space. He gathered in his power, attuning his mind for the complex patterns of space and time. He transfixed his destination within his thoughts, utilizing quantum mechanics to manipulate the power to open the portal. A minute window to his world started to grow before him, yet his attention wavered as a nearby door smashed open.

The door was the side emergency exit to the building where Cameron had worked. Immediately he felt a foul taint in the morning air as evil stepped into the alleyway before him; the black malevolent shape of an Azael moved with deadly grace. Tamlyn rose quickly to his feet, his swords held before him. He stood ready to engage his steel with this deadly creature. The headless demon was the size of a tall man; its black body armor glistened like the wet scales of a snake. It glided towards him; its own black scimitar gleamed with a malicious intensity ready to spill his blood. As silent as death they moved into battle then swords clashed in mind blurring speed, magnificent skill and ferocity, like Titans of war. Sparks filled the alleyway every time the blades connected like a showering display of fireworks. Fury and hate aligned with skill and speed, as centuries old enemies sought nothing less than the bloody death of their adversary.

Tamlyn believed that the Azael might have been drawn to the portal he just formed. Those of his kind were trapped here on this world. Cameron had destroyed the crystal matrix that allowed them to create portals of their own and travel across the stars to other worlds. They had enough power to create smaller portals-gateways to travel upon a world, but not for any great distance. The Azael lived here still and through the ages hid in the darkness, hunting humankind. Tamlyn had hunted them and others of their world relentlessly. They were a foreign infestation, not part of the natural order of this planet. The Azael were deadly creatures and finding and killing the Elf would grant them darker powers. If they could kill Tamlyn they would re-animate him into a Reaver; a soulless creature with all the skill and magic he possessed but with the mind in full control of the Azael.

Tamlyn's thrust tagged the creature upon its left shoulder, its black blood flowing through the wound, slowing the creature as the Elf scored another hit, this time upon its sword arm. The Azael danced out the next strike and smashed its mailed fist fully into his mid-section, staggering Tamlyn with the blow. The Demon moved back from its enemy as if weighing whether it had bitten off more than it could chew. The Elf had the greater skill and it hesitated briefly then ran into the shadows and disappeared, living to fight another day and on better terms.

Tamlyn set himself to track the creature, yet his keen hearing picked up the distant wail of sirens. The wail was building in its intensity, coming closer with each passing second. His battle here had lasted only a brief few moments and not likely to arouse the attention of those outside the alley. Its sound worried him; this was the building where Marina and Morgan worked. Morgan was Cameron's 'replacement' on this world; the path Cameron's soul had taken in this new plane of existence. The presence of the Azael and now the sirens getting closer to the building the Azael just vacated turned Tamlyn's worry to fear. He cast the outwards illusion of himself to that of a smartly dressed executive and raced towards the front of the building.

He was indeed correct as the ambulance had stopped in front of the building and the EMT's were busily pulling out the gurney and equipment through the growing crowds who were hoping to get a glimpse of the action. Tamlyn pushed his way further into the crowd, following behind the EMT's.

"Over here! Here!" He heard the voice of Morgan's large friend Jim calling them, concern mirrored in his voice.

"Come on people, back off! Give them some room!" That was Morgan's other friend Rob, who immediately went to the side of a woman kneeling on the floor beside the prostrate form of a man. Tamlyn knew the woman was Marina even before he saw her tear streaked face, desperately trying to keep hold of Morgan's hand.

"Come on Marina let the paramedics do what they have too," Rob said worriedly as he helped her to her feet. Tamlyn saw Marina's tawny haired friend Lynne Brodie comforting her.

"He will be ok, really he will," she said with encouragement yet her eyes mirrored the same fear as Marina. Morgan's friends Rob and Jim stared bleakly at the scene unfolding before them.

"Are you his wife, can you tell me what happened?" one of the EMT's asked as two police officers now entered the scene, one went to aid the EMT's, the other was moving people out of the way.

"Yes… I don't know what happened. He was fine one moment, he said his head was hurting then he just collapsed and went into seizures," Marina said through her tears.

"Does he have a history of seizures? Is he taking any medications, drugs?" the EMT asked as he was taking Morgan's vitals, then Morgan started shaking as another seizure took hold of him. "OK, here he goes again, you got his head?" the EMT asked his partner, with a nod in acknowledgement, they comforted Morgan as best they could.

Horrified Marina watched on. "No he has never had them before, for as long as I have known him, no drugs or any medication," she finally got out.

The EMT nodded. "Any history of epilepsy in the family?" he asked as Marina just shook her head.

"No, no!" she replied.

The EMT nodded again. "Did he hit his head on the floor?" he inquired while waiting for the seizure to dissipate.

"No he didn't I caught hold of him and helped him to the floor," Marina said as they moved him on to the board then strapped him in on the gurney.

"Do you want to come with us to the hospital?" the EMT asked Marina and she nodded in reply.

"Marina I will be right behind you?" Lynne said anxiously.

It was then Tamlyn stepped up beside Marina taking her hand in his own. "Marina?"

"Tom, what are you doing here?"

"I had some business here today," Tamlyn replied in his guise as Morgan's old time friend from college. He sent her warm feelings of support through his hand to hers, her fears lessened in their intensity pushing the fear and panic to a calmer state. "Go with him, I will be there at the hospital soon as I can," he said releasing her hand as she followed the EMT's to the ambulance. Lynne's anxious look caught Rob's attention as he squeezed her hand. "C'mon with us," Rob said nodding, towards Jim as he waved at both of them to follow while he pulled out his cell phone. He was cancelling his meetings for the day as they rushed to the parking lot and piled into his jeep, speeding off after the ambulance.

Tamlyn watched them go, breathing a quick sigh, for he had feared something far worse after his battle with the Azael. When he saw Morgan on the floor, he thought the Azael had somehow taken its revenge and killed him. He scanned the area were Morgan went down. It was directly parallel to the alleyway where Cameron had dissipated. He was certain, almost to the inch that he could draw a straight line from where Cameron had last stood to where Morgan had fell in the foyer. He saw the emergency door the Azael had went through, it was by a darkened corner beside the stairwell going up to the mezzanine above. Tamlyn went over to the exit. From there, he looked back to the area where Morgan collapsed. The Azael would have a clear line of sight from here to the foyer of anyone waiting for the elevator. He stared at that exit, thinking it through and could not believe it as coincidence. Tamlyn could find no more answers here, he would need to get to Morgan and follow up through him. This situation troubled him deeply; he could not say what triggered this attack on Morgan. Was it the Azael, did it launch some sort of assault, biological or a psychic attack or was this something else? The proximity to Cameron's dissolving also seemed terribly disconcerting and the possible ramifications frightened him.

Tamlyn, still in his executive's guise, flagged a cab. He could have opened a portal, but he wanted to conserve his power for what lay before him. "University Hospital, please," he said to the cabbie, and jumped in the backseat of the cab. On the way, he wondered if it *was* the Azael, what type of attack had it launched upon Morgan? What would cause the seizures? How did it know who Morgan was to begin with? Even if it was at that battle outside of Achnashellach, and survived all these centuries, how could it have known that Morgan was Cailean reborn? So many questions kept coming at him, but knowing that only a thorough scan of Morgan's mind would provide sufficient answers, he would have to show patience and wait for his opportunity.

Tamlyn was still in deep thought when the cabbie interrupted him. "We are here my friend, it's twenty-one fifty," he said as Tamlyn gave him twenty-five. "Keep the change," he said as he left the cab and walked into the hospital. He did not need to inquire where Morgan was, Tamlyn could locate him with but a single thought. He walked into the emergency ward, and followed the path directly to Morgan's bedside. Rob and Jim both sat outside with Lynne still comforting Marina.

"Any word yet?"

Marina looked up towards him. "No… nothing yet. The doctors are in with him now. He had another seizure while he was in the ambulance," she said as her tears began to flow again. "He's never been sick a day in his life, I just don't understand this."

Tamlyn knelt down in front of her, taking her hands in his own again. "Morgan will pull through this. He will. I promise," he said staring into her dark brown eyes, her beautiful face flooded with worry. Tamlyn smiled confidently at her and through his touch he was about to put her into a deeper state of calmness to stem her fears, but he recoiled slightly. He sensed a new spark within. Marina was newly pregnant, so he carefully put forth his power to ease her anxiety. The effect was immediate on the inside and gradual on the outside to avoid arousing suspicions. It was then that the curtain surrounding Morgan slid away as nurses rolled him through the hall and into another room.

The attending doctor approached them. "Mrs. Hamilton?"

Marina and the rest stood up. "I am Mrs. Hamilton, what's going on, where are you taking him?" she asked quickly.

"X-ray and for a CAT scan, we need to see if there is any damage to the brain and if necessary a spinal tap. Blood-work will take a little time, for now we have him on IV with benzodiazepine. He has had no further seizures since he was in the ambulance. The EMT's said he achieved baseline when he went into the ambulance, before the last seizure?" he asked.

"He...he did come around, just for a few seconds he was confused," Marina answered.

The doctor nodded. "That's normal; we will have to monitor him closely. If the seizures come back we may have to induce coma."

"Coma…. I don't understand. Isn't that a bad thing?" Marina asked, her voice re-taking on the fear that Tamlyn had tried to bury.

"Coma in this case would be a way to protect him, to protect the brain; seizures can cause terrible damage if allowed to go on repeatedly. Now you said he was on no medication of any kind, what about drugs, or drug abuse?"

Marina shook her head vehemently. "No Morgan is a health nut, he has never done drugs. He's always been healthy."

"What about alcohol?"

Again Marina shook her head. "Nothing extreme, wine with meals, beer on the weekends with the guys. Doctor, what's causing this, what's happened to my husband?"

The doctor looked to her friends and then back to her. "Seizures can be a result of a stroke, an infection, metabolic disorders, trauma or a fall, but the x-ray, CAT scan and preliminary blood-work will help us rule out some things, a full toxicology report will take some time. He needs rest right now, I will keep you posted on his condition and will tell you as soon as we get anything helpful," the Doctor said comfortingly, as he followed off after Morgan. Lynne helped ease Marina back to her chair.

Rob and Jim looked at each other in disbelief. "What the hell Jim? This is fucking for real. Morgan? C'mon, now if this was me, yes. The amount of bad shit I have put in my body! This is insane that this is happening to Morgan, coming out of fucking nowhere!"

"Will you put a lid on it? You're not helping," Jim said nodding towards Marina, his huge powerful frame was intimidating, but he felt as helpless as the rest. His words shook with the same fear as Rob.

"Sorry Marina, I…I just can't believe this is happening, this is freaking me out, and I know it's even worse for you…I…I'm sorry."

Marina took Rob's hand and she gave it a comforting squeeze. "Morgan will be ok, he has to be," she said with a courageous smile.

Rob forced a laugh. "Damn right he will be ok, I will kick his freaking ass if he is not."

It was a few hours later when the doctor sought them out. "Well I can tell you what it's not. We have done more tests, and we have concluded that there were no signs of a stroke; it is also looking like we can rule out meningitis or encephalitis. His heart is strong, on the preliminary blood-work everything came back negative; a full toxicology report will give us more to go on but that may take weeks. The only thing that came up on the CAT scan was an abnormally high amount of activity in the limbic center of the brain, off the charts actually. That in it-self is a cause for concern and something to monitor, we can get an MRI done to look at it more closely," the Doctor said as Tamlyn interjected.

"Limbic center is associated with memory…" Tamlyn said in wonder.

The Doctor looked at him, nodding in agreement. "Yes memory, emotions, mood, pleasure, pain, it connects the higher and lower brain functions," the Doctor went on with Marina but Tamlyn was deep in thought. *Memory, memories? Cameron? Not the Azael, this is Cameron's soul, the overflow of Cameron's memories pouring into Morgan unchecked. The memories from all of the reincarnations from Cailean to Cameron that never existed because of the different path history took, suddenly dumped into Morgan who already possesses reincarnations of his own past.* Tamlyn realized quickly what maybe the cause of Morgan's illness; he had not thought that this was possible. He believed himself prepared for many different scenarios for when Cameron returned to the future. Tamlyn did not anticipate any immediate risk to Morgan. He needed to be sure, he needed to get to Morgan and delve into his mind to confirm his fears. He had to find out if this was only a one-time thing, or would the merging cause lingering damage that would affect his mind and his life.

††††

Hours melted away. Rob and Jim, after much encouraging from Marina went home, but only after strong promises to keep them posted on any change. Tamlyn and Lynne stayed longer and almost had to force Marina away to eat an evening meal, for she had eaten nothing all day. Tamlyn insisted strongly that she needed to keep up her strength for Morgan and she grudgingly agreed. Later in the evening Marina convinced Lynne to go home, again with promises to let her know of any changes in Morgan. They moved him into a private room, still hooked up to an IV and oxygen, and a host of other monitoring equipment. The nurses checking up on him assured them that Morgan was resting comfortably, and they sat around his bed in more comfortable chairs. Marina held his hand and kissed him on the forehead, her presence stirred something within Morgan, he shook his head slightly–his eyes still closed. "Gone … they are all gone … wiped from existence, my….my fault," Morgan said in a painful whisper.

"Morgan, honey who is gone?" Marina moved closer as she lovingly stroked his hair and his cheek.

"My… my son … Conner … Conner is gone, my fault. My life … gone. I am nothing, no-one … I don't exist anymore, I am nothing," tears rolled down his cheeks, as she looked to Tamlyn in confusion.

"He is delirious and confused, the doctors said this may happen," he said hoping to convince her, yet the moment he spoke there was an instant recognition by Morgan to Tamlyn's voice.

"Tam …help me … my head is bursting … everything inside is chaos … all confusing, Tam … Tamlyn help me …" Morgan said the last in a whisper as Marina looked to him for answers he could not divulge, as all she could do was hold his hand letting him know he was not alone.

Tamlyn sat silently studying Morgan and Cameron's plight. Staring upon Morgan's face, he noticed how much the two men resembled the other. Morgan shared Cameron's dark brown almost black eyes. The same brown wavy hair and strong brow yet Morgan had the sharper face and cheekbones. Cameron had the more commanding chin while both men were of the same broad muscular frame and height. So alike they were, yet their subtle differences spoke volumes. Tamlyn had waited until Marina fell asleep; judging his timing to be right, for the nurses would not be back on their rounds for a little while yet. He placed his hand upon Morgan's forehead; a quick scan was all he needed to confirm his fears.

It was as he suspected and what Morgan had said in his delirium: chaos ruled in his mind. Normal electric synapses were supercharged, almost on complete overload, memories of so many lifetimes, all trying to dominate. It was as if the careful protective walls of the subconscious had completely broken down. Tamlyn knew Morgan's mind well and sought to untangle the mess. He knew it would be almost impossible, but he would do what he could and poured healing energy into Morgan's mind, to restore the walls of the subconscious. Tamlyn drove deep downwards through the layers of his mind attempting repairs, but it was like a finger in the dyke; what he had done would not hold off the chaos for long.

The affect however was immediate. Morgan stirred awake, he took in his surroundings, holding up his arms to see the IV and the monitors placed upon him.

Seeing Marina sleeping at his side he looked confusedly towards Tamlyn. "Tom, what the hell? How did I get here, what happened? The last thing I remember was waiting for the damn elevator and now I am here in this freaking hospital bed."

Marina woke instantly upon hearing his voice. "Oh thank God Morgan, you're back … you're back," she said as tears of joy and relief welled up in her eyes. She took his hand and squeezed it tight.

"Of course I am babe, I'm right as rain, it's gonna take a lot more than…whatever this is to keep me away from you. Umm, what did happen?"

Marina smiled warmly at him. "You just collapsed in front of me, then…then you started having seizures, several of them," she replied and the memory truly frightened her yet she was trying to be strong for him.

"Seizures, seizures, wow that's nuts. Did you take a video of it?" he asked with a straight face, as Marina teasingly punched him on the shoulder.

"You asshole!" she said laughing as Morgan smiled with that classic smile that would charm a beggar of his last coin. "Seriously you scared me to death you jerk."

"Sorry, I will try not to do it again. Man am I starving, I'd give my right arm for a couple of burgers right now."

Tamlyn smiled at him. "Let me find a nurse to see if it is ok first." Taking to his feet, he left to give them some time to themselves.

"Can you also find out if they can take all this shit off me, looking at its' gonna make me hurl," Morgan shouted after him.

Tamlyn found a nurse on duty and informed her of the change in Morgan's condition, smiling in relief she followed him back to Morgan's room. "Well look at that, back with us I see! How are you feeling?"

"Hungry," Morgan replied.

"That's good. We can see about getting some food into you then."

"Big Mac, Morgan?" Tamlyn knew his friend well.

"Two please, you are the greatest Tom."

"Marina, would you like something too?" he asked but Marina shook her head no. Tamlyn smiled back and went out of the hospital to the twenty-four hour McDonalds around the block. He placed his order and waited patiently for the food, knowing that waiting meant it would be good and hot. Once he had his order, he made his way quickly back to the hospital and to Morgan's room. It was good to see both the IV and the oxygen removed when he got back.

Morgan's face went bright at the site of the food. "Tom I could almost kiss you," he laughed as Morgan opened up the paper bag and just inhaled. "Oh my god that smells so good," he dove into the fries and filled his face with the first Big Mac.

"Morgan, you are impossible," Marina said to him as she watched him devour his late night meal.

"What are you talking about, this is perfect, my comfort food. You eat what you like and let me eat mine," he said with a grin as he started on the second Big Mac.

Tamlyn waited for Morgan to finish his meal, "What did the nurse say?"

"I'm stuck here for the night," Morgan said grumpily as Marina finished for him.

"You have to see the doctor in the morning before they let you go home, to make sure you don't have any further seizures. Hopefully then we may have some answers as to what is wrong with you," she sounded relieved that the worst was over but Tamlyn was not so sure, and he needed more time to think this through if he was to be of any help to Morgan.

It was just past 3am when Morgan and Marina dozed off again. Tamlyn quietly left the room; he wanted to think this out as he paced the hallway outside Morgan's room. The more he tried to sort out the problem the more he knew he needed help; he knew just who to ask, but how to get Morgan there was a bigger problem. He tried thinking of a way to tackle that little conundrum when he heard a door close by the far end of the darkened hallway. He turned to see who was coming toward him and his inner senses screamed in warning while his eyes saw a female nurse stop suddenly. She looked at him. Her grey eyes glared evilly at him. She turned quickly, entering an empty room with Tamlyn right on her heels. She darted towards the open window pushing out the screen and jumped; they were on the fourth floor. Tamlyn raced to the window but in the darkness his eyes could only make out a large Raven flying out into the night. *Shape-shifters, what are they doing here? Is it me or Morgan that they are hunting?* Tamlyn thought to himself.

Over the centuries he had done his best to eradicate many of the creatures from that hellish planet, but there had been so many portals opening all over the world during that time that he had no way of knowing just how many survived to this day. He thought that the Azael may have sent the shape-shifter to track him after their battle in the alleyway; it was too much of a coincidence. He would stick close to Morgan, and was thankful that he did not use the traveling crystal to take him home or he would have never known about this new situation and its effects on Morgan.

†††††

It was early in the morning when the doctor came in to see Morgan. He was making his rounds and he was encouraged with Morgan's progress. More tests came back negative and Morgan was scheduled for a MRI that morning. Tamlyn took Marina for breakfast at the hospital cafeteria while they waited for Morgan to return from the MRI.

"Thank you so much Tom, for me and for Morgan," Marina said with a grateful smile.

Tamlyn smiled back at her warmly. "Morgan would do the same for me, anyway it's been slow in the antiquities business so I have some free time on my hands, which was why I was coming to see Morgan in the first place," he said to her.

"Tom I'm scared for Morgan. These seizures, what if…"

"No 'what if's' Marina; the doctors are doing the best they can, they will figure this out, he will be OK. Don't fret until there is something to fret about, alright?"

She smiled again. "That's exactly what Morgan would say you know," she said with a laugh, and he smiled back at her encouragingly.

"Who do you think I got it from? C'mon we should head back upstairs, do you want another coffee?" he asked.

"No I'm ok for now, thanks." They both took their trays to the garbage, then headed back up to Morgan's room. Both Morgan and the doctor were waiting there for them.

"The MRI preliminary results look promising, no inflammation, tumors or lesions but still showing a heightened synaptic activity in the limbic center. Keep him home for the week, if he has any further seizures bring him right back here and follow up with his family doctor as soon as you can, we will send the toxicology report to him. If something important comes up we will contact you. Look, these tests may only reveal something while a seizure is actually taking place otherwise everything shows normal. Don't get too discouraged, it may take a while to find the root cause. Sometimes these things are stress induced, the body's way of saying 'too much'. If the seizures come back we can try different medications to limit them or stop them from ever coming back, it is just a matter of finding the right drug and right dosage to manage it. For now I will have to say no driving for 6 months seizure free, for your headaches you can take aspirin for now."

"Six months. Doc, you're killing me, seriously?"

"Sorry Morgan, it's the law, we can't have you behind the wheel when you could have another seizure," the doctor replied, and Morgan knew the doctor was right as much as he hated the fact. "Remember, any more seizures he gets back to the hospital fast, we can't risk damage to the brain. And follow up with your own family doctor right away, OK? Then you are free to go."

"Thank you very much doctor," Marina said, appreciating all the doctor's efforts.

"Yeah, thanks Doc, hopefully you won't see me back here," Morgan said with a devilish smirk as he started to get back into his own clothes.

"You're welcome, and yes I don't want to see you back either," he laughed as he left them to see to his other patients.

"If it's alright with you Marina, I would like to tag along, I can help keep an eye on him while you can rest or take care of whatever you need to do," Tamlyn asked, as she smiled with relief at the added help.

"Hold on, I don't need a freaking baby-sitter. No offence Tom," Morgan piped in as he saw Marina's face already accepting the help.

"Thank you Tom that would be great. I could use an extra pair of eyes on our clever little escape artist," Marina smiled deeply at her husband.

Morgan gave in. "Fine, fine you can both knock yer-selves out watching me sleep and watch TV."

"Good then it's settled. Tom can watch you while I call your mom and your brother and everyone else to update them on you, and make your appointment with Doctor Brennan." Once they signed out of the hospital, Tamlyn hailed a cab while Morgan had sent several texts back and forth to both Jim and Rob that he was going home, and for Rob to drive their car back as it was still in the car park at work. Marina had left him the keys to do just that. Rob lastly texted back, *'glad yer ok shit-head, will bring yer car back tonight. c-ya then.'*

"Rob's going to bring the car around after work tonight, Jim's coming over too," he said as they piled into the cab.

"Great, that's one less thing to worry over. Can you take us to 1255 Forest Glen Drive please?" she asked the cabbie.

"Sure thing ma'am."

CHAPTER TWO

Sleepyhollow

IT WAS A quiet ride home into the newly built sub-division; their house was a two-story brick home, spacious and warm. Marina opened the door for them, then turned off the alarm, and proceeded into the kitchen, depositing her purse upon the large granite island. "Morgan, Tom, I'm going to make some coffee, would you like some?"

"Yes please, thank you Marina," Tamlyn said and Morgan smiled warmly at his wife.

"You read my mind hon. Going to grab some aspirin first though, heads a little sore still," he said as he grabbed a glass and poured some water to get the pills down easier. Morgan rubbed his eyes and took a seat in the family room right beside the kitchen.

Marina watched him as she made the coffee, and took out some hamburger and pork from the freezer. "If Rob and Jim are coming over I'm going to make spaghetti, OK?"

Morgan with eyes closed smiled. "You're the best wife ever Marina, I love your spaghetti. I'm so glad I annoyed you so much in college that you dumped that duffus boyfriend and married me. I don't know how I could live without you," Morgan said as he looked at his wife adoringly.

"Yes you did annoy me then, but after bringing me a rose every day until I agreed to go out with you, I just couldn't say no to those big dreamy eyes," Marina smiled at her husband as she placed his coffee on the table beside him then kissed him on his forehead. "I guess I didn't want you spending all your money on roses, being a 'starving student' and all, you never did tell me how you paid for them anyway."

Morgan looked to Tamlyn who sheepishly held up his hand in defeat. Marina looked to Tamlyn and laughed. "I should have known."

"Well you could have said yes a lot sooner instead of making me wait two weeks," Morgan said in his defense.

"I just wanted to see how long you were going to keep it up," Marina laughed and went into the study to contact her office and see what work she could do from home, leaving Morgan and Tamlyn alone.

"How's the head?" Tamlyn asked worried that Morgan's mind might push through the band-aide patch he installed and force another seizure.

"Not bad really all things considered, just a bit of a head-ache. I'm sure the aspirin will kick in soon enough, I'm just going to rest my eyes for a bit. My laptop is on the table there if you need to use it for anything," he offered as Tamlyn nodded in reply.

"Thanks, I just may do that later." As the minutes melted by, he sensed Morgan fall into a deep restorative sleep, while Tamlyn worked out possible methods to aid Morgan.

It was about an hour later that Marina came back into the room. Smiling at Morgan sleeping away comfortably, she draped a blanket over top of him and whispered to Tamlyn. "I have booked him in to see his family doctor tomorrow and called his mom to let her know he's home and doing OK. She is four hours away there is no need for her to come unnecessarily. I got in touch with his brother Alex; he is coming over for supper. My work knows I am off the rest of the week and will reroute anything major here. I called Lynne also, she will likely drop by tonight too. How is he doing?"

But before Tamlyn could answer Morgan sleepy-eyed piped in. "He's doing well, thank you for asking...ssshhhh." Marina laughed and gently caressed her husband's face lovingly.

Morgan ended up sleeping right through the afternoon, Marina herself laid down for a short nap as well. She woke around three and started on some work on her computer after a quick check on Morgan. Around five thirty Rob pulled up in Morgan's Optima and Jim followed behind in his jeep.

Tamlyn waited for them at the front door. "How is he?" Jim asked right away.

"He slept most of the day away, he's awake now and eager to see you two." As Morgan's two friends came into the family room, Morgan took to his feet and gave them both warm hugs in greeting.

"Here's your keys back, man that's a nice car," Rob said as he tossed the keys back to Morgan.

"Yeah well if Marina didn't need it, I'd let you borrow it for a few months, the doctor's say I can't drive until I'm six months seizure free."

"Ouch man that hurts, but probably the smartest thing to do for sure," Jim said.

"Come on, let's head down to the man-cave. Marina we're heading downstairs OK?"

Marina smiled and nodded. "No video games!"

"Ya, ya ya," Morgan said as they followed him down. He headed to the bar and opened up the fridge. "Beers?" Morgan asked with a chorus of 'yeses' and 'sure' he pulled out three and grabbed a ginger-ale for himself. "Here you go."

They took their seats on the large recliner-sectional. "So what's up, what did the doc say?" Rob asked quickly, his normally mischievous face became all too serious.

Morgan shook his head. "Nothing really, said it wasn't a stroke, tumor, meningitis or something else, heart's fine, but they did an MRI and CAT scan, with nothing conclusive, all the other tests they ran will take a few weeks, so hopefully by then we will know more."

"Hey, was talking to yer boss Anderson, he raved about your work on the Peter's account, saying you saved the company from losing a major client. He said take all the time you need, just come back healthy," Jim said as Morgan nodded gratefully.

"Thanks man that's good to hear."

But Rob didn't care about that. "So what do you remember, that morning, like did you feel anything before it happened?"

Morgan looked towards his friends then looked to the stairs, making sure Marina was still upstairs. "It was weird, like maybe it started on Sunday night around eight or nine, I felt kinda odd, and had this stupid headache, anyway I just went on as if there was nothing happening but the morning was kind of a blur. I remember dropping off Marina to grab some coffees 'cause I didn't sleep so good. I parked the car and waited for her in front of the building. She was talking to some guy, I called to her and she passed me my coffee, we went inside and waited along with everyone else for the elevator and..." again he looked up the stairs. "Then it went really weird. I don't know why but I was looking over to the stairway to the second floor mezzanine and I think I saw the guy from that movie *Sleepy Hollow*."

Rob was expecting something more. "You saw *Johnny Depp?*"

Morgan shook his head. "No, the bad guy the...the headless horseman."

Jim cocked his head questioningly. "You mean *Christopher Walken?*"

Again Morgan shook his head. "No not the actor the guy, the headless horseman." Tamlyn looked hard at Morgan, as Rob jumped in. "You saw a headless guy on a horse in the lobby of our building. No wonder you had a seizure; me I would have pissed my pants."

Morgan put his hands on his face, shaking his head laughing. "No you idiot, let me finish, no horse just the headless guy. Then my head started to pound, I remember the elevator ringing and people climbing in, I just stood there letting them pass, I guess Marina thought I was being polite, then I blacked out; waking up in the hospital to Marina and Tom and as hungry as hell."

Rob laughed. "Even without the horse I would have pissed myself if I saw that guy." They all laughed, all except for Tamlyn who smiled as he again wondered why the Azael was there after all this time.

It was then Morgan's younger brother came down the stairs. "Hey bro. Marina filled me in," he said as he hugged his brother warmly. Alex had the same dark hair, dark brown eyes and well favored looks as his brother; he was just a hair shorter, he carried a leaner muscular build than his brother, more like Rob.

"You want a beer?" Morgan asked.

"Sure, but sit down I'll get it. Sorry I am late I got detoured by the cops. You remember hearing about those murders with the victims heads missing? There looks to be another over at Greenfield Towers, that's the apartment complex Marina's friend Gina lives in, Marina is on the phone with her now. Check it out its all over the news," Alex said as he grabbed the remote, turning on the TV and changed the channel to the local news. There was a female reporter standing in front of the police taped off front entrance to the apartment building.

"Again here are the facts as we know them. Fifty six year old Martha Shaw murdered in her apartment here at 150 Greenfield Towers. The building's superintendent Peter Johnson found her during a routine fire inspection with her head cut off and it appears missing from the crime scene. This is the third such victim in less than a year. So far the police have no confirmed leads until now; there was some footage from a lobby camera of a male asking to be let up into the same apartment the night before. The Police are to release more details as the investigation proceeds. Back to you Mike."

Tamlyn knew who the person in the footage would be; he knew that same apartment in a different path of fate used to belong to Cameron MacLean, and that footage would reveal Cameron who was only trying to go home. Martha Shaw's murder was the work of the Azael. It had to have been the one who took the photograph from Cameron's apartment, delivering it to him 750 years into the past. When it returned to the future, history shifted and the apartment once belonging to Cameron now belonged to this murdered woman. Cameron it seems is a murder suspect that the police will never find because he does not exist.

"Wow. That's sick, it looks like we have a serial killer out there now that collects heads; that is so fucked up," Rob said being serious for once.

Jim followed. "For once I am in total agreement with you there," as he took a deep swig of his beer.

"Hey, maybe its Morgan's headless horseman that's taking all the heads, didn't he do that in the movie?" Rob said jokingly, which forced Alex into a confused look as Morgan explained. "Don't listen to him, I was telling them about a hallucination I had just before the seizures happened, I thought I saw a headless horseman in the lobby at my office, don't tell Marina ok?"

Alex smiled although there was concern reflecting in his eyes. "Sure, no problem, hopefully you won't have them anymore."

Jim raised his beer. "Cheers to that!"

"Cheers!" the rest replied and clanked their bottles together. Silence took over the room as they watched the footage of the horrific crime unfold while other news reporters added their two cents and talked about the two previous victims. The first was a female, Michelle Clarke, an archeologist specializing in rare medieval weapons who had only just returned from a dig in the North of Scotland. The second victim was a male investigative reporter named Timothy Reynolds. The news reporters seemed to think there was a connection to the two victims: that Timothy Reynolds was investigating the murder of Michelle Clarke, perhaps finding something that made him the next victim, although the police would not comment on the issue. They were also trying to figure out a connection with the latest victim, a retired schoolteacher.

"Hey Tom, did you know the archeologist, Michelle Clarke? You deal with historical stuff," Rob asked, putting together a connection all his own.

"Yes I did. It was several years ago, she wanted me to donate some ancient weapons to the local museum, but the artifacts already had a buyer in place so I had to decline. I believe that was the only time I had actually met with her, the rest was through email about sales and museum events," Tamlyn replied truthfully, yet not sharing the fact that Rob's bizarre theory was dead on and that the Azael, Morgan's headless horseman was indeed the killer.

"Wow, that's freaking unreal. Wonder if she pissed someone off enough for them to chop her head off with one of those rare weapons, like a sword. It could even be someone you know in the business, eh Tom?" Rob suggested as both Jim and Alex nodded at his hypothesis as credible.

"You never know, I have heard of this before were the victim and killer could have travelled in the same circles," Tamlyn said, yet inside he wondered what Michelle had found that caused her to be murdered by the Azael, and Reynolds could have been collateral damage, he may have stumbled upon something he should not have. He would have to look into this himself: if the Azael were gearing up for something, he needed to find out quickly. But first things first, he needed to make sure Morgan was safe. He was certain that the chaos in Morgan's mind would eventually resurface–he just had no way of knowing when. Tamlyn felt helpless, all he could truly offer Morgan was but a brief respite in the war raging within his mind. He didn't know if the seizures would get worse or hopefully with either time or the right medication could effectively treat him. He was getting more and more frustrated, for he knew who could help him, but getting Morgan there was something else entirely. He had no time to ponder it further because Marina called down. "Is anyone hungry?" and as one they all took to their feet; Marina's spaghetti and meatballs was legendary.

As they piled around the table, she grabbed Alex. "Would you mind cutting the bread for me?"

Alex smiled. "Sure, no problem."

Morgan's eyebrows shot up. "Isn't that supposed to be my job, Marina, I'm not a total invalid." Marina's sharp look along with tightened eyebrows was enough, Morgan knew better than to fence with her.

"You are supposed to rest and do nothing with any concentration or sharp objects."

"Can I keep my knife?" he cracked a mischievous smile.

"I haven't decided yet. Let's see how well you do first, you're lucky I let you feed yourself," she shot back at him with another glare that said 'don't push it'. Conversation resumed as if it was an ordinary night, of work, sports, weather and crude jokes. Marina felt she was at a table with a bunch of kids really. But the topic eventually turned, taking more of a grim path.

"Alex told you of the murder at Gina's apartment complex?"

Morgan shook his head. "Yeah scary stuff. He said you were talking on the phone to her, how is she handling it?"

"She's pretty spooked to say the least."

"I bet. It would freak me out, and I can handle myself," Rob put in.

Jim laughed at him. "You can handle yourself huh? A crazed maniac wanting to chop your head off and you can handle yourself?"

Rob with a serious look. "I run very fast." They all laughed at him as Rob laughed himself. "Ya, well laugh it up, but all of you would be running yer asses off too," Rob got a chorus of nods in agreement.

Yet Tamlyn knew them all probably better than they knew themselves. They would find courage whenever necessary, no matter what the odds. He had found the race of humanity adaptable and resourceful; bravery and courage always came from the unlikeliest of places.

"Tom was saying he knew one of the victims, the Archeologist. Small world, huh?" Morgan said to Marina.

"I'm sorry to hear that Tom; was she a good friend?" Marina asked with a sympathetic tone.

"No not a friend, a business associate. However, it's still disturbing when it's someone you know, a sad loss to her family and to the Museum she was part of," Tamlyn said, as the rest quietly agreed.

"Marina, you never disappoint. Again I don't know how you do it; this spaghetti is amazing," Alex said with a smile to change the topic. Marina blushed slightly as everyone complimented her on the meal.

"She even beats Spaghetti Betty's, hands down," Morgan said proudly.

"Thanks hon, I know it's your favorite," she said, her dark brown eyes shone with love and concern at the same time.

Once the meal was done, the guys took over. "Marina, you and Morgan take it easy. We'll clean up here," Rob said. He that hated cooking anything but was always the first to jump in with the cleanup. He had figured out long ago if he at least cleaned up the mess after the meal, he would be more often than not invited back for another. So all the dishes, pots and pans were all cleaned and put away; the table, counter tops and stove all wiped down to a sparkly clean.

Not long after, Lynne and her husband Aaron arrived. Lynne hugged Marina then Morgan. "I'm so glad your home and back on your feet. You'll do almost anything to get out of work!" she said with a warm kiss to his cheek.

"I have no idea what you're talking about!" Morgan said with a devilish grin as Aaron stepped in to give him a warm handshake. "Glad you're ok Morgan."

"Me too, I've got five mother-hens watching my every move. I can't take a leak without someone knocking on the door every two minutes making sure I'm alright."

"Ohhh you poor baby," Lynne said pinching his cheeks. Lynne and Morgan were childhood friends, more like a brother and sister as she too showed worry in her eyes.

"He's not out of the woods yet, the doctor's still haven't found a cause for the seizures. The toxicology report is not due back for weeks; hopefully that will tell us something that the CAT scan could not pick up. We go see his family doctor tomorrow, hopefully we can find out what the future holds for us," Marina said, sounding less than convinced. She was not expecting any answers from this visit tomorrow, only more questions and most likely more tests.

They all moved into the family room, Tamlyn staying quiet and observing all the interactions before him. He compared Morgan's life to Cameron's; how fate took the soul of one man down a different journey; how similar Morgan's life was to Cameron's, sharing the same friends and acquaintances, the same job and most of all the same incredible love of the same woman.

Tamlyn had followed the soul of Cailean MacKenzie through the path of reincarnation for over seven centuries, though similar, there were variations. The Goddess' who sent Cameron back in time to relive that life as Cailean MacKenzie, to be with his soul mate had manipulated him and altered history. Cailean was fated to have killed that Viking but only after his rape of Kerry. Cailean had married Kerry quickly to protect her honor, but mostly out of love. In Cameron's reality, that rape produced a girl child Meaghan whom both parents loved despite the horrible event. That child would grow up strong and healthy, a beauty like her mother, and would never know her true parentage. When she was old enough she married Eoin MacGhillean, son of the chief Ghillean that would become the source of clan MacLean. Meaghan, along with her brothers and sisters, were at Cailean's bedside when he died. Kerry had passed away a few years before and Cailean was never the same afterwards, a ghost of his former self. It was only a few weeks after his death that Cailean's soul was reborn within Meaghan's womb. That child was the next reincarnation that would eventually lead to Cameron MacLean.

That path disrupted and Tamlyn followed Cailean's soul upon a new path, one that would lead to Morgan Hamilton. It had been an interesting journey indeed following Cailean's soul, but one he knew had to do. Not only because Cailean had saved his life and so many others, but also to wait and watch for Cameron to reappear back into the world and to find a way to save him, to help if he could. There was some small comfort in this for Cameron, for in this timeline the soul-mates that lived long ago in Cailean and Kerry, had found each other once again in the present as Morgan and Marina and that was a rare happenstance.

CHAPTER THREE

Questions

I
T WAS LATE in the night and Morgan was looking exhausted. Tamlyn knew he had taken more pain medication, for he could not hide the signs of a bad headache from him. Lynne and Aaron were the first to go, followed by Rob and Jim and lastly Alex. The brothers hugged at their parting, an underlining fear of the unknown passed between them. For Alex, it was the fear of something bad happening to his brother; Morgan would never show any weakness to his brother. Their father had died when they were young, which forced Morgan to become more than just a brother to Alex. The long hug was enough to convince Alex that his brother was afraid, and it caused his own heart to skip a beat.

"Keep me posted alright, of anything. I'm only 15 minutes away," he said as he felt the tears well up in his eyes and a lump in his throat as he nodded to his brother to do what he asked.

"Sure, no worries baby-bro. I'll be right as rain," Morgan replied with a reassuring smile. Alex kissed Marina goodbye and was gone.

"Man its bed for me, my head is splitting apart," Morgan said as he watched his brother drive off.

"Tom, could you stay? I have the guest bed all set, just in case something should happen," Marina asked.

Tamlyn nodded in reply. "That would be fine, thank you. Morgan, I would like to take you up on your offer for your laptop, I need to go over a few things, if you don't mind?"

"Sure, knock yourself out," Morgan answered as Marina ushered him off to bed.

"Goodnight Tom, and thanks," Marina said. She turned out some of the lights, except for the one Tamlyn used on the kitchen island as he powered up the laptop. Tamlyn wanted to do some research, to check out for himself these murders and why the Azael wanted them dead.

He searched out the investigative reporter that was murdered, Timothy Reynolds. So far nothing out of the ordinary; he had graduated in journalism, also had a degree in history, worked for some prestigious magazines and had won several journalism awards. Tamlyn read some of his work, yet none of it would make him a target for the Azael. He was about to give up, when his research turned up something interesting. Reynolds had been working on a missing person's case, a young teenager, Carla Simpson who was a runaway. She had been in and out of youth shelters, which by itself was not setting off any alarm bells for Tamlyn, until he picked up that Carla at the time she went missing was seven months pregnant. The angle Timothy Reynolds took was that no one was actively looking for her. The police had not done much about it feeling that she may have simply moved away as she had broken all ties to her family. It seemed the logical explanation, but Reynolds had found a pattern of missing women that had been pregnant at the time of their disappearance; in fact, over the last ten years there had been thirteen missing pregnant women and twenty-four over the last twenty years. Reynolds was convinced there was a serial killer out there preying on pregnant women. When he took his findings to the police, they took notice and a surge of cold case missing persons opened up. So far, nothing had been found, no trace of any bodies or of the women surfacing in any part of North America.

Reynolds even went back so far that he found over last hundred years 136 missing pregnant women. He had proposed that a serial killer had passed on his killing appetite through his offspring or some sort of apprentice. It was then that the police stepped in to discredit him, accusing him of trying to start a panic and sensationalizing the case. He was looking to make a book of it, and making it out to be an *X-file* type of case. After that, his career took a turn for the worse. He struggled to find work, until he started working on the murders involving missing heads. He had gone back over the last ten years, and found over a dozen cases involving murder victims with missing heads across the country. Tamlyn wondered if Reynolds had ever connected the two types of murders to be the machination of one evil creature. He did not know if the Azael watched TV or read the newspapers, but perhaps they would notice someone getting too close to discovering their existence or their diabolical eating habits.

Tamlyn wanted to follow up with some of his friends and colleagues, perhaps find out anything the police may have missed. He also emailed a colleague in reference to Michelle Clarke, to see what she was doing in Scotland that had forced the Azael to silence her.

His colleague Jeffrey Laurent was an antiquities dealer like himself and knew Michelle fairly well. Tamlyn received back an immediate reply from Jeffrey

Hello Tom,

I see you heard on the news, there was another of those dreadful murders, which made you think of Michelle. I understand your professional curiosity...As I told the police, she had been working on a dig in the northwest of Scotland, north of a small village of Strathcarron. She came across what she felt must have been a battlefield dating back to the 13th century. She found some peculiar and interesting pieces that should not have been there. As I know you will ask about the 'peculiar pieces' they were Saracen like weapons, curved daggers and scimitars that were remarkably well preserved. Normal period weapons were also found but were in conditions indicative to what you would normally expect. All I know was she was extremely excited about having the weapons composition tested, but all the weapons were missing along with all her notes.

Jeffrey.

Tamlyn cursed. That was a battlefield he knew well, having been in it. The Azael were covering their tracks, concealing themselves. He did not want Jeffrey himself to draw their attention so he wrote back.

Thanks Jeffrey for getting back to me so fast. There may be a logical explanation for the Saracen weapons found there. You recall the Templars fleeing persecution in Europe were granted safe haven in Scotland by Robert the Bruce and Primate Lamberton; it is not farfetched that they would have Saracen weapons with them, probably as trophies or souvenirs from the Holy lands. You know of the stories of their vast treasure perhaps bandits and thus the battlefield and those artifacts.

Tom.

Tamlyn hoped that would stem Jeffrey's curiosity in this case, not wanting him to end up another victim. Jeffrey was quick to reply.

You are right, it would make the most logical sense. Although it was never really proven that the Knights Templar did in fact have their vast treasure with them

in Scotland, perhaps this was what excited Michelle.
I hope her murder was not about some lost Templar
treasure trove...

Jeffrey.

Perhaps Jeffrey stumbled upon a theory that all of the Templar conspiracy theorists would drool over. However, they would be all going in the wrong direction, as this was only the Azael destroying any evidence that they exist in the shadows of this world. Tamlyn turned off the laptop and turned out the lights. Within the darkness he closed his eyes tight and extended his other senses forward. He searched out the night, his mind sought for any disturbance no matter how remote. His hearing tuned for anything unnatural, even the silence would tell him something. Nature going silent was the usual prelude to the presence of these beasts.

Tamlyn could find no trace of his enemy; the shape-shifters would stay away in fear of him, only a full pack would try to take him on and reluctantly at that. Only the Azael would have no compunction in attacking him, one would be wary like the one he wounded yesterday, two or more would do anything to kill him. What bothered him was their interest in Morgan. They had been a nuisance in Cailean's time and for a few generations after. It must be something to do with Cameron returning to the future perhaps through him they felt a connection to their home world. The portal from their world opened up just recently after so many centuries, it would be like a shining beacon to them. Of all the creatures from that dying world, only the Azael and the Fuathans lived for centuries, the rest of them lived relatively short life spans. Perhaps the shape-shifters lived longer than humans did but Tamlyn was not certain. The giant hairy Fuathans tended to live in remote areas, well away from humankind, living generally in small groups and had no further dealings with others of their home world. The Bogils lived very short lifespans, they were voracious eaters of flesh yet as far as Tamlyn could tell the great plagues wiped them out long ago, and he felt it unlikely that any still survived. Other creatures from that dying world had crossed over before the end: Fachan, Sirens, Furies and more still lived to plague humanity, spread out all over the world, surviving on the edge in the darkness. Tamlyn quietly sympathized with their plight but knew that they could have gone to different worlds to sustain them. It was they who chose inhabited worlds with a multitude of prey, yet the prey on these worlds fought back, forcing them to live in the shadows hiding from the race of men.

CHAPTER FOUR

Azael

TAMLYN WENT INTO the guest room and lay on the bed. He required little sleep, but he used the time to plan his next moves. He had some hunting to do. One hundred and thirty six pregnant women missing over a hundred years could mean at least 137 or more Azael were out there. He had witnessed before at least five Azael at a single grizzly feast. Gorging upon the embryonic fluid and the unborn child allowed the Azael to clone themselves–making perfect copies equipped with the same strength, skill and memories of its original. It was quite possible there could be hundreds of them out there. In the past century, Tamlyn had found and killed sixty-two. Their feeding habits did not always include pregnant women; another delicacy they enjoyed and what had piqued his curiosity about these murders with the missing heads. Azael were almost insect like in nature; when they materialized their heads they had a proboscis which they injected a venom type cocktail into the skulls of their victims. This toxic cocktail liquefied the brains, the longer it sat a strange fermentation took place, creating a ghastly delicacy that could sustain them for some time. Tamlyn had wrongly assumed that over time there were not a rash of murders with the heads missing reported to authorities. He had always felt that a lack of reported victims was a measurement of how few Azael were still alive on this world. Yet the Azael were clever creatures, never drawing attention to themselves unless they were ready to completely overwhelm their victims. More and more he was convinced he needed help, but he needed to go home to a world he had been away from for more than seven centuries to find it.

It was so long ago that he and three companions took up the Blood-hunt. His brother Finn, Marek and Conn all took the oath and chased the Azael across the stars. The Blood-hunt was an ancient oath of the Warrior Cast used rarely and not for thousands upon thousands years, when his world was a much different place. It was a call to vengeance that gave one certain benefits and when taken it would last until the oath was fulfilled. When the Azael and their brethren came to his world in their thousands, the Ljosalfar had been completely overwhelmed from the very start. The Warrior's Guild was not large in numbers, typically his people trained there within the guild before choosing another profession. Being immortal, they often chose many different guilds to enrich their lives. Tamlyn and his companions were Guild Masters, teachers of their craft and almost never chose any other guild thereafter.

There were no large cities on his world, only communities that number in a few thousand individuals. The attack upon his world was swift and terrible, entire communities fell quickly in those first few days. Sensing the evil upon their world, the Warrior Cast acted swiftly to engage the foe. The battle was terrible, but ultimately they won some small reprieve … until they realized the sheer size of their enemy. New attacks came in with greater and greater frequency. It was then with great malice, that the Azael unleashed their most insidious of weapons: The Reavers, re-animated soldiers turned by the Azael. Although dead, they possessed the same strength, speed, skill and agility as when they were alive. These undead warriors were totally under the control of the Azael and as hard to stop as their headless masters. The Warrior's guild was fighting its own dead soldiers. Reavers inflicted terrible carnage upon the Warrior Cast, while the rest of the Demon hordes were feasting upon its people.

Every soldier within the Warrior's Guild was conscripted into action. Tamlyn's own wife Jenna, pregnant at the time but still far from her due date, was a deadly fighter and would not stay out of the wars. She fought in Tamlyn's company that was led into a trap by the Shape-shifters. They were quickly overwhelmed; most were taken alive as prisoners for food. Those that had died in the struggle were re-animated into the Reaver legions.

All of this Tamlyn saw in incredible disbelief. Beaten, bloodied, and restrained by his captors, he could only wait for the slaughter. Finn, Marek and Conn, all of them wounded and helplessly bound, were restrained by Reavers and Shape-shifters. They could only watch as the Azael fed upon Jenna and her unborn child. Five Azael stabbed at her stomach, penetrating her womb with their proboscis, injecting their deadly venom. It liquefied their unborn child, digesting it along with the embryonic fluid while Jenna was still alive screaming in unbearable agony until she died. Tamlyn, held secured by the Reavers, screamed in rage at seeing this horrific feast of his wife and unborn child. When the spark of her life force expired, the five Azael glowed, giving birth to exact clones of themselves; their skin distorting, expanding outward, they slid out of themselves, like a snake shedding its skin.

It was then the Azael were at their weakest. Their control over the Reavers briefly faltered, Tamlyn's rage broke his bonds and he destroyed the Reavers that held him. He freed his companions and they flung themselves at their enemy. Four of the newborn Azael in their weakened state fell quickly, but the fifth newborn was shielded by the fully recovered parent. Tamlyn in his fury killed several Azael, while the others Marek, Conn and Finn fought Reavers and Shape-shifters and destroyed them. It was a terrible struggle as their rage fueled them through terrible wounds.

The Reavers however had given the Azael enough time to recover to make good on their escape. Tamlyn and his companions destroyed the Reavers and full of rage and anguish they took up the Blood-hunt. They were so utterly consumed in their vengeance that they had invoked the ancient oath. Finn too the oath for his brother's sake and because he was Jenna's brother-in-law twice over. Marek and Conn because Jenna was their sister. When the Guild discovered that they had taken the oath they were deeply saddened, for the outcome was always fatal.

The Warriors Guild, now fully aware that their entire world was in peril, coordinated their efforts planet-wide to the danger these creatures represented. Communities armed and backed up with battle-hardened members of the Warrior's Cast. Although these creatures could open portals anywhere upon their world giving them the advantage of surprise, the Ljosalfar could tune in to their presence, sensing when they were near. As always, the Azael used Reavers in the forefront of every battle to protect their own; these walking dead warriors were so terribly hard to stop. Only the creative efforts of the Science Guild that developed incendiary weapons had helped turn the tide of the wars. In the years that followed, wars pushed the Ljosalfar to the brink and through it all Tamlyn and his companions managed to track down and kill many Azael.

Tamlyn had learned much about his enemy from reading the residual traces of the Azael's mind from captured and restrained Reavers. Only bits and pieces, yet it was enough to put together at least the 'why' behind this war. Their home-world had suffered some tragedy and using portals they had visited many worlds, sizing up potential food sources. On three different worlds, they had hunted all the inhabitants to extinction, and Tamlyn's world it appeared was next. It had been sorrowful years for his kind, continuous hit and run raids from the Azael armies, their only purpose was to capture any alive or dead, it seemed relentless and without gain on either side. Moreover, the enemy unleashed other horrors from their world: Kelpies, Banshees, Furies, Sirens, Ghouls and other creatures that spread fear and terror. Kelpies turned lakes and rivers into killing zones. Banshees were invisible, riding within darkened winds until they attacked, ripping victim's apart, limb from limb. Furies flew night skies, scooping up victims on their vast bat-like wings and carried them to dizzying heights before dropping them and then feasted upon the smashed corpses. Siren's sang songs to lure in victims to their deadly embrace, then devoured the flesh. Ghouls crept everywhere feasting on both the living and the dead.

All of this was but a distraction, as these creatures were few in number but caused the Ljosalfar to concentrate on remote areas. It was then the Azael had orchestrated their attack upon the largest of the Ljosalfar communities, a massive army of Reavers, Bogils, Fachan, Fuathan, Shape-shifters, and Furies all with Azael, leading the assault. The community itself fell to the Demon hordes, yet it had held out long enough to engage the enemy with the largest force the Warrior Guild had ever marshaled at one place.

Tamlyn led a legion of Guild Masters under his command, all sent for one major purpose: to destroy as many Azael as they could. The Azael were the masterminds of their race. They were the ones that controlled their armies, opening their portals wherever they wished, by destroying the Azael the threat would be over. The battle had been long and terrible; vastly outnumbered yet the skill and speed of the Warrior's Guild prevailed, with hundreds of Azael destroyed. The cost had been devastating, for the ranks of the Warrior's Guild were decimated but it had achieved its goal. The Demon hordes pulled out of the Ljosalfar Home-world. Their defeat showed them that this world would not be taken easily and decided to move on to easier pickings. They did not know how close they were to destroying the Ljosalfar; they must have believed the Ljosalfar still had more legions to combat them.

Tamlyn and those that remained of his legion could not let go of the Blood-hunt so easily, it drove them on to pursue relentlessly the Azael and its army to three other worlds, all of which gleaned lifeless by the Demon hordes. They chased them down across the stars, following through portals of their own. Time and again they lost more and more of their legion, until it finally took them to Earth. By then it was just the four of them, Tamlyn, Finn, Marek and Conn: only those that had taken up the Blood-hunt. The oath they took endeared them with a greater strength than their brethren to achieve their task, no matter what the cost. The journey to Earth had taken its costly toll, Marek, Conn and then Finn fell against the overwhelming numbers of the Demon hordes. Tamlyn too would have perished, his oath unfulfilled, if not for Cailean and his gallant Highlanders charging into the battle.

It was from that moment on he was caught up in the saga with Cailean and Cameron. Once he discovered Cameron was somehow within Cailean's mind from a future that wasn't dominated by the Azael, he knew that he must stay and see how these strange set of events would unfold. Tamlyn quickly surmised that somehow Cailean played a pivotal role in their destruction. The sending of Cameron back in time was a scheme to have it all come to ruin. Ultimately, they still achieved the destruction of the Demon's home world. The unfortunate consequences of that event had trapped many of those terrible creatures upon this world. Through the centuries, they had proliferated in the shadows, always watching and waiting, feeding upon humankind.

For better or worse Tamlyn made his choice to follow Cailean's soul through the ages. He waited for Cameron's possible return and until then, he hunted those vile beasts, always believing he was successful in this task until now. His fate seemed now tied with Morgan as it was with Cailean. This new dilemma with Morgan and Cameron had to be rectified. For now, all he could do was wait and see how Morgan would hold up; if the mind of Cameron could only integrate itself without causing further damage then he need not force Morgan to the truth. If that failed, he would have no choice other than to get aid from his Home-world, heal Morgan and finish the eradication process to destroy the Azael and all its brethren forever.

CHAPTER FIVE

The Sword

Dawn heralded a new day. Tamlyn heard Marina get up to shower while Morgan grumbled that his head still ached. Tamlyn went downstairs to start a pot of coffee, then grabbed a glass of water, the bottle of aspirin, and knocked on Morgan's bedroom door.

"Hey, catch!" he said as he tossed the pill bottle, allowing Morgan to catch it before he passed him the glass of water.

"I guess you heard me? Sorry to wake you."

Tamlyn only smiled at him. "You are not the most quiet person I know, but I was awake anyway," he replied while Morgan shot him his most pathetic grin.

"Hey is that coffee I smell? You are the best Tom. Are you sure you don't want to work as my butler or something? I know you already have a cool job and all."

Tamlyn grinned at him. "You couldn't afford me."

"Ya, I suppose your right," Morgan replied getting out of bed as Marina walked into the room in her bathrobe, toweling her auburn hair dry.

"Right about what?" she asked, while her smile showed playful curiosity.

"I tried to hire Tom as our butler but he said I couldn't afford him," Morgan replied.

Marina laughed. "Yum, coffee, how is it you always make the best coffee Tom?" she asked while Tamlyn winked at them.

"Just a little trick I know. I'll meet you downstairs," he said, leaving them to get dressed. He went downstairs to pour a cup for himself, *If and when I ever return to my world I will miss this coffee,* he thought as he savored the aroma before taking a sip. Marina poured a cup for herself and Morgan as she made some oatmeal for herself and put in a couple of bagels in the toaster for both Morgan and Tamlyn.

They ate their breakfast while watching the morning news; the police had released the apartment building footage of Cameron trying to get the superintendent to let him into the apartment of the murdered woman. It was grainy and dark, hard to make out specific details. Tamlyn knew it was Cameron; the police were calling him a 'person of interest' at this time, as the footage only put him on the scene the day after the murder.

Marina looked hard at the footage. "He kinda looks like the guy I ran into at work while I was bringing you coffee Monday morning," Marina said, watching the footage with great interest.

"Seriously? Hon, that's scary stuff. Was he bothering you?" Morgan asked his face pinched now with concern.

"No, not at all. Even if it was him on that footage, I don't think he is the killer," she answered confidently.

Morgan looked at her confused. "What do you mean?"

She looked at him, eyes locking each other with sureness. "It was just in his face, his eyes, something familiar, he actually reminded me of you Morgan. He looked lost, in pain; there is no way he could be the killer."

Morgan studied his wife for a brief moment, then with a warm smile. "If you say so hon, I trust your instincts." Marina reached over to him and comfortingly squeezed his hand, her smile reflected love and trust to the very core.

Once breakfast was done, Marina got after Morgan to hurry up for the doctor's appointment. Morgan, although he still carried that headache, was of a mind that all of this was a waste of time. He didn't feel sick, and felt confident that the seizures would not return; he would rather chalk it up as a 'really bad day' and go on as normal. Marina was of another mind entirely: not convinced that the seizures were done, and wanted answers as to why and what the future would hold for them both. Marina herself was feeling off. She had been putting it down to a slight case of the flu or stress; she had been too worried over Morgan lately to look into her own wellbeing.

The wait at the doctor's office did not take long; Tamlyn said he would stay in the waiting room. Dr. Brennan had a warm smile as he came into the room, a slim frame and piercing blue eyes that continually looked over his eyeglasses as he scanned Morgan's chart. His grandfatherly appearance always put Morgan at ease; after all, he had delivered Morgan into this world.

"Wow, Morgan you have been busy, haven't you?" he began as he put down Morgan's file.

"Yeah well, it's more of a pain in the ass, if you ask me," Morgan replied with a sarcastic grin.

"Well that may be easier to treat then your brain," Dr. Brennan replied with a wink to Marina. "So we are waiting for the toxicology report I see. The seizures you had are Generalized or Tonic-Clonic seizures, once called Grand mal seizures. Now a lot of things can trigger seizures, and if you have seizures, it doesn't mean you have epilepsy. Also, this may be a one-off type circumstance due to a chemical imbalance, sodium or sugar; the toxicology report will give us more to go on. If it is that, then a diet plan may be all that is required." Marina and Morgan both nodded, as Dr. Brennan continued.

"Now there may be something or nothing on that report, I can give you a fancy medical term that simply means 'we don't know' what might be causing these seizures, most of the biggies have been ruled out at the hospital. I just do not want you to be discouraged if we don't get an answer to this right away. It may take even more tests to discover what's behind this," he said while giving Morgan a comforting pat on his shoulder.

"For the meantime, if you continue to have more seizures, keep a record of them. Maybe we can pin point any curious trends. If he has several episodes without coming to, or if he hits his head in a fall, get him to the hospital. Otherwise, just make sure he is comfortable, allow him to rest and sleep it off. Take a few weeks off work to see how things are progressing. I can give you a prescription for carbamazepine; only have it filled if he has more seizures. Keep me posted, we may have to tweak the dosage a bit. Some of the side effects can be fever, weakness, nausea, skin irritation, urination changes, confusion, and hallucination. I can go on and on, just let me know if any of these pop up," he wrote out the prescription and was about to hand it to Morgan, but changed his mind and gave it to Marina.

"Better to give it to the reliable one," he said with a grin. "And how are you doing, Marina? You look a little tired and pale. I suppose Morgan's the cause?"

"Isn't he always? I've just been a little tired of late," Marina replied as Dr. Brennan just nodded with a smile.

"Well don't worry about him, he will be ok, he's always pulled through before," he gathered up Morgan's file and said his good-byes.

"See a total waste of time!" Morgan said smugly, yet Marina only shook her head holding up the prescription.

"No it's not, weren't you listening? We just have to wait and see what happens next. If the seizures come back we have this prescription to use, if the toxicology report gives us more to go on, like if your sodium or sugar levels are the cause, then we can get you on the right diet," Marina repeated to him a little more edgy than she intended.

"Great, just great. So I have something to look forward too, let's see, drugs that will make me dizzy, make me pee a lot, breakout in rashes, oh and hallucinate or go on a lousy diet eating tofu and bean sprouts. See? I was listening," Morgan said, feeling a little pissed off as to what his future was possibly going to be like.

"You can be such an ass, Morgan. Those are possible side effects only; you may never have any of them. And as far as the diet is concerned, it may not be as bad as you think," Marina replied just as testily.

Morgan shrugged his shoulders, and hugged his wife. "I'm sorry babe, I'm being selfish. I have put you through hell these last few days and I am sorry. I love you more and more each day, it's just this has freaked me out; all my life I have always been in control of things. Now it's like I have no control whatsoever and it scares me hon," he said as he kissed his wife tenderly.

"I know Morgan it scares me too, whatever this is, and as cheesy as it sounds, we are in this together."

"Yeah, that's cheesy alright."

"Jerk!" she said with a loving smile and they kissed again.

Hand in hand they met up with Tamlyn in the waiting room. "Well?" Tamlyn asked as they moved in beside him.

"I got drugs!" Morgan said with a twisted smile.

"Only if the seizure's come back," Marina added. "But nothing new; a hopeful prognosis, we just have to see how he does going forward. Oops, sorry that's my cell," Marina said opening her purse, talking as they walked to the car.

"… OK, I'm on my way. Tom would it be alright if I drop you two off at your place, that way you can get your car? I have to drop in at work," Marina asked.

"Sure, that's sounds perfect to me," Tamlyn replied as they hopped into the car. It was a fifteen-minute ride to Tamlyn's building downtown on the river-side; a one-time shoe factory converted into ten high-end two-story lofts. Tamlyn punched in the door code in the front foyer to get into the building, and they both took to the stairs up to the third floor to Tamlyn's end unit. He took the key from a chain around his neck, and opened the door.

"You know most people carry their keys in their pockets," Morgan said with a grin. Tamlyn just smiled back, opened the door then immediately shut off his house alarm system. A spacious foyer opened up in front, expensive artwork hung upon the walls and down the hallway like a small gallery. At the end of the hallway it opened up to a stylish kitchen on the right, wonderfully polished concrete countertops with a large island. To the left was a staircase to the second floor that had a spacious bedroom, bathroom and walk in closets. On the main floor across from the kitchen was a large table and chairs, opposite that was a leather sectional placed in front of a massive fireplace. The French doors beside the stairs opened up into the office and study and another bathroom. All of it was well lit with east facing floor-to-ceiling windows overlooking the river.

Tamlyn stopped at the island and picked up a large manila envelope addressed to his landlord, who had permission to let himself in once every six months to collect his checks. This envelope, however, would have a note to have him mail another envelope inside it to the Lyon's Corp, the corporation Tamlyn worked at. There were instructions for the trustees to sell all of his assets and to distribute the funds to various charities; there would also be a sum of money to go to Morgan and Marina. Tamlyn did not believe he would still be here after Cameron returned. He knew he had failed to find help for his friend, assuming that Cameron would dematerialize along with his world. Knowing that he had done all that he could, his guise as Tom Fletcher would no longer be needed and so these instructions were to be followed a full year after the Trustees received this letter. It would say that he had gone off on a solo sailing trip across the Atlantic Ocean. It seemed an easy yet not out-of-character way for him to disappear.

"Man, Tom this place is amazing. Do you mind if I grab a soda or something?" Morgan asked as he stood in front of the island.

"Yes sure, go ahead," he answered, thinking about the envelope and its contents.

"Um Tom, do you actually ever put food in this fridge?" Morgan asked, snapping Tamlyn's attention to the present. He laughed as Morgan noticed that besides a case of coke, the fridge was empty.

"I have been out of the country, I haven't had a chance to get to the market," he replied. Morgan nodded and followed him into the study. He looked around in wonderment, taking in the floor to ceiling oak bookcases filled with very old and very expensive books, and stopped at a full suit of armor.

"Wow, this King Arthur's armour?" Morgan asked joking.

"Hardly. That dates to 1510, its German Maximilian, named after the style of armour of Emperor Maximilian the First," Tamlyn replied, tossing the envelope on his desk.

"That was my second guess," Morgan said with a smile, as he moved over to a glass-encased sword. "Tom this thing is huge."

"The two handed swords normally are. It dates back to 1573, from the State Guard of the Dukes of Brunswick, and no, you can't play with it," Tamlyn said with a sly look.

"You know how to spoil a good time, don't you?" Morgan said laughing, as he sat in the chair in front of the desk. A wooden antique box piqued his curiosity, and he leaned over to see what was inside. "Holy Jesus Tom, you have all the coolest toys," Morgan said, almost drooling over a pair of dueling pistols and all its accessories. "So what's the story on these?" he asked.

"Oh, they are early nineteenth century, made in Versailles by an exceptional gunsmith named Nicolas-Noel Boutet during the Empire of Napoleon," he said and gently slapped Morgan's hand away from that box.

"Yep, that's what I was thinking too. So what is all this stuff worth, like everything you have here?" Morgan asked, still being nosey.

"Well, based on Sotheby's last estimate about 30 million give or take, you can't always be sure at auctions," Tamlyn replied, watching Morgan's chin slide to his knees. "Well you asked!"

"Yeah, but I thought maybe a cool million. Holy crap Tom, you did alright for yourself," Morgan said in awe.

"Well, I was in the right place at the right time," Tamlyn said with a warm chuckle. He noticed that his answering machine had been blinking, and hit the play button, listening to the messages while Morgan finished his coke. Morgan's attention was diverted to a bureau that had a Scottish targe laid upon it. It was chipped and battered, but what was under it caught his eye: a broadsword, its pommel and hilt worn with use, the scabbard old cracked leather, plain yet well made. Morgan's hand touched the hilt.

"Morgan! No!" Tamlyn shouted and lunged towards Morgan, who all but collapsed in his hands, eyes rolled back and seizures took over. Tamlyn held him through the attack until the seizures abated.

"Easy Morgan, easy..." he said as Morgan was finally coming around. Tamlyn blamed himself for this new seizure; he should have anticipated certain triggers with Morgan's condition. The sword that had saved this world and many others, Cailean's sword, the sword that destroyed the crystal matrix upon that hellish planet would be a powerful trigger. Tamlyn had kept it all these years as a reminder of what Cailean had done, never realizing it would prove to be something dangerous to the reincarnated soul of its original owner. With the turmoil of Morgan's mind, Cameron's recent return, the sword would immediately bring to the forefront Cameron's persona and unleash the seizures once more.

As he held Morgan thinking about that matrix it gave him an idea, a possible plan, a slim chance but it was something. Morgan steadied himself–sitting on the floor, his right hand flat upon the floor; the left ran through his hair and then rubbed his eyes.

"Tamlyn…where am I?"

Tamlyn stared in disbelief upon his friend. "Cameron? How is it you have come forth?"

"Yes, it's me. What are you talking about and where the hell am I?"

"This is my home here on your world. I had to live somewhere; you didn't think I lived in the alley ways, did you?"

Morgan's face smiled. "No I guess not. So what in God's name happened to me? The last thing I remember is fading away, and you telling me that my soul lived on in this world, that it is happy? Does that mean I am somehow with Marina?"

Tamlyn's face remained calm yet inwardly he grew terribly concerned. "Yes, you two are married in this life. I could not speak of a happier couple, you were meant for each other as soul-mates, it is as it should be."

"Then what happened, how are we having this conversation? I thought I was dead and gone," he said, his face grew worried.

Tamlyn could only shake his head. "I am sorry Cameron, I don't understand the cause, but it seems when your physical form faded, your consciousness jumped into your living persona upon this timeline. The body you inhabit belongs to Morgan Hamilton, he met Marina in college just like you did, but Morgan is more like Cailean, he doesn't really take no for an answer."

Cameron seemed to be thinking it through smiling. "Good for him…uh…me. Fuck this confusing. Why does my head feel like it's gonna explode?" he asked as his eyes bulged and squinted at the pain of it all.

"I am uncertain, but I believe that two consciousnesses are trying to reside in the same brain. All of what you once were as Cameron, all your past reincarnations are competing with those of Morgan's. It's causing a form of epilepsy within you. Normal electrical synapses are overloading, like a thunderstorm within your brain," he said, though his voice stung with worry.

"Great, just great! How do we make it stop?" he asked, while both hands massaged his forehead.

"I don't know Cameron. I feel like that is all you are getting from me; I am out of my league here, I need more information and I need help," Tamlyn said as Cameron's attention went over to the sword.

"My sword, I mean Cailean's. You kept this all these years?" he picked up the familiar blade, drawing it from the scabbard. "This sword shattered those glowing crystals," Cameron said as he stared blankly upon the ancient weapon. "It should be in a museum somewhere, for all to see, the sword that saved mankind. But here it sits on a shelf…gathering dust," he said, his voice trembled in pain. "I miss her so much Tamlyn, I miss Kerry. Oh how it hurts inside Tam, it hurts so bad," his eyes brimmed with tears. "Get me back Tamlyn, get me back or kill me, do something to make this right."

Tamlyn's eyes darkened with concern for Cameron, and with his own frustration that he could not help more. Morgan's body staggered, grasping his head in pain, falling to his knees and the seizures took over once more. Tamlyn could do nothing again but wait and ride them out. Once they had abated, Tamlyn scooped him up, taking him into the living room and laid him on the couch. Tamlyn sat on the chair beside him his hands together resting under his chin, studying his sleeping charge.

He was deciding on contacting Marina to let her know of the seizures, perhaps the medication could help Morgan's condition. He was at fault for triggering them, but was contemplating whether or not the drugs would do more harm than good in this particular situation. He had to see if, perhaps with time Morgan and Cameron could somehow co-exist. He dug out Morgan's phone from his pocket and called Marina.

"Hi Marina it's Tom. I'm sorry to say that Morgan had another seizure here at my place. He is ok, just resting now."

"Oh no! Ok, well it is what it is, I guess. I will get the prescription filled and will contact Dr. Brennan to keep him apprised of the situation."

Tamlyn could hear the concern in her voice. "I will bring him home once he is back on his feet," he said.

"Thank you, please Tom, thank you so much. I just have to tie up a few things here and I will be straight home," she replied gratefully.

"Don't worry Marina, we will get him through this, I promise," Tamlyn said, hoping to reassure her. But he knew that at this point nothing other than the seizures stopping for good would give her any peace inside.

Tamlyn let Morgan sleep while he went back into the study and took up Cailean's sword, gazing upon the ancient blade. His thoughts were of the battle just outside of Achnashellach. He had kept the portal open between the two worlds, allowing Kerry and the others to escape from that hellish place. Cailean stayed behind, smashing the matrix with this very sword. That matrix that allowed the Azael to use the portals to travel anywhere in space had also powered the protective shield that kept their world alive.

Tamlyn remembered clearly Cailean diving through the portal with sword in hand, glowing red from the power within the crystals. That critical moment, the jumping through the portal, separated Cameron from Cailean. What had haunted Tamlyn was looking back through the portal to find Cameron still trapped upon that evil place.

Not even with all his incredible power could Tamlyn break through to bring Cameron back.

"Tamlyn! It's over with, done! The magic they used to travel about with is destroyed. Forbye there is no reason to go back there. That entire place is shaking apart. Trying to go back is foolhardy!" Cailean shouted at him as Tamlyn's portal diminished, closing from the other side by a power far stronger than his own. His last look upon Cameron's face was of despair and fear knowing Cameron had been abandoned to his fate.

Tamlyn had no real time to ponder any of it, as the enemy was still in control of the battlefield, even with the reinforcements to the Highland army; almost two thousand strong from Achnashellach had come charging to their rescue. They had formed a defensive ring trying to hold off the murderous creatures. The survivors upon that field wounded or otherwise barely held on. Bogils and Black-dogs darted into the ranks of defenders and snatched out their prey to be cruelly devoured. MacKenzie and Ross clansmen formed a defensive perimeter around a score of armored Knights, who in turn shielded the wounded Earl of Ross and his wife along with the other women folk. The Highlanders bravely held their ground with targes, spears, axes and swords as Cailean, Tamlyn, Coll, Tynan and Kerry fought their way towards them.

Giant Fuathans tried to break the Highlander's line with massive war-hammers as hundreds of Bogils scurried into any breaches to tear into flesh. Azael upon their deadly war-horses encircled them making sure no one could escape. Then as one they suddenly stopped. Their gaze peeled towards the heavens, letting out terrible screams. The Azael realized that they had somehow been cut off from their home-world. It was then Tamlyn watched in horror as across the battlefield dozens of portals failed, trapping the Demons on Earth. Closing portals sliced through flesh and bone neatly, leaving a gory pile of severed limbs and torsos. The effect was immediate. The Azael fled the battle while the rest of the demons watched. Confused, they decided it was everyone for themselves. They disengaged the Highlanders and disappeared into the wild. That day although it was seven and a half centuries past it was all still fresh to Tamlyn as if it had just happened.

The sword which Tamlyn now held, Cailean had chosen to put away almost like a treasured talisman never to be used in battle again. As Tamlyn studied the blade, he could see a slight redness to it where it had struck the crystals, and upon close inspection found tiny red crystal shards fused into the sword's ancient edge. He slid the weapon back into its scabbard then walked to his bookshelves. Pressing a hidden trigger, he stood back as the bookcase opened to reveal a hidden storeroom. Tamlyn carefully placed the sword there, out of sight; no longer would it trouble the soul of its one-time owner.

CHAPTER SIX

Zombies

T AMLYN WAITED WITH determined patience until Morgan finally came around.

"Oh don't friggin tell me, another seizure?" he asked as he swung his legs on to the floor and gingerly sat up.

"Afraid so. Are you ok? What was the last thing you remember?" Tamlyn curiously asked.

"Um … in your study, looking at the pistols … um you telling me you are sitting on 30 million in treasure, and that's about it," Morgan replied.

Tamlyn nodded with a warm smile; *At least he doesn't recall the sword.* "Well I can't say I have had anyone react quite that way before about my holdings," Tamlyn laughed at him.

"I'm glad I can still amuse you. My phone? Did you call Marina or did I just dream that?" he asked.

"No dream; she will get your prescription filled and meet you at home. If you feel up to it I can drive you."

"I'm fine, just a little light headed is all," Morgan said, more annoyed at the situation than anything else.

"Alright then take your time, there is no rush," Tamlyn told him. After a few minutes Morgan nodded that he was good to go and kept close beside him so Tamlyn could catch him if he fell. Tamlyn set his home alarm and locked the door behind them. They took the service elevator to the buildings old docking bays, now converted to a climate controlled car park. Tamlyn clicked his remote to unlock the car doors of his black 911 Porsche Carrera.

"Man I love this car. I guess the way things are going for me I will never get to drive it," Morgan said, a little disappointed.

"Maybe one day," Tamlyn said as they both jumped in. Tamlyn started it up and the engine purred in response, he drove to the automatic doors and waited until they were sufficiently high enough then sped out down the exit ramp. Tamlyn glided expertly through traffic, and it wasn't too long before he pulled into Morgan's driveway. Morgan, now more recovered, let himself and Tamlyn into the house. His headache would not relent so he went straight to the sink, poured himself a glass of water and downed a couple of extra strength aspirin.

"Do you want anything Tom?" he asked as he turned on the TV then sat in his chair.

"No I'm good Morgan," Tamlyn replied worriedly and sat down beside him. The news was on and it went through the weather and sports, then back to local news, but Morgan was fading fast, the seizure had taken more out of him than he cared to admit, and Tamlyn let him sleep.

About an hour later Marina came in, she put her purse and some grocery bags on the kitchen island with Morgan's prescription. He stirred as she sat down beside him, and opened one eye to smile at her. Marina took his hand and squeezed it comfortingly.

"Yum, is that rotisserie chicken you picked up?" Morgan asked.

Marina smiled. "Well at least your nose still works. Yes I decided to pick up dinner and all the fixings to make it easier for us tonight. Tom, you are more than welcome to join us."

Tamlyn nodded. "Thank you I would like that very much."

Marina smiled; she was glad for the help. She went over to the kitchen island taking out Morgan's prescription and returned to his side, opening the pill bottle. "Hon, you need to take two of these, twice a day," she explained. Morgan sat up, taking the pills from her and picking up the glass of water beside him to wash them down. Morgan smiled at her then closed his eyes; it was not long before he fell into a restorative sleep. Marina sat beside him watching, worry lined her beautiful face.

"I'm exhausted myself just watching him, I'm going to make some coffee. Tom, would you like some?" she asked as she headed back to the kitchen.

"Sure Marina, that would be grand," Tamlyn got up and sat on the island to join her.

"So what happened?" Marina asked. She needed to understand more about what was going on with Morgan and these seizures to discover what may be triggering them.

"He was being his normal nosey self," Tamlyn informed her.

Marina laughed. "That's my Morgan. He didn't break anything did he?" she sounded a bit worried, remembering another time they had been with Tom at an antiques show and Morgan almost dropping a vase once he was quietly informed how much it was worth.

"No, he was looking at a 13th century sword, although he doesn't seem to recall it right now," Tamlyn said truthfully, in case Morgan did start to remember.

"Did he say or do anything just before?" she asked.

"He just finished a coke; that was all he had," he replied as Marina nodded.

"Dr. Brennan said these seizures could be a chemical imbalance, sugar or sodium. Maybe it was the sugar in the coke; I don't know, I'm grasping at straws here," she said, sounding frustrated.

"It's ok Marina, we will find out one way or the other. It's just going to take a little time that's all." She nodded, knowing he was right. Marina knew there was nothing either of them could do but to sit tight and see what the next day would offer.

Morgan slept through the rest of the day, and Marina had to wake him for dinner. The chicken, potato wedges, coleslaw and a warm apple pie for dessert satisfied the hunger quite sufficiently. After they ate, Marina gave him some more pills to take.

"So what's the deal with these things anyway?" Morgan asked.

"They may take a while to take effect. After the first week you are to increase the dosage to six pills, then to eight the following week. The pharmacist said to see how it goes, how your body is adjusting to the medication. He said each pill is 100mg and the maximum dosage is 1200mg, if nothing changes and the seizures are still happening then to contact Dr. Brennan," Marina replied, hopeful that this course of action was best for him.

"Fine, and the side effects?" he asked. Marina handed him the documents that came with the prescription of the carbamazepine. "Wow, fun times ahead!" Morgan said as he read it through.

By the end of the night Tamlyn decided to head home. "Keep me posted Marina. You have my home phone?"

"Yes I have it on my phone, not your cell though," she said expecting him to provide it, then Morgan piped in.

"He doesn't have one, he doesn't believe in having one."

Tamlyn smiled at him then winked at Marina. "I'm old school, I find my home phone suits me well enough."

Marina laughed at him and kissed him on the cheek. "Thanks for everything Tom."

"You're quite welcome," Tamlyn said as he then hugged Morgan in a strong embrace. "Take care of yourself my friend," he said as Morgan simply nodded. Tamlyn smiled and with a departing wave he went to his car.

Tamlyn backed out of the driveway and followed the road to another destination. He headed up to Reservoir Hill, just outside the city. It was a haunt of young lovers and stargazer's alike. Tamlyn often came here to think and gaze at the stars, one always in particular, the star that his Home-world orbited. It was a world much like this one, a green and blue marble in the vastness of space. The planet itself was bigger than Earth, maybe one and a half the size, with the same tilt of the axis, the seasons were similar but it held a larger moon almost a deep red in color. He had been gone so long; he wondered how his world fared after the wars, of what changes had taken place and what had stayed the same. His mission here was not done, he would see it through to the end no matter how long it took; the debt would be paid. Tamlyn truly longed for home, alone on this world he could not help but pine for the sights and smells of home. Try as he might to fit in here, he always felt an outcast; his friendships had been fleeting and painful. The lifespan allotted to the race of men seemed to fly by in the eyes of an immortal being, the sorrow he felt each time was always difficult to bare. He endured it all as he knew he must, marking as well as he could the changes in the timeline's and to wait for Cameron's return.

††††

Morgan fell asleep as soon as his head hit the pillow; even with his head still pounding, the tiredness won out. Marina curled up beside him listening to him breathing, eventually letting it lull her into a restful sleep. When Friday morning came Morgan felt refreshed, but still the headache lingered and he took even more aspirin to make it at least bearable. He took it easy for the day, allowing Marina to get some work done. He even made dinner for them both: marinated pork-chops, nicely grilled, a side of applesauce, with perogies and a mixed greens salad.

"How are you feeling? No side effects from the pills?" Marina asked.

"Nope no problems so far, but this freaking headache doesn't seem to wanna go away anytime soon," he replied as he put the dishes in the dishwasher and filled the sink full of hot soapy water to soak the pans in. They both sat down and watched some TV to pass the time.

"Hey hon, you feel like a soak in the hot-tub?" Morgan playfully suggested.

"Sure I would love that. It would be just the thing," she answered with a wink. They both went upstairs to the bedroom, removed their clothes, wrapped themselves in their bathrobes and headed back downstairs to the back deck. Morgan undid the buckles that held down the hot-tub cover on his side while Marina undid the ones on hers. Sliding the cover to the side they hung up their robes and stepped into the hot-tub naked.

"Oh I love this," Marina said as she lay back in her seat letting the hot water and the jets relax her.

"Me too," Morgan said as he sat back and let the jets and the heat sooth his body. After a few minutes, he moved closer to Marina and kissed her.

"Yumm," She purred as they kissed now fully and more passionately with hands caressing each other in spots that only they knew how. They carried on until the jet cycle turned off.

"You want to carry this on upstairs?" she asked.

"You read my mind," he said with his most seductive grin. They jumped out of the tub, put on their robes then tossed on the cover and clipped it down. Marina led him inside, holding his hand as they made their way to the bedroom to finish what they started. They made love with tremendous passion: the days of tension, worry and fear surmounted into a climax for them both.

"Wow!" Marina said through deep breaths, as they were both wonderfully spent.

"Damn right, wow!" Morgan added with a laugh.

"Oh, how I love you, Morgan Hamilton."

"I love you too, in this life and in the next, until the end of time," he said. It was as if he was speaking from within a trance like state, staring into her eyes. He swam into those depths, somehow knowing that all of this had happened before in a different time and a different place.

As the weekend rolled by, the headache never fully left Morgan. Sometimes it was a dull throb and at its worst it was like a smash-up derby going on inside his head. He suffered another seizure on Sunday, Marina held him until well after it ended. When Monday morning arrived, he still felt tired from the seizure and decided to take more time off work. Marina stayed home with him, working from home, fielding phone calls and texts from friends. Morgan's mother arrived that afternoon to stay with them for a few days. Alex came by to check up on his brother and visit with his mom. With her there, it allowed Marina to go to work and get caught up on all she needed to get done. On Wednesday, the day he was to increase his medication dosage, he had another seizure; his mother was with him at the time and put off her leaving for another day.

"Mom look, I will be ok, I'm sure once I hit the right dosage they will be all over with," Morgan said, but she could hear the frustration in her son's voice. She went with him back to Dr. Brennan and he prescribed something stronger than aspirin, Naproxen. He also had Morgan's toxicology report but it showed nothing unusual, which again Dr. Brennan said, could happen. He also mentioned if the carbamazepine doesn't work out he would refer him to a specialist. This step would likely lead to hospitalization for a ten day period while hooked up to several monitors to better see what is going on in the brain while the seizures are actually happening. All of this put Morgan into a bad mood, he was hoping for the toxicology report to give him some answers.

On Friday his mother left reluctantly, after having Morgan and Marina promise to let her know if there was any change in his condition. Rob and Jim came over that night to watch the game on

TV and keep Morgan's mind off his situation. The rest of the weekend was seizure free, so he decided to get back into work for half days.

His boss, Mr. Anderson was there to welcome Morgan back. "How are you Morgan? I'm glad to see you back," he said, his eyes showed concern through his thick eyeglasses as he gave Morgan a welcoming pat on the shoulder.

"Doing ok for now, itching to get back to work and the daily grind," Morgan replied with a reassuring smile.

"That's great to hear. I have a couple of small accounts for you to go over, nothing too urgent, just enough to get your feet wet," Anderson said. He pointed to Morgan's desk at the assignment already there for him, and left Morgan alone to his work. Morgan quickly glanced through the file and started into the work.

Immersing himself in his job seemed to be the best thing for him. The day blew by, ending with Marina dropping in at noon to get some lunch and take him home, and that was what the rest of the week seemed like. He had only one further seizure on Thursday night, which upset him: he thought that because he was now at the full dosage of carbamazepine the seizures would stop. Morgan could not help but feel disappointed, he wanted so badly for the medication to work. Marina saw it in his face and reassured him to have patience that the medication would help.

It was around that time when Marina noticed he was getting a little paranoid. He would keep checking the locks on the doors, and double and triple checking the home alarm; he would keep going downstairs saying he heard something in the basement, but nothing was ever there. Friday morning he still seemed odd to Marina, but she put it off as just her imagination and walked him to his office.

"Morgan, are you alright?" she asked as he sat down at his desk and picked up some of the files.

"Yep, I'm good," he said with an odd kind of smile. She looked at him for a moment.

"Rob is going to drop by this morning for coffee, ok?"

He smiled. "Oh that would be nice," he said and started going through the paperwork so Marina left, closed his office door and went over to the elevator. She thought she heard a 'click' that sound like a lock on the door but did not think much of it. She took the elevator up to her floor and texted Rob to remember to check up on Morgan.

Around 10:15am Rob made his way to Morgan's office. He tried the handle but it was locked. Confused he tried again. "Nope locked, he must have gone out," he said out loud to no one in particular. He knocked, when heard movement inside.

"Morgan open up. It's me, Rob."

"Keep your voice down!"

Rob was now totally confused. "Why?"

"They will hear you," came the reply.

Rob smirked. *Ok I can play this game.* "Who will hear us?" he asked, intrigued.

"The Zombies!"

"Zombies? Morgan open the friggin door! There're no zombies out here."

"They are all over the place. I can see them on the street; there are hundreds of them."

Rob glanced out the window, looking down at the street just in case. "Morgan those are not zombies, they are just regular people. Will you let me in?"

"No! What if you're a zombie?"

Rob heard what sounded like Morgan sliding things around in his office. "I'm not a zombie! Look, do zombies talk?" Rob figured he had him there and it seemed Morgan was thinking it through.

"You could be on their side, trying to fool me into letting you and those zombies in here," Morgan finally said.

"Enough already. If you don't let me in, I'm calling Marina!" Rob threatened as he pulled out his cell phone. The door remained locked.

"Hey Marina," Rob said when she picked up. "You better get down here fast. Morgan's locked himself in his office because there are Zombies everywhere."

"What?" Marina replied. "Alright, I will be right there!" she said as she hung up. Grabbing her purse, she took the stairs at a run. When she got there Rob was still trying to get into Morgan's office.

"Morgan, it's me, Marina," she said, knocking at the door. "Let me in, please." She heard him giggling. Rob looked at her as Morgan started talking with someone in there.

"He's alone isn't he?" Marina asked.

"How should I know?"

"Morgan who are you talking to?"

"An elephant. He wants me to go to a party. Can I go Marina? What? Oh it's a birthday party," he said, and Rob started laughing.

"Those are some good drugs he's got there."

Marina could not help but laugh too. "Um no Morgan, you're not well remember?"

"No I don't have any party favors. Look, I'm sorry you're sad," he said softly.

"Who's sad Morgan?"

"The elephant!" Morgan shouted back, and Rob started laughing again.

"Look Morgan, I'm going to come in now ok?" Marina said as she took out her own key to his office. She unlocked the door but could not open it; with Rob's help they pushed it open. It was blocked by his desk that he pushed up against it.

"So where's the elephant?" Rob could not help but ask.

Morgan simply looked at them. "It went to the party Rob, you are such a dumbass," Morgan said seriously. He was holding his umbrella like a club while looking out his window down at the street, fear radiating from his eyes. Marina was trying to get him to sit down as she called Dr. Brennan's office. Rob sat with him, telling him jokes as

Marina was explaining the situation to Dr. Brennan's office assistant, who then got Dr. Brennan on the phone.

"Hallucinations can be one of the side-effects, he's been at a proper dosage level, and you say he had another seizure last night? Ok then this isn't working for him, they should be under control, this may or may not be epilepsy; these may be NES seizures. We can try a different drug in the meantime, no more carbamazepine. It will take a while to get out of his system so you will have to keep an eye on him for a few days," he said with a little worry in his tone that they still had not figured this thing out.

"Thanks Dr. Brennan," Marina said.

"No problem. Why don't you bring him in tomorrow? Come any time, I will squeeze him in somewhere," he replied and Marina again said her thanks.

"So what's the plan?" Rob asked Marina while she grabbed Morgan's meds off his desk.

"Well he won't be taking these anymore. I've got to get him home," she said. Her tone reflected the helplessness that she felt deep inside.   She smiled to cover it up, watching Morgan holding his umbrella ready to smash in any zombies head.

"Yeah, home may be the safest place for everybody. Let me text Jim to come down, that way we can keep the Zombie slayer from hurting anybody," Rob suggested and Marina nodded, knowing that would be the wisest course.

It was only a few minutes before Jim showed up. "Hey Morgan you ready to go home? You will be safe there," Jim said trying to be helpful.

"Are you sure that is ok? I mean we need guns, lots of guns!" Morgan said. He was growing more and more anxious about leaving the apparent safety of his office.

"Look Morgan, I will take the lead and Rob will follow right behind you and Marina, we will be safe. You know that zombies only attack if you look them in the eyes, so keep your eyes on my back then you will be fine," Jim said. Morgan seemed to roll that around in his head.

"OK but only if you're sure."

"I'm positive; it's in all the zombie manuals, right Rob?"

"You bet! I always keep one of those handy in my desk so I'm up to date on how to deal with zombies," Rob replied with a smirk, but Morgan still seemed unconvinced.

"That's not what they do on 'The Walking Dead.'"

"That's a TV show Morgan, trust me this will work," Rob said confidently, and Morgan reluctantly agreed to go. They took the stairs; Marina held his hand as Morgan stared right at Jim's back. They made it to the lobby as Marina started to detect a bit of panic in her husband.

"Jim I looked at one!" he shouted in fear.

"It's ok it didn't see you, we're still good," Jim said as he kept on going through the crowds.

"OK," Morgan said with a panic tremble in his voice and kept on going. They made a strange procession heading to the parking lot, but they knew they had made it ok once Morgan was safely seat-belted in.

"Thanks guys, I don't think we could have made it without you. I was worried Morgan might bash in someone's head," Marina said with a forced smile.

"I know that seizures are not funny, but I can't help but laugh at these side-effects of his meds," Rob said to her.

"Well we can always look back at this and have a good laugh," she replied.

"Let us know you made it home safe," Jim asked and Marina nodded back.

"I will." She got into the driver's seat and went home.

Morgan only came out of the car once the zombie walking her dog was safely out of range. He waited patiently while Marina set the home perimeter alarms and checked the basement while he exchanged his umbrella for his baseball bat.

"The basement is all clear," Marina said as she came back up the stairs. Morgan nodded quickly.

"Good that may be the best place for us to hide then," he said as he started to rub his eyes and forehead.

"Morgan? Are you OK?"

"Umm no the headache is back, it's really starting to hurt," he answered, the pain was clearly evident on his face. Marina knew she needed to be strong, to not give up, that he would get through this.

"Do you want me to get the Naproxen–you have some left still?" Morgan nodded in reply. She went upstairs to the medicine cabinet in the master-bathroom. By the time she returned Morgan was once again on the floor having a seizure.

CHAPTER SEVEN

Restoration

THE DAY AFTER Tamlyn left Morgan; his night's vigil on Reservoir Hill convinced him of two things. Firstly, he needed to learn more about Morgan and Cameron's condition and secondly he needed to find the Azael. To do both he needed a Restoration: he needed to be at his highest energy levels both physically and mentally. He would have to leave Morgan alone for a couple of weeks, by then he would see how he was doing with the seizures and know for certain what more appropriate steps to take with his friend.

He opened a gateway to the far side of the world. Tamlyn stepped through and the lush earthy smell of a forest pleasantly overwhelmed him. He was in the remote area of Henan province in China. The tall Elf stood upon on a cliff face overlooking a majestic hidden valley that held a secluded Shaolin Monastery. This particular monastery unlike its well-known counterpart in the same province; was truly a hidden refuge. Deep in the mountains, tucked inside a narrow gorge and habitually shrouded in a gloomy fog, very few knew of its existence. Tamlyn took to his true form, for the monks knew him and of his mission. He walked the ancient mountain pathway into the narrow valley and up to the gates of the temple. The massive gates were closed; he pulled a small cord that was attached to a bell on the other side of the gates. He then stood patiently before them motionless, his impressive height and striking features poised and relaxed in harmony with the serenity all around him.

He did not have to wait long until the great gate opened inwards and two monks approached him. Tamlyn bowed in greeting and they in turn bowed to him. Speaking in fluent Mandarin, he explained his purpose and desire to see the Abbot. They politely bowed again in silence, beckoning him to follow them into the temple. He followed through the ancient courtyard and to a bench under a cherry tree where the Abbot was sitting.

The aged monk smiled at the sight of him. "It has been a long time my old friend."

Tamlyn smiled in return and bowed his head slightly. "Yes Zhi it has been at least fifteen years," Tamlyn replied as Zhi offered him a seat on the bench beside him.

"You are still here on this world. When last we spoke you felt the timing was close at hand that your friend would soon return. Either you were wrong or something happened?"

Tamlyn nodded, his face serene and calm. "You are very astute Zhi, as always." The old man bowed his head with a comforting smile. "It happened just a few days ago. He came into this world as we suspected and discovered on his own the change in the present, the path the world had taken. I drew him towards me in his confusion and despair, I confirmed his situation."

"Did he fade away?" Zhi asked.

"Yes it all unfolded as we thought, yet something unexpected happened: the soul transferred into his body of this timeline. Now it causes turmoil from within, two consciousness and subconscious trying to exist in the same brain. The effect is like epilepsy."

"This is unexpected, bad, very bad, it will kill him if not removed; two minds in constant struggle. His suffering will grow worse unless they can find a way to co-exist. Even I do not know if that is possible,"

Zhi said, his voice tinged with sadness and seeing in Tamlyn's face that he too had come to the same conclusion.

"There is more; the enemy is still among us, perhaps in greater numbers than we first thought," Tamlyn's face tightened with concern.

Zhi tilted his head to the side and nodded. "The enemy will be hard to find, always in the shadows, darkness and fear work in their favor. They hunt you as you hunt them. If they manage to capture you and turn you to a Reaver, then they will have the ability once again to travel across the stars," Zhi said, and Tamlyn nodded. That constant threat was always in the back of his mind, but he took the chance for Cameron.

"I need the chamber, Zhi. I need to be ready for them," Tamlyn said and Zhi nodded in understanding.

"Then it shall be prepared. Twenty Shaolin Temple monks will stand watch at all times while you are there." Tamlyn took Zhi's hand in trust, for in the chamber he will be vulnerable.

"Give us one hour to have it ready for you," Zhi said and Tamlyn nodded his head in acknowledgement. Zhi left him alone to make the preparations.

Zhi was as good as his word, as an hour passed he approached the tall Elfin warrior. "Tamlyn, it is time." Tamlyn took to his feet and followed Zhi down to the temples catacombs and through hidden passages with only a small lantern to guide the way. The tunnel came to solid stone door that opened to a lightened chamber. Twenty Shaolin Temple monks stood ready, these elite warriors, deadly proficient in martial arts and masters of the weapons they held.

"These are my best warrior monks. They are cognizant of the powers and the evil the enemy presents, they will defend you to the last man," Zhi said as Tamlyn glanced at them, following his path into another chamber beyond. The door there was also solid stone, made carefully that when closed it would look like part of the wall.

Tamlyn went inside and pressed a hidden lever, the stone door slowly closed shut; once closed it could only be opened from the inside. In the middle of the room was an elongated box like sarcophagus, the lid was open and it was filled with water. Tamlyn lightly sighed as he was sealed inside the room in total darkness. He placed his swords on the floor and disrobed. He stepped into the sarcophagus and lay within, floating on the water as he slid the stone lid in place to seal him in. Several air holes lined the side of the sarcophagus just above the water line.

In complete darkness, he moved himself into a trance like state to begin the Restoration. The sarcophagus was a sensory deprivation chamber that allowed him to make the transition into the Restoration cycle. The timing could take as little as a week, sometimes two, depending on the depth of restoration. He will be at his most vulnerable, thus his need for the Shaolin monks. They would protect him while he completed the cycle. Two squads would stand guard; for twelve-hour shifts they would not let anyone in except their relief shift, and then only after the code word was given. Once long ago Tiangou, the Shaolin name for Shape-shifters; tried to gain entry to this temple. One Tiangou was careless in omitting a scar upon the face of a monk it had taken the shape of which revealed them and their malicious intent. That attack had led to eight Shaolin monks dead and four dead Shape-shifters. The Azael, (called Xing Tian in this region) that lead the Tiangou killed six more before it was hacked to pieces.

That had been the only time the Xing Tian and Tiangou had breached the temples walls and that was over 500 years ago. It was during the Ming Dynasty that the Azael looking for a hidden refuge attacked this monastery believing it was poorly defended, yet the skill of the Shaolin monks showed them otherwise. The monks had driven off the enemy but not before they suffered significant losses of their own. Tamlyn himself had come to their aid, for he had been a guest in their main temple near Dengfeng in the Song Shan mountain range, he was with a troop of Shaolin monks that were tracking Tiangou that had devastated several small villages in the region. With his aid they were able to defeat the Azael and their Shape-shifter army.

Tamlyn had befriended several different cultures, some in desperate need of his aid and others for his sanctuary. The Shaolin had been both. The Blood-hunt oath constantly turned him to pursue his enemy, to hunt them relentlessly. The enemy was spread worldwide, every land gave them different names but their goal was always the same: spreading fear and terror wherever they went, building their numbers quietly in the shadows, feeding upon flesh of man and beast alike. Tamlyn was always hunting them, sometimes with aid, sometimes without. Some of his greatest battles against his foe had been with strong allies, the Shaolin monks, the Samurai, the Mongols, the Turks and the Inca; all had fought battles against the Azael and their hordes. Though he was grateful to them all it was the Shaolin monks and the Samurai that he felt the most akin to, for they were so much like the Warrior Guild on his Home-world. That had been his life in-between following the soul of Cailean. Not always was Cailean's soul reborn immediately after his death, sometimes it took days, months, or even years before being born into the world again.

While he was in Restoration all thought would be set aside: his mind would remain completely focused to the absorption of energy, filling his spiritual cup to over the brim. This would be the deepest restoration he would ever undergo in order to prepare for what was to come. There was no essence of time within this state; his body would awake once it could hold no more. Lying still, floating in the blackness, his heart rate and breathing lowered to almost nothing, similar to hibernation. When he emerged he would be stronger, faster, his senses sharper, his mind heightened, all his abilities would be enhanced. It would mean leaving Morgan alone and vulnerable but it was a gamble Tamyln had to take. If Tamlyn could successfully complete a full Restoration, the benefits would greatly outweigh the risks

†††††

Tamlyn's normal heart rate and breathing slowly returned, bringing him back to a conscious level as he could feel the Restoration nearing completion. When he was ready he slid the stone cover down so he could ease himself out of the sarcophagus. He stood within the darkness of the room, his eyes adapted well in the dark. After toweling himself off, he dressed and replaced his swords upon his shoulder harness. Taking a deep breath Tamlyn pressed the hidden lever opening the doorway to the lit chamber with his twenty Shaolin monks. They escorted him upward to the main temple grounds, where he was seated by a small pond of koi fish swimming tranquilly within.

Zhi came up to him with a warm smile, followed by young monks with food, rice, steamed vegetables and fruit, for Tamlyn was famished as he was with all completed Restorations. He ate quietly while Zhi sat beside him.

"How long was it?" Tamlyn asked when he was finished all the food.

"Thirteen days. It has been quiet here, nothing unusual or out of the ordinary," Zhi answered, smiling at the Elf and Tamlyn nodded. He was happy that there had been no move against him or the temple.

"What of the outside world; have our contacts come up with any viable information on our enemy?"

Zhi looked a little worried and puzzled. "Some little things, but it may be nothing; best for you to decide on your own. Unofficial reports are indicating several different thefts at different military bases around the world, mostly high-powered explosives. All went unnoticed by the military at first; security footage only shows power outages for short durations, no more than a few minutes. It was the same at each facility, with no sign of break in. Each believe it was what they say 'an inside-job'. Chinese, Russians, Americans, Israelis, British, Iran, North Korea, India and Pakistan all seem to be aware of their own thefts and not of the others. Obviously they do not want each other to know of the thefts."

Tamlyn took it all in. "It could be the Azael, they still can use gateways, just not across any great distances, a hundred miles at best. The power outages could be caused by the discharge from the gateways opening. I wonder what they are planning, for this seems highly unusual for them. They normally distrust weapons of men; they like to be very personal with their victims. We cannot afford to be wrong here. As you say Zhi, it may be nothing but I need to find them and discover what they are planning once and for all."

Tamlyn hugged Zhi in parting. "Thank you my friend, for all that you have done. It is my hope that in the days to come I can discover the enemies plans and what, if anything, they have done to Morgan. If they have some sort of agenda, perhaps we will learn of it in time to thwart it. But to that end I must find them, and I know a good place to start," Tamlyn said, his face held strong with determination. Here he would embark on a journey that would see the end of his enemy, or of himself. It was the legacy of the Blood-hunt, always demanding, never relenting. It would press him to completion whatever the cost.

"Good journey my friend. May you find the peace you worked so hard for, for all of our sakes," Zhi said with a bow. His eyes reflected an inner sadness, for he knew that should the Elf fail it would mean Tamlyn's death. Even if successful, Tamlyn would have no further need to stay on this world. Zhi could see it always in the eyes of the Elf, the longing for home. Zhi knew this was the last time he would see Tamlyn, for that the friendship of such a being was beyond words to the old Abbot.

The Elf bowed in return. He stepped away to the open pathway and gathered his will, opening the portal beside him. Zhi could see that it was nighttime on the other side, of gentle rolling slopes and water in the distance, with one last look and a smile of reassurance Tamlyn stepped through and closed the portal behind him. Zhi watched on with wonder, as the goose bumps reseeded upon his flesh,

"Good luck my friend," he said and he prayed.

CHAPTER EIGHT

The Spear

TAMLYN STEPPED INTO the dimness of the Scottish Highlands. He was back in the hills just northwest of the town of Lochcarron. It was not quite midnight, dark but not too dark on a summer night this far north. The ground felt familiar, as did the taste on the wind. He walked down towards the village, the lapping waves–growing louder the closer he got to the loch. It all brought a sense of coming about in full circle. Here his quest had led him to these gentle hills–the richness and the beauty over awed the darkness, violence and death that had once tarnished this serene landscape. He passed the stony outcrop of Cailean's keep, a few boulders and stones grown over with grass and moss. Nothing much was left of that stalwart keep that once housed great heroes, their love, their laughter and their sorrows upon this rocky ground. All that Tamlyn could see now was the lights in windows of houses that lined the shores, perhaps holding descendants of those proud clansmen that Tamlyn felt so honored to have fought beside.

He walked further south, towards the loch and its sandy beach. Here was where Cailean fought a battle of wills against the vile Kelpie. Here they captured it and here Cailean slew it with the Azael spear. Tamlyn's mind drifted back to that day, to the Kelpie's screams filling the air along with the smell of its burning flesh. The sun would have killed it but it would have been long in the dying. Cailean, acting more out pity than his burning desire for vengeance, had taken up the evil Dulachan's spear with Tamlyn at his side.

"You said no earthly metal could harm this beast?" he asked the Elf, the pain showed in his dark eyes; he held up the dark weapon. "This black blade, vile to the touch, cruel and truly evil in its making perhaps shall know goodness in mercy!" he thrust with all his strength into the chest of the Kelpie. The black blade bit deep and hot red blood ushered out of the wound, igniting into flames as it came in contact with the sunlight. Vengeance had been met. Nevertheless, the pain had endured for some time, Tamlyn saw it long after residing within Cailean whenever he thought of his brother. For days after the Kelpie slowly burned to ash, all traces eventually carried away upon the wind. In the early hours of the morning Tamlyn took up the black spearhead, the shaft had burned along with the Kelpie but the vile blade remained. It was the spearhead that he needed and had come across the world to retrieve.

His feet took him further away from the town to a gentle hillside overlooking the loch. Time had since vanished all traces of two grave markers: Cailean's brother and foster brother, but only one grave held ancient bones for Anselan's body had never been recovered, he had been another victim of the deadly Kelpie. Only the remains of Ian MacKenzie, his foster brother could still be felt below the soil and the preserving peat. Tamlyn had never met Ian but wished he had. He had been a true and loyal friend, a valiant fighter and a bit of a character. Cailean, along with Drostan, Coll, Tynan and Kyle would regale the Elf with tales of Ian's exploits when filled with drink. He saw in their eyes the love these men bore for him and the pain of his loss in their voices when speaking of him.

Tamlyn stood before the grave as he gave greeting, his fingers gently touching his bowing forehead then presented his hand before him palm open. "Hail Ian MacKenzie and well met," he stood silent for a few moments out of respect. "You will forgive me for disturbing the grave beside that you have protected all these years, but I come for something I left long ago." Under the soil Tamlyn dug and pulled forth the Black Spearhead. Although encrusted with dirt, Tamlyn knew the blade, when cleaned would look like it had just been buried. The metal that it was forged with would not have eroded like any earthly metal. Evil it was and still it reflected that essence, for captured within was a Dark Elemental. A vile spirit that fed only upon death and pain, the Elemental still rippled in shades of black and radiated coldness and despair. Tamlyn wrapped up the blade with a protective cloth; its emanations would not affect him but its evil sharpness would try its best to cut him. The poison within the Elemental would not be strong enough to kill him, but it would surely incapacitate him for some time. He took to his feet, looking back towards the land he had lived in for many years, a land and people that gave him refuge, showed the upmost kindness and every courtesy: he never lacked for anything within this tiny corner of the world. He was very glad to have called this place home for a time and saddened at his leaving. Knowing that no one was near, he opened a portal, this time it was back to his apartment and to Morgan.

Stepping through the portal to the front foyer of his home, his warning senses went into overdrive. Quietly he placed the spearhead upon the bureau facing his front door. Drawing his two swords from their scabbards upon his back he moved as stealthy as a hunting cat. He stepped silently down the hallway past his kitchen and saw nothing there. Tamlyn turned to his right and saw the French doors to his study were open. He heard crashing and things being overturned; he stepped in, swords held ready. Two Azael were ransacking the study, one going through his desk and the other had opened the hidden room behind the bookcase it held Cailean's sword. Its scabbard discarded upon the floor, the Azael was studying the edge of the blade–Tamlyn's heightened senses could see the tiny red shards reflect off the dim light. The Azael saw him and as one they drew their weapons, but so soon after a full and deep Restoration he moved far quicker than they thought possible. The one that had Cailean's sword threw it at him, yet Tamlyn's speed surprised it. Ducking under the thrown sword, his swords moved in quickly, slicing off the throwing arm and cut clean through the torso before it had a chance to defend itself. The other was on him before its companion hit the floor; swords clashed with tremendous force, blades moving with eye wrenching speed. Tamlyn forced the Azael backwards, its downed companion's severed arm had sensed something near, sliced the Achilles tendon of its partner instantly causing, its leg to go out from underneath it. Tamlyn's blade removed both sword arms then its remaining good leg just below the knee. His foes were defeated, although their thrashing limbs still sought anything within reach.

Tamlyn opened another portal, this time the terrible heat from Kilauea's lava lake was akin to a blast furnace; he tossed limbs and torsos, a small rug and a couple of towels soaked in blood with the Azael's weapons into the molten magma and quickly closed the portal. He scanned his study, looking for anything that they may have been after but there was nothing here that they could want. He walked over and picked up Cailean's sword. Long he stared at the ancient blade, his eyes scrutinized every inch of the old sword; the red crystal shards were tiny, almost undetectable to the human eye.

'What were you seeking upon this blade?' Tamlyn delved the tiny crystals, residual traces within the shards. He looked at this from the Azael's perspective. He cast forth his magic upon the crystal shards, and what he felt surprised him: amid these tiny fragments, the last few moments of their existence played out before him. It was over seven hundred and fifty years ago, but they held onto the moment of their destruction: perfectly clear for one who knew how to read them. It could be the Azael needed to know what had happened upon their

Home-world, to perhaps, understand why they could no longer travel across the stars and to know why they were trapped upon this world. It had been a terrible dread since the very day he came to this world that the Azael and their foul brethren would feed upon humankind, replenish their vast numbers and go back to his world to finish what they started. Tamlyn knew his race was slow in reproducing; having offspring for immortals was not often necessary. The population was diverse enough to not overwhelm the planets resources; for a world that was somewhat larger than the earth a population under a million lived in harmony with nature. The war with the Azael had most likely reduced that number by more than half. Given time, the Azael would have more than enough numbers and totally overwhelm his Home-world.

That was not Tamlyn's immediate concern, for here and now it worried him that they found his domicile; he had always been careful to hide his presence from the enemy. They had to have found a way to trace him, and been confident that two Azael would be enough to defeat him. Tamlyn stirred it around in his head; perhaps it was by accident they found him. He had gone to great measures to hide from their unique senses, but Morgan had no such protection. If they had traced Morgan's steps, it would explain why the Azael had found him. That snapped his attention back to his true task. He found his phone upon the floor and dialed Morgan's phone number. On the second ring Marina answered.

"Hello?"

"Hello Marina, its Tom. How is Morgan? How is he coming with the medication and the seizures?" he asked and she started to laugh.

"I'm sorry Tom. Um it's a long story, the short of it is the medication has not helped but it has provided wonderful hallucinations and a great source of comic relief for a good long time," she said.

"I see. Would it be ok for me to pop over in a while?" he asked, feeling that perhaps some of these hallucinations may not be so drug induced until he heard more about them.

"No problem Tom. We are home safely locked up, Morgan has been Zombie proofing the house," she replied jokingly.

"OK that's good to hear. Will see you shortly then," he said, and he noticed flashing lights outside. Tamlyn quickly went to his window; two police cruisers pulled up to his front entrance, he could see them rushing out to his front lobby entrance.

"Damn the alarm!" He cursed after running to his front foyer. He turned off his alarm, then picked up the spear head carefully, taking it back to the study and placed it into the room behind the bookcase, moving books off the floor so he could close it again as he heard the knocking upon his door. He called forth his magic to take on the illusion of Tom Fletcher once more. He rushed to the doorway and heard keys being used to open his door. Tamlyn opened it first to the surprise of his superintendent Mr. Franklin, along with four police officers.

"Mr. Fletcher, oh thank goodness it's you, your alarm went off and I feared a break in!" Tamlyn smiled and allowed them all to come in. It was standard procedure in case of a potential hostage situation for the police to enter and check the unit.

"Well as for a break in it truly was, but I was able to fight off the intruder," Tamlyn said with a smile that piqued the police officers curiosity.

Tamlyn could not hide the mess in the study. "It was my fault entirely. I left the window open slightly, but it was enough to let a raccoon work his way in. When I came home, I heard a crashing sound from inside and fearing a break in, I didn't turn off the alarm. With my baseball bat I managed to surprise him and chase him out of my study and back out the window he came in, but not before he had some fun in my loft," he said. Raccoons had been responsible for similar occurrences.

The officers laughed at the situation but they did still check through the unit. "Well it's all clear. Looks like you have quite a mess there to clean up, nasty critters those raccoons. You got off lucky, normally they would destroy a room like that, and with the merchandise you have in there it would be expensive, I'd say," the officer said with a polite nod. "Have a good night Mr. Fletcher," he said and they left with the superintendent.

Tamlyn locked the door behind them and went back to the study. Picking up the contents of his desk from the floor, he set about putting things back in order. The rest of the room he stood looking at then decided to get to it later; Morgan was far more important. He walked out of the study, closing the French-doors behind him. He picked up his car keys, reset the alarm, locked his unit door and headed to his car.

The drive to Morgan and Marina's house was quick, and as he pulled into the driveway, figuring out with a smile how to circumnavigate Morgan's zombie security measures. He rang the doorbell and Marina answered the door; she looked happy to see him, but he instantly saw tiredness reflected in her eyes.

"Hi Tom, glad you could stop in. Morgan is resting; another seizure knocked him out for a while."

Tamlyn nodded. "They are not getting better with the medication I take it from our talk on the phone?"

"No, they haven't stopped in frequency. He is off the medication as of today, and he had a good conversation with an elephant in his office while barricading himself in there because of all the zombies," Marina said with a slight grin that didn't fool Tamlyn. She was worried but she was trying to bury it in the craziness of the episode.

"What about the headaches, have they gone away?" he asked and could tell right away by her face that she was just as concerned about the headaches as the seizures.

"No, the headaches seem to be getting worse from what Morgan says. His doctor is pulling some strings to get him into a specialist as soon as they can. Morgan is on the strongest medication for headaches right now, there is not much more they can do other than morphine. When he has a seizure it seems to be like a computer reset; he comes out of it tired and confused but he seems fine for a little while before the headache comes back. I'm worried Tom. Dr. Brennan says Morgan's condition seems out of the ordinary, especially with all the test results coming back negative. I just don't know what I would do if I lose him, I…" Marina could not finish, and Tamlyn hugged her.

"Hey not to worry. Morgan will pull through, I promise," he said with an encouraging smile. She nodded with hope in his promise and the sincerity in his eyes.

"Come on in, Morgan's crashed on the family room sofa. Would you like some coffee?"

Tamlyn smiled. "Yes please, thank you very kindly."

"Sure no problem, I was making some for myself anyway," Marina answered him as she led the way into the family room and kitchen area. Morgan was sleeping soundly with a baseball bat still locked into his secure embrace.

Tamlyn looked upon him. "Is it safe to come close?" Tamlyn asked jokingly.

"I don't know, just don't stand to close when you wake him," she warned.

"Will keep that in mind," Tamlyn said with a grin. He nudged Morgan awake and sent a peaceful, healing energy into his comatose friend. "Morgan, hey, it's me Tom, are you in there?"

Morgan stirred as one eye opened lazily, seemingly in trying to figure out where he was. "Heeeyyy buddy, what's going on?" Morgan asked sleepily and realizing with some confusion that he was sleeping with a baseball bat.

"Here let me take that," Tamlyn said as he took the bat from Morgan's grip. "I'll put that with the rest of your zombie assault kit," he said jokingly while Morgan only looked at him even more confused.

"Oh no way, I thought that was some freaky-ass dream. Marina?"

"Yes babe? Here is your coffee Tom," she said, trying very hard not to laugh.

"Jim and Rob? They were in it too… they walked us to the car?" he said trying to grasp what had unfolded at the office as Marina nodded with everything he said. "Oh no! That was real? Those two clowns will never let me forget this, and the elephant? This just sucks, it really does. For the rest of my life I'm going to get elephant and zombie jokes," Morgan groaned as both Marina and Tamlyn just smiled at him.

After a few hours Morgan was nodding off again and Tamlyn decided he should let his friend get some much-needed rest. "I should be getting back home, let me know how he does at the doctor's appointment tomorrow," he said as he shook Morgan's shoulder comfortingly, sending more healing energy through that brief contact. He hugged Marina.

"We will," she said still in his embrace and followed him to the door. Tamlyn climbed behind the wheel of his Porsche, he cast out his senses, seeking for any trace of the enemy yet there was nothing to find. Satisfied he started the car and headed for home.

Once home he went into his study and retrieved the Spearhead. Bringing it into the living room, he placed it upon the coffee table and undid its cloth wrappings. Lighting some incense, he sat on the floor in front of it, his legs crossed; and started into a song of power. The black rippling of the spearhead intensified; a battle of wills with an ancient Dark Elemental as Tamlyn sought to pull out the Elemental from the spearhead. For thousands of years the evil Spirit was magically bound within that blade. Savoring death and pain, feeding upon it and poisoning those who possessed the blade, only the Azael were immune to its power.

Tamlyn's strength was formidable and he overcame the Elemental's will. The blackness of the blade left the spearhead as a black mist and hovered in the air above it, trapped in Tamlyn's power. Tamlyn forced it to reveal the hiding places of the Azael, for though the Azael had not touched it in centuries, the Dark Elemental was always inextricably bound to its masters. Their contest of wills had lasted through the night. Satisfied that he had obtained all that he could from the horrid entity he transferred it back into the blade. Tamlyn carefully wrapped it up again and placed back on the shelf behind the bookcase in his study.

Tamlyn went into the kitchen to open a bottle of red wine and poured himself a goodly amount. He enjoyed the bouquet before taking a sip, and savored its taste. The sun was just about to break in dawn's early light. He watched the sun crest upon the horizon in the distant east, letting its nourishing rays fill his soul with light and stir the burning powers within. The Azael had hidden themselves deep underground in their hives, thousands of them, in four major concentrations. They were indeed gearing themselves up for a major attack against this world, and if successful it would be devastating to the race of men

The dark Elemental had shown Tamlyn what they were planning, the thefts of the munitions was indeed the work of the Azael. They were preparing to attack multiple targets worldwide. Their goal was to destroy major power plants and power distribution centers all over the world, plunging this planet into darkness, then allow the chaos to unfold. Communications would be disrupted; emergency response teams would be over extended to a point of uselessness. Food in major cities would quickly run out, mass riots of hungry people would roam the streets and in the night the Azael and their brethren would feed upon humankind with impunity. Fear and terror would add to the chaos, it would be a massacre. Humankind is so dependent upon communications and electrical power that without it they would inevitably turn upon each other, governments would try to hold on with their military but the masses would outnumber them tremendously. Soldiers would abandon posts to protect family and loved ones. Every night Azael would be stalking their prey, claiming their gory trophies and packs of Shape-shifters would take on their most terrifying forms to hunt humankind. The race of man would be returned to the dark-ages and no longer at the top of the food chain.

Tamlyn stood staring into the sun, his eyes unaffected by its light; for creatures of fire, its radiance was everything. He wondered if in the chaos of the Azael, humankind could survive and adapt. He found the race of men resourceful and in times of conflict they have endured and grown. He almost laughed at the thought for all of mankind's accomplishments, their dependence on technology may well be their undoing. He thought that the men of Cailean's time would be better suited to deal with this threat than men of today. He finished his wine, holding the empty glass against his thigh; he had to formulate a plan before the Azael executed their strike. He was one lone warrior against thousands of Azael deep underground, in what appeared to be old abandoned mines. The stolen munitions stockpiled with them, enough to obliterate all the nuclear, coal, natural gas, solar, wind power plants and power transfer stations all over the world.

Moving into the kitchen he poured himself another glass, placing the stopper into the bottle he smiled, and took another sip as his plan laid out in his mind.

CHAPTER NINE

The Weapons Deal

T AMLYN FINISHED HIS wine as he formulated his plan. It was rather simple in design, but those were always the best. He had to investigate what type of mines these were and logged into his laptop on his kitchen island. Tamlyn knew the location of the Azael's underground hideaways courtesy of the Elemental, and with geographical research on the type of mine he was confident in his plan. Situated in Tennessee, Ukraine, England and Japan, all confirmed abandoned coalmines. Tamlyn smiled; for once luck was with him. He knew of coal mine disasters of the past, accidental explosions had caused veins of coal to burn for years underground. If his timing was right he could catch the Azael off guard, destroy their plans and wipe out thousands of these demons.

He needed to get his hands on some powerful explosives; C4 would fit the bill, lots of it. He knew just the man to help him out with that little problem. Tamlyn logged off his laptop and went up the stairs into the bedroom and into the master bath. There was a hidden switch above the top of the medicine cabinet; pressing it opened the cabinet fully to expose a hidden wall safe. He dialed the combination and opened the door, revealing a good quantity of world currency. Tamlyn selected several bundles of cash and felt he had more than enough. He re-locked the safe and closed the cabinet.

Tamlyn headed back downstairs, he went into the study and pulled out an envelope from his desk and placed the cash inside. With the travel crystal firmly in his hand he opened a gateway. Across the world he traveled to early evening in a remote village in northern Iraq.

It was a cool night with a beautiful glowing moon shining over an arid landscape. The lights from the village gave off a warm glow as Tamlyn casually walked towards it. He navigated the little warren of twisted streets and alleyways to his destination. The door opened to his friendly knock, a small man's bearded face lit up with a big smile when he saw who it was.

"Tamlyn my friend! Welcome to my home," he said, taking Tamlyn's hand in greeting.

"Thank you Ahmed, I am sorry for disturbing you," Tamlyn said as he ducked down entering through the doorway. He was immediately swarmed over by Ahmed's five children all shouting his name in excitement.

"You are always welcome here, always my friend," Ahmed said, his face booming with pride. Tamlyn used his true appearance here as he did with his friend Zhi. It was far better to be himself, within these walls, trust went a long way to get what you need and live to walk away.

"Tamlyn show us some magic! Yes please magic Tamlyn. Please! Please!" came from the kids' happy faces. Tamlyn could not help but smile and five glowing bulbs appeared before each child, hovering in front of their faces. One child touched it as it bounced in midair; the balls moved with each child forward or backward. The youngest one took off running as the ball chased after him. Another went to reach for hers as it deftly evaded her grab and she laughed; while another took hold of his and threw it at the youngest girl, but it stopped short of hitting her and bounced off the ball she had. They all took off all over the house laughing as the glowing bulbs chased them joyfully around. Ahmed bowed to Tamlyn in appreciation.

"Not to worry, the orbs will not hurt them and as each one falls asleep tonight it will dissipate."

Ahmed laughed. "I was never worried my friend," he held out his hand for Tamlyn to follow him through the house, through the enticing smells coming from the kitchen. Ahmed's wife saw them and smiled.

"I thought that you were here. Those glowing balls worried me for a moment, I thought we had a Djinn lose in the house," she said with a warm laugh that illuminated her beautiful face.

"The orbs will keep them quite occupied Fatima," Tamlyn said with a grin.

"Then I thank you so very kindly. Perhaps they will tire them out and I may be able to sleep in tomorrow," she said hopefully.

"For you Fatima I hope so," Tamlyn said with a slight bow of his head.

"Would you like some tea?"

"Yes please that would be most kind," Tamlyn replied. Ahmed led him farther into the house and behind a stout door, into a large storeroom. It was well lit and filled with floor to ceiling shelves of weapons: guns of all sorts, RPG's, grenades, mortars, and explosives of every kind. Working on a large table, three of Ahmed's brothers called in greeting. Tamlyn bowed his head in return as they went back to work cleaning and repairing assault rifles and machine guns, the family business.

"So my friend how can I help you?" Ahmed asked as Fatima came in carrying a tray of tea.

"I need about forty pounds of C4 and four timers," Tamlyn said, watching Ahmed's brows tighten up in curiosity.

"Forty pounds, I have twenty here," he replied, going over his supply in his head. "Ali, go to Darwish. See him directly, I need twenty pounds of C4," he asked his brother, who jumped up at the request and left to see his neighbor.

"I have the timers here. This is strange you are asking for this. Have you found the enemy my friend?" Ahmed asked.

Tamlyn inclined his head and sipped some of his tea. "I have traced the enemy, deep underground they are hiding, thousands of them, but they have not been idle. They are planning a massive strike against the race of men."

Ahmed shuddered as he took his seat at the table, piecing it together in his head. "The military thefts, it is they that are behind it then?" he said slowly. Tamlyn nodded, and Ahmed went on. "You are aware of this already my friend? The enemy has taken much, enough to cause terrible damage. Do you know what they are planning?"

Tamlyn stepped closer to him. "They will plunge your planet into darkness. They are going to destroy power plants all over the world." Ahmed absorbed what he just heard, thinking it through.

"This will be very bad for the cities. In less than a week most will run out of food and water, riots will take over; men will turn on each other. They will then head to the smaller villages, taking everything. It will be chaos," Ahmed said, his fear became clear for him and for his family.

"That is not the half of it. In the night terror will run free, the demons will openly hunt men. No longer will they skulk in the shadows hiding their actions, they will actively hunt humankind. It will be a massacre, a virtual Hell on earth." Ahmed and his brothers stared in horror as they understood fully what that future would be like.

"We cannot let this happen. Anything you need I will give you; men, weapons anything you need." Tamlyn bowed his head in appreciation.

"I need only the timers and the C4, the rest I can do far better on my own," he replied as he took out the envelope of currency.

"No my friend I cannot take this. It would bring me much dishonor," his face reflected that dishonor.

"Then take it for the children, the poor perhaps. The money means nothing to me; see that it does some good," Tamlyn replied, and smiled warmly.

Ahmed finally nodded. "It will go to the poor to help in whatever they need. You my friend, you are truly God's angel on earth."

Tamlyn laughed. "Those are some very big boots to fill." It was then Ali came in with the other twenty pounds of C4 as one would be carrying in groceries from the corner market. Ahmed put it all together for him, the forty pounds of C4, detonators, and timers he assembled into four ten pound units, showing Tamlyn how to set them.

"Are you sure you do not need any help? I can come with you. Surely two of us would be better for this?" Ahmed asked, wanting so much to help. Tamlyn only gave him a warm smile and a comforting squeeze upon his shoulder.

"You are one alone against thousands. You have fought for the race of men for centuries, a hero, a true champion, I thank you from the bottom of my heart," Ahmed said.

Tamlyn shook his head. "It is not I you should thank, for my contribution but pales in comparison to the true hero of this world. A long dead Scotsman heroically destroyed the heart of the enemy, tore down their ancient machinery, and stole their ability to travel across the heavens. If not for him the race of men would not be as it is," Tamlyn said and Ahmed smiled.

"Then I shall pray to the soul of this Scotsman, the 'true hero' then, to give you and all of us the courage to defeat this terrible enemy," he said.

Tamlyn bowed his head and departed, walking out into the night. His thoughts lingered again upon Cailean, the Highland Chief of MacKenzie. Cailean, the *true hero,* who had played the most crucial role in all of this so long ago, it all started with him.

CHAPTER TEN

Cailean

SCOTLAND 1263

I T WAS AN exceptionally hot morning in mid-July on the shores of Loch Carron. Cailean Mackenzie was walking the sandy shores with a giggling toddler on his shoulders, his little hands over his father's eyes. Cailean feigned blindness as he twisted around and around and went splashing knee deep into the cool sea, making the toddler laugh even harder. Cailean roared merrily in his predicament, lifting up the child off his shoulders and twirled his son around so that his feet and legs splashed into the water. The child screamed in delight as Cailean tossed him in the air only to catch him in the last instant before landing in the water. The High Chief of MacKenzie was truly as happy as any father could be.

His lands and his people had seen relatively peaceful times; the Norse raiders had diverted their attentions to easier coasts. Even though they brought unruly Iceland finally under the Norwegian crown, they had stayed far away from MacKenzie lands. England in the south was in civil war. King Henry and his son Prince Edward were on the losing end against Simon de Montfort and the Barons of England. Even Ireland had seen its share of conflict as the Irish had recently risen up in arms under Brian O'Neill, High King of

Ireland against the Anglo-Norman lords. The battle that took place was Irish against Irish for very few Anglo Normans took part; their army made up entirely of Irish clans and mercenaries. They fought the King's forces at Druim Dearg where Brian O'Neill was slain, his short rein over. Ireland was for now ruled by the Normans, as they were themselves ruled from England.

Closer to home Scotland was in peace; young King Alexander twenty-two years of age, now ruled the kingdom without the need of powerful regents. One of his first moves was deciding to finish what his father had started in reclaiming the Hebrides. Cailean and his clan had led some local campaigns against the Norsemen in Skye and King Alexander had launched assaults on Norse held territories in the Western Isles. It would be sooner than later that Haakon, King of Norway would act for there was more than one rumor floating about that the Norwegian King was to assemble his fleet of dragon ships against Scotland. Alexander had tried to buy the Hebrides from Norway, as did his father yet the Norwegian King refused them both. For Cailean, that was up to Kings to decide. He would play his part when called upon; he and his clan were ready against all things.

Even now, the attacks from the Dulachan (the Azael as Tamlyn called them) and the rest of their foul brethren were reported of less and less in his lands. This brought great relief to Cailean for his nightmares had finally started to fade from his dreams. The memory still stayed strong in his mind even as the creatures from that hellish place had almost disappeared from his lands. Tamlyn's own personal mission to wipe them out was an obsession. Cailean often felt he left a part of himself on that awful world; it was a feeling he could never truly shake.

Those creatures had taken so much from him his brothers Anselan and Ian, and too many of his friends. The battle near Achnashellach had been disastrous, hailed as a victory for he had retained the field, the evil fiends fled once they realized they could not get back to their home world. The memory of it was still frightening to recall. Cailean remembered Tamlyn helping him to his feet after jumping through the portal, back home to Scotland from that dark world. All around him was death and ruin. His sword was glowing a deep red, as if straight from the forge. And then strangely Tamlyn had turned back towards the portal, trying to get back through.

"Tamlyn! It's over," Cailean shouted at the Elf Lord. "The magic they used to travel with is destroyed. Forbye there is no reason to go back there, that entire place is shaking apart; trying to go back is foolhardy," he shouted while holding Kerry protectively. Cailean quickly scanned the battlefield. The MacKenzie host had been reinforced by men from Achnashellach who had come to their aid, yet still they were outnumbered. Ross clansmen, William the Earl and his wife and a few Comyn Knights had formed a small box around the women. Of that proud host perhaps only a thousand remained, most wounded, as all around the Black Dogs and Bogils, Fuathan and Fachan, along with Dulachan hemmed them in.

The battlefield was littered with the dead and dying, all being savagely devoured by the foul beasts as the survivors could only watch in horror at the ghastly feast. They had to close their eyes and their hearts to the screams of the wounded that filled the glens. Black Dogs darted in upon the survivors, dragging out anyone that was within their reach kicking and screaming as they ate them alive; the others could only watch and wait their turn.

All of this Cailean watched in stark horror, as his small party fought their way to the ring of survivors. The Dulachan were certain of their victory, but suddenly stopped in their tracks. They stared into the heavens and screamed in terrible unison as they realized their world was destroyed. Their brethren stopped their gory feasting in fear and confusion, watching the Dulachan abandoning the field. They too bolted into the fastness of the glens, leaving the living staring at the carnage in total confusion at their sudden turn of events, worried that at any moment the evil creatures would return. With his beloved wife in his arms, Cailean watched the fleeing enemy, then looking to Tamlyn who simply nodded that what Cailean's eyes were showing him was true. The enemy was done on this field. He kissed Kerry upon her forehead.

"It's over," he whispered, then he said again, louder. "It's over!" he shouted and again even louder for all to hear. "It's over! They are fleeing! We have destroyed their home world. No longer can they travel back and forth from that evil place. No more can they bring to our world their armies!" Cailean shouted as the spirits lifted, hope returned.

"Cailean! Cailean!" A woman's voice shouted through the press of survivors.

"Isa? Isabel!" Cailean shouted. His heart lifted as the people opened up for her to get through. Her face and clothes were dirt covered and tears tumbled down her cheeks as she ran into her brother's embrace. Sir Andrew Fraser stoically followed at her side, his armour dented, his proud surcoat was torn and covered in blood, his sword still tight in his hand. He placed his free hand upon Cailean's shoulder in greeting, his face grim but his eyes shone in amazement.

"I was too far away to join you, I am sorry. Isabel... you must understand I had to stay, to protect her," the knight said as Cailean shook his head.

"You did right my good friend, you did right. I would nae have it any other way. Your honor is intact, for that I am truly grateful."

Isabel turned to Kerry. "Ach, I thought we lost you when that terrible Dulachan took you, Cailean chased after... after Jean...." She held her hands to her face and started crying again, reliving the murder of her dearest friend. Kerry comforted her as best she could, yet Isabel could not stop. Cailean felt truly saddened; he had to choose between Jean and his wife. It tore at his soul the look in Jean's face;

the pain of abandonment, the shock and disbelief in her eyes would haunt his soul until his dying days.

It was mirrored in his face as Sir Andrew bore witness to it all. "There was nothing you could do, you could not save both. Going off after Kerry was your only choice. To go through that portal on yer own without a care of what you would have faced on the other side and knowing you had no way to get back…." A look passed between the two warriors. It would have been the same choice he would have made if it had been Isabel who was taken. Andrew would have done the same; his only thought would be to die together.

"What happened there Cailean?" the knight asked yet Cailean shook his head as exhausted as he was he would not relay the tale here.

"Later, my friend. We must see to our wounded to get them ready to travel as best we can to Achnashellach and see to our hurts there," he said. Both Coll and Kyle quickly nodded and shouted out Cailean's orders, while Tynan stayed glued by his side. It was a haunting vision as Cailean took in the grizzly scene around him, blood seemed to be everywhere; flesh torn from bones so unlike any other battlefield he had ever seen. Those that were with him gazed upon the gruesome battlefield; although they survived this nightmare the memory of it would forever mark them.

Though the years had passed, and those creatures were scattered, there was always rumors of them haunting dark roads and forests in the blackest of nights. Once any rumors came this way, Tamlyn was off hunting them down. Cailean always worried when Tamlyn went off on his hunts; for there was some deep need within him to relentlessly pursue those beasts.

Those few years ago seemed like another life, and now, deep in his lands, he was truly happy. His son Conner, almost three, was a testimony to that. The boy was hale and strong, full of energy and totally without fear; Kerry constantly reminded Cailean, he had too much of his father in him.

Cailean and Conner were under careful watch upon the beach. Kerry was nursing their nine-month-old daughter Matilda, a group of ladies sitting with her. The only other male part of this entourage was Tynan, who watched constantly for trouble and his keen eyes caught just that.

"Cailean! Cailean, westwards, approaching fast!" he shouted as specks on the horizon grew into four Dragon ships, heading directly towards the village of Lochcarron. Kerry and her ladies took to their feet in alarm, yet upon the wind that powered those great sails he heard the sweet music of the pipes.

"Friends I'd say, for the Norsemen dinna care for the pipes overmuch," Cailean shouted to ease everyone's fears.

"MacLeod, by the emblem upon their sails," Tynan returned, and Cailean nodded at his friend's assessment.

"Come let us greet them more favorably, before someone in town over-reacts," Cailean said as he again tossed his son upon his shoulders and headed off towards the beachhead of Lochcarron. As the ships drew closer those upon the upper decks became more recognizable.

"Unca Drostan!" little Conner shouted in glee as they waited upon the sandy shores with hundreds of fellow clansmen wary and ready for action, yet the pipes and the recognition of friendly faces put the locals at ease.

"Cailean!" Drostan shouted, his booming voice easily heard over the din. The giant bear of a man jumped into the water as the lead dragon ship drove into the beach along with a few others. Cailean's cousin smiled heartily as he snatched little Conner and launched him high into the air with the lad screaming in delight.

"Ach laddie tis good to see thee," he gave the toddler a smothering hug then lifted him up so that his furry face touched the boy's belly and the big man blew for all he was worth, sending gales of laughter from Conner. Once Conner had finally recovered, he placed the boy upon his shoulder.

"So what brings you here from Applecross in MacLeod ships?" Cailean asked his cousin while taking in some of the others that followed Drostan. One was a face he had not seen for a very long time. He was like Drostan, a big man dressed richly in a Viking tunic with a fur-trimmed cape and a gold belt encircled his waist with gold beaten armbands to match.

"Sweet Jesu, I dinna think you were still alive!" Cailean laughed aloud.

"Aye, still alive and still wi' enough fight in me to piss on Haakon's grave!" the Viking said with a dangerous smile. Paul Sigardsson was well over twice the age of Cailean and then some, yet still he was a man to be feared. He was a full Viking and onetime foster father to both Drostan and Coll in their youth. Drostan and Coll's father, Magnus Magnusson was his cousin who had lorded in Stronoway on the isle of Lewis in the Outer Hebrides. Magnus sided with Earl Skule Bradsson in his attempt to hold the Norwegian crown. Skule lost against Haakon and all of Skule's adherents paid a terrible price. Most were hunted down, cruelly slain as a stark message to all who went against Haakon. Magnus, forewarned, had prudently hidden Drostan and Coll with Paul who had kept them safe in his lands of Rodel. It was not long after that Magnus and his wife Mary, Cailean's aunt were savagely burned alive in their own home. Paul fostered Drostan and Coll and changed their names to MacKenzie to keep them hidden. They were the age of six and five when they were bundled away in the middle of the night, rushed off across the ocean to a grandfather they had never met. Haakon's spies were seeking out rumors that Magnus' sons still lived; Sigardsson secretly brought his entire household with him to Lochcarron. The Lord of Rodel stayed for a year before venturing back to his own lands. Drostan and Coll stayed behind, growing up with Cailean but always knowing their parents were evilly murdered. It was no wonder Drostan and Coll had taken great pleasure in killing any Norsemen who sided with Haakon.

Cailean took the Lord of Rodel's arm in greeting as two other men joined them. Both were dark in coloring, with great down turning mustaches, dark brows, and strong chins. Both men well favored in looks bore a striking resemblance to each other, for indeed both men were the sons of Leod, Tormund and Torquil, chiefs of the MacLeod's of the isles of Harris and Lewis. Having these men here only confirmed Cailean's concern in Haakon of Norway; if they were all here, it meant trouble was coming. Whispers were already spreading, for those of his clan upon the beaches jumped to dire conclusions; Cailean forced a friendly smile to stem their fears and embraced the newcomers in greeting.

Cailean laughed aloud as Kerry fell in beside him. "My Lord of Rodel, tis with great pleasure I introduce my wife Kerry Matheson MacKenzie." Kerry smiled warmly at the big man who instantly withered from a great and ferocious bear to a cuddly puppy; he took her hand gently and brought it to his lips.

"My Lady, tis truly an honor to see the face that sent our greatest hero's after ye to that dark and terrible world. For I too would have followed on after you to Hell and back, I say," Sigardsson said. None there doubted the elder warrior's courage, some said he would proudly go where Angels and hero's fear to tread.

Kerry blushed. "It was enough for those heroes that did go; champion's all. I owe them my life and that of my son's." Paul Sigardsson looked to Conner and ruffled the lad's hair with teary eyes; the warrior was above all an emotional man who heard of the Dulachan's vile feeding habits, knowing all too well the fate that almost befell them.

"Let us move on to my keep for food and refreshment. Kyle, see to their men, make sure that they have all they need. Come My Lords!" Cailean ordered as Kyle his steward saw to the disembarkment of the

Norse and MacLeod's fighting men. Cailean and his party made their way up into his keep into the main hall as he waited patiently for all to be seated and ample food and drink to be served. Two of Kerry's maids took away the children as Kerry remained with the men.

"Where be my other foster son Coll?" Sigardsson asked as he scanned the hall.

"Coll is on his way here. He was in Kintail hunting along with Tamlyn, sniffing out rumors of Demon's still running loose in the Highlands," Cailean said. He often had ventured on those hunts, but lately Kerry insisted that as Chief, he need not always be in the forefront of every confrontation.

Paul looked towards the MacLeod's and added. "We have fought them as well, the Black Dogs, the Shape-shifters, a score of them were feeding in remote areas, eating our people in the black of the night," his eyes were dark with wrath.

"A pack of them spread terror through my lands. I cannot imagine what an army of them would do," Tormund said, who was chief of Macleod's upon the island of Harris.

Paul nodded. "We slew them all, a merry chase they led us; we lost many brave warriors in our hunt yet they trouble our lands no more."

Cailean looked grim, as this was not new to him; reports always came in of the evil doings of these creatures. He knew that as hard as it was to hear, it could have been far worse. Tamlyn had so often pointed out that had Cailean not destroyed the Demons ability to travel across the stars his world would be overrun with these creatures. The destruction he caused allowed the human race a chance to survive otherwise it would be the end for them all. The evil creatures would have spread unchecked, their hunger would wipe out all life upon this world and then on to other worlds to continue their wretched survival. He had hoped that it was not news about these evil creatures that had brought these men here.

"So my friends, what has brought such valiant warriors to Lochcarron?" Cailean asked eagerly to get to the point of this visit.

"Haakon! What else? The bastard has put out the call; he is assembling his fleet as we speak, some say 250 ships others say 300. He wants the Hebrides and he will take them. From there he be joined by Magnus of Man, they will grab the Hebrides and take Ireland from the Normans and then march upon Scotland. With Scotland, Ireland, Man and Norway behind him he will move against England as its lords fight with their King. Haakon sees himself as some Emperor of the North," Paul said, his voice dripping with hate towards the Norwegian King. Cailean took it all in, assessing the facts and realizing what he knew a few years ago: that Haakon would move south.

Now with the true scale of the Norwegian King's plan laid out before him, it all seemed so frightfully clear. Haakon's vision was simple in its design and easy to accomplish, only as long as he was victorious in each step. The Hebrides could not stand against Norway; the MacDonald and the MacDougall, the decedents of mighty Somerled could not hold against such power, even united they would have no chance. Haakon's fleet could overwhelm the entire seaboard; no one upon the coasts would be safe.

"You are sure? The last we had heard is that Alexander was in negotiations with Haakon, to buy back the Hebrides," Cailean said.

Paul snorted in disgust. "Bah, your King may think he can buy the Hebrides, but it is all a ruse to hide that Haakon is assembling his strength. The King of Norway sees resorting to this haggling as a weakness in the Scots and will take back what he thinks is his. He will kill Alexander for what he feels are insults to his retaking the Isles. I come here today to warn you, for he also mentioned that he would destroy the MacKenzie clan for all you have done against his raiders."

Cailean looked to Drostan, whose hate was as strong as his foster father's towards the Norwegian King. Drostan's face enlightened in dreadful eagerness, the anticipation of a confrontation was a dream come true to his bear-like cousin.

"This is a bold move; I have not the strength to withstand Haakon. His captains yes, but not the entire might of Norway. This is far bigger than our corner of the kingdom, we must warn the King. Perhaps Alexander's army and the Hebrides marshaled against Haakon will be enough to stop him," Cailean said, knowing that they still had a chance.

Paul was quick to disagree. "The descendants of Somerled will do nothing, they will stay neutral. I have sounded them out already, they have no choice. To take King Alexander's side would have them open for attack. One by one each island in the Hebrides would fall against Norway. No, they will neither help nor hinder our cause," Paul said and his hand slapped the table hard. "Warning your King will do no good, we must go to him. You, MacKenzie he will listen to. Only you will his cronies let through to have a private ear with the King," the Viking said, laying out what he was truly here for. He would use Cailean's influence to speak with Alexander, it was clear that his earlier attempts had failed. Scotland was Sigardsson's best hope at defeating Haakon. Cailean was the key to his plan in more ways than one, for Cailean spoke both Gaelic and Norman French, which was the dominant tongue at Alexander's court. It is said that Alexander himself had learned Gaelic, yet it was the Scottish nobles, Normans all, that blocked Sigardsson attempts before.

"Cailean, you have fought the Norsemen well enough to be of great value. You know how they think and how to fight against them. Your friend, the Elf Lord, he has great magical powers they say, will he help us?"

Cailean shook his head. "Tamlyn will not fight against the Norsemen or any man unless he has no choice. He is only here to hunt the Creatures. His magic is to be used solely against them. For him to use it here in a conflict of man against man go against his principals nor would I ask it of him, we owe him too much already," Cailean said. Sigardsson looked to Drostan; the look said that they had had the same discussion with the same results.

"I understand his position; it is for only the lives of the innocents that I was considering it. For I have heard he can open portals to anywhere upon this world, we could lead a party of warriors to kill Haakon in his bed and perhaps end this before it begins."

Cailean marveled at the Viking's plan. It was creative, yet perhaps that would work against them fuelling the next King of Norway into swift and deadly action.

"We will go to Alexander, your ships and mine will sail south to the King at Stirling. Now let us feast well and get our rest, for the days ahead will be trying to say the least," Cailean said and with that, Paul Sigardsson had smiled for the Lord of Rodel, this is what he truly wanted, his war with Haakon was here at last.

CHAPTER ELEVEN

The Journey South

L ATER IN THE privacy of their room, Cailean waited for the backlash from his wife. He could tell she was bursting at the seams but perhaps waiting for the right moment or the right words to come to her. Cailean realized it would be far better for him to start before she had finally assembled her thoughts on the matter.

"You know I must go; Paul is right about this," he said as she stopped undressing and sat upon their bed.

"But I dinna have ta like it! I know you must go. I see it as do you, but I like it not a bit. Why is it that when the world needs savin' it's always Cailean MacKenzie that must rally to the call?" her cheeks flashed red in frustration as he knelt in front of her, taking her hands in his own.

"Lass you know I love you with all my heart; to protect you and our wee bairns I must do this. The threat is real, if I do nothing we are all as good as dead. If Haakon wins, we would have nowhere to go, we would never be safe," he moved his hand and caressed her cheek tenderly. "I have to convince the King to assemble his strength. Only Scotland united, north and south, can hope to stop Norway. If we can defeat Haakon it will take the pressure off my lands and bring us peace," he said while a single tear trickled down her cheek; he watched it carefully as it passed her lips to her chin. "I will be back soon I promise," he said. His charming smile and mischief in his eyes forced a smile back into her beautiful face.

"See," he said lifting her chin up gently with his hand. "Forbye, that is why I will be back as soon as I can. That is the smile that will hold up the heavens and nothing on this world or any other will keep me from seeing it again," he kissed her and she returned that kiss with a hunger that turned their insides to fire. Kerry ripped his shirt off in her passion as he pulled her top over her shoulders. Her hands were adept at loosening the belt that held his kilt. Quickly she slid it off his lean muscular frame. Their kissing enriched their drive, eager tongues caressing, fueling desire, each seeking to devour the other.

Cailean made his way down her neck vigorously with hungry lips while caressing hands found sensually pleasing trigger points that further escalated his wife's primal passions. He kept on making his way down to her perfect breasts. There he made sure he pleasured them equally. His lips slowly yet progressively made their way further downwards. Lips pressed tightly against her belly as his hands now caressed her hardened nipples. Kerry moaned with pleasure and anticipation as her husband went down even further. His lips and tongue ventured between her legs and sought to devour her as she pushed his head deeper into her most precious of places. Her moans, her heady aroma and her wonderful wetness spurred him on until she screamed in climax. Convulsing in total ecstasy she shuddered in spasms that only he could provide.

"Oh my love, my love!" Kerry said in a joyous whimper. She pulled him up to kiss him again as he gently pushed himself inside her. A devilish smile smeared upon her face as he slowly built up his momentum until she was climaxing again just as he too burst his seed within her. Both covered in sweat from their pleasure, they resumed their kissing as their passions carried them through the night. Both gave everything for they knew that in the days ahead they would be apart, neither knowing if they would ever see each other again.

They awoke in each other's arms to the hungry calls of seagulls just outside their window. It brought old memories to Cailean, back to when he first rescued Kerry, awaking together in each other's arms for that first time. The seagulls' calls had awoken him then as if to herald in a new chapter in his life. Perhaps now again they were doing the same. So much had happened from then to now that they could scarce believe it was only four years ago. He rubbed his eyes to get the sleep out while trying to suppress a yawn but it did no good. Kerry lay there watching with a loving smile.

"Tired you out did I?" she asked with a sultry laugh.

"Ach aye, you did at that, I know not what came over you," he said with a wink as she reached up for his head and kissed him with the same hunger. "You keep this up and I shall never be able to get outta bed," he added and Kerry finally released him.

"Cailean will you see Isabel, talk to her?" That brought him back to his mission at the King's court in a hurry.

"Isa….Isabel. If she is there I will try."

"Cailean it has been two years since you last spoke with her," Kerry said as sadness touched her voice.

Cailean took her hand and squeezed it. "She could not be at peace in the Highlands anymore. The ghosts of Anselan and of Jean Ross haunted her; she needed to remove herself from those memories. I know not if seeing me will do more harm than good. She is happy with Sir Andrew; I have no wish to bring her further pain," Cailean replied sadly, for the absence of his sister troubled him greatly.

Until now he had not thought of Isabel or the possibility he would visit her while at court. She had become one of the Queen's principal ladies in waiting, being the wife of the Sherriff of Stirling.

"She will wish to see you. It has been long and the memories will have faded enough," Kerry said with encouragement, as she knew how deeply her husband missed his sister.

"Aye, well we shall see. But for the now I must get ready, men and supplies must be gathered. I hope Coll and Tamlyn arrive back soon."

It was the next day that Tamlyn and Coll returned with their warrior's and trackers. It had been a successful hunt. Some two score of Bogils and a Fuathan would trouble the Highlands no more. Coll was thrilled to see his foster father as the two giant men exchanged hugs and greetings.

"God's blood, you and your brother would have made fine raiders. Had I a score of you I would rid my seas of those cowardly pirates!" Paul bellowed as Drostan greeted his brother just as enthusiastically.

"Wi' you both here are we finally getting our war, brother?" Coll asked eagerly and Drostan's face shone with anticipation as he slapped his younger brother jovially upon the shoulder.

"Haakon is coming south, the bastard himself is coming," Drostan returned. Long ago, the brothers had sworn an oath to avenge their parents when fate brought them the opportunity. Content they always were under Cailean's command; their home in the Highlands they would protect most feverishly. Yet given any opportunity to engage Haakon in the field was something entirely different.

Paul Sigardsson's eyes bulged at the introduction of Tamlyn, hearing the tales of this being and now seeing him in the flesh was a different matter altogether. The tall Elf Lord brought his fingers to his forehead then brought his hand down, palm open in greeting.

"An honor to meet you, My Lord of Rodel," Tamlyn said as the Norseman returned Tamlyn's gesture of greeting.

"I know not who to thank, Odin or by Christ for this meeting; truly you are Alfinn from Alfhiem. Our grandfather's spoke of such beings like you and that grace always favored those who were friends to the Alfinn. I could die a happy man for this meeting my Lord Tamlyn, but today I must carry on my fight. I go to war and my foster sons will join me and it shall be glorious," Sigardsson said, his eyes shone with a feverish glow. Coll looked to Cailean his chief for acceptance in joining Sigardsson. The vengeance that he and Drostan sought after was finally before them, yet it was for Cailean to decide.

"We were waiting for you. I will take four fully manned ships, with my lord of Rodel and of the MacLeod's, eight ships in all. We go to the King come morning," Cailean informed them of what Sigardsson had told him about Haakon's plans, and that Scotland needed to rally behind its King to save the country.

They had a busy day and night getting men and supplies fully equipped for the journey south. It was approaching nightfall when they had finished, the skies were clear and the heavens shone with an angelic-like glow.

"Tamlyn, a word please, if you will?" Cailean asked.

The Elf Lord finally broke away from the gaggle of children that followed him. "Off to your homes lest the Black Dogs pick up thy scent." The children looked to each other and took off running at the warning. The Elf smiled at their chaotic departure.

"That was a wee bit cruel was it not? You would give them nightmares, you will!" Cailean said in jest.

"Perhaps. Making them wary will cause no harm; their dreams however are their own," Tamlyn said with a straight face, yet his eyes reflected the humor they shared.

Cailean patted his arm warmly. "I know not to ask that you come with me in what is clearly a conflict between nations. I solely would wish for you to stay here and watch over my family. Kyle stays here with a strong force but he will need your help should enemies call while I am gone. I can feel some ease knowing you are here keeping my family safe," Cailean eagerly requested of him and knew full well what Tamlyn's response would be.

"I will guard them with my life," he said to put the MacKenzie chief at ease. They both walked back to the keep.

"I should be gone perhaps a few weeks at best–then I will return to gather in my power for when Haakon comes south. We will wait to see where he takes his fleet," Cailean advised the Elf Lord who looked intensely upon him, his eyes amber hue cast a wary shade as he saw a glimmer of fear upon Cailean's face.

"When do you think Haakon will come?" Tamlyn asked, his eyes searching Cailean's face.

"It will be weeks yet I say. To bring in that many ships, men and supplies is a vast undertaking. Launching a major campaign will take much planning and preparation." Tamlyn nodded at Cailean's assessment and understood Cailean's fears.

"I do not think that Haakon will strike at your lands, you have said yourself that for his campaign to be successful he needs to win every engagement. If he decides to start against MacKenzie, he will give away his advantage of surprise. You could easily bog down his army until help arrives from your King. This Haakon will probably take an important base in the south along the coast to create safe harbor for his shipping while he recruits allies of the Islesmen and the Irish as he goes. You, my friend, need not worry about your lands and people for on the greater scale of things you are only a minor part of this venture," he said as he grasped Cailean tightly upon his shoulder.

"I thank you my friend, it sets my heart at ease. In the weeks ahead I need my wits about me, I canna do that wi' worry about my wife and the wee bairns," Cailean said as he embraced the Elf warmly in thankfulness.

"You need not thank me I point out what is the most logical direction for the Northland King. I too have a request of thee, one that Kerry is sure to agree with." Cailean looked to him with puzzlement as Tamlyn continued. "You must play the commander and not the soldier in heat of battle. You need not endanger yourself when your wits can suit you far better in directing your men instead of being in the front lines."

Cailean nodded. He had seen more than his share of blood and battle, perhaps it was time to play the general. He had his wife and children to think of. If he fell in battle, what would become of his family? What would befall his clan with him gone? That was what had truly bothered him these last few days.

"I will do what I can, but I make no promises," he said and laughed. "Come, it is to bed for me, for the morning we leave at first light."

††††

First light did not truly come; the gray-black clouds filled the skies, letting no light through its thick canopy. Winds were unfavorable and the seas choppy, yet nothing would deter Paul Sigardsson. Cailean had said his good-byes to Kerry and Conner, Matilda still asleep in her mother's arms oblivious to all. Kerry watched his departure from the keeps battlements, her eyes never left her husband's ship until it could no longer be seen on the horizon. She sent forth hopeful prayers that he would return both safe and sound.

Eight dragon-ships, fully loaded with 1100 men and provisions, sailed westwards out of Loch Carron, around Plockton and into the Inner Sound. The seas did not improve but grew worse as the dark clouds opened upon them and lightning and thunder joined in the chaotic chorus. Cailean could hear Paul Sigardsson laughing on the upper deck of his ship; storms meant nothing to this hardened seafarer.

They travelled in a tight formation: the Lord of Rodel and Cailean's ship leading the way, both Drostan and Coll in command of their own ships, as did the sons of Leod. The seas settled somewhat in the tight confines between the Isle of Skye and the Kyle of Lochalsh then down into the Sound of Sleat. It was hard going–high seas with no sails to aid for the winds were against them. It was all muscle power as crews of rowers switched on and off in shifts to provide the best speed possible.

Tynan scowled constantly. He disliked sea travel and storms did not improve his demeanor. "This storm is a bad omen," he said after a massive wave crossed their bow.

"Speed is essential here. We cannot afford to wait for better weather," Cailean replied while the winds slowly turned in their favor soaring them over the waves with fantastic speed. There was a brief respite in the high seas when the Island of Eigg sheltered them while they passed it on their starboard side, as did the Isle of Muck shortly after. They sailed til late in the day on such terrible open seas that it was with great relief the Isle of Coll appeared as the darkness of night smothered them in its black embrace.

Their ships finally ventured into the sheltered harbor joining scores of ships already beached upon the sandy shores. Tired crews were glad to have their feet on solid ground once again. The inhabitants of Arinagour eyed them warily, but the Chief of MacDonald was there in person to greet them.

Angus MacDonald son of Randal, despite his intimidating appearance of piercing blue eyes, dark swarthy hair and beard greeted them warmly. "My Lord of Rodel, Sons of Leod, and Cailean Fitzgerald MacKenzie, the slayer of Demons, welcome to the Isle of Coll," he said, eyeing them all with a grin. The newcomers were all soaked to their skins and looked the least illustrious. The MacDonalds saw to the crews, providing shelter, heat and food to them all. Their commanders accompanied the Chief of MacDonald to the hall house, where hot food and roaring fires soon brought the warmth back into them.

The isle of Coll was not the principal seat of the MacDonalds that was Islay further to the south. Sigardsson prearranged this meeting weeks ago and gained permission from the MacDonald chief to rest their crews on this journey to the King. The Lord of Rodel would have brought his fleet to Coll even without consent yet he was here with his own mission and the Norseman was not long in stating his demands.

"Now Chief of MacDonald, Cailean is with me, he has promised all his strength, when we go the King can we not tell him MacDonald is with us?"

MacDonald's blue eyes sought out them all, accessing what he could. "My heart says to follow you, but my head says otherwise. I cannot join you, my power is the Isles," he said as he then nodded to Cailean. "You, MacKenzie, can fall back into your lands and that I canna do; Haakon can cut me off from all. Nay even all the sea power of Scotland combined could break through three hundred ships. I am truly sorry."

Cailean understood and sympathized with the MacDonald, but Sigardsson was a different man. "Somerled will be turning in his grave at those words. Should he be here today he would not take that stance!" Paul all but spat in his contempt, yet the chief of MacDonald was not as hotheaded as the Lord of Rodel.

"So you say he would take the side of the Scots and the Normans who had murdered him?" the chief asked levelly.

"It is different times and you know it," the Norsemen countered.

"Perhaps, but I say Somerled would just as likely have let Norway and Scotland fight it out between them. The Isles was an independent nation then, why fight when you don't have to? Now my fleet is but half that of my great-great grandfather. I can assemble perhaps fifty ships, Ewan MacDougall could have the same, perhaps more, yet even he is even less likely to join you. Why fight when I don't have too?"

Paul Sigardsson smiled a dangerous sign. "Because I know Haakon as you do not. He will come to you and treat you warmly like a brother. He will make you add all of your ships to his fleet. He will use your men in the forefront of every battle, keeping his own in reserve. All the while he has you held closely at his side. To all it will be as if you joined him of your own accord, yet you will truly be a prisoner in all but name. Even if he wins you will not see his favor. No, you he will quietly remove and give your lands to one of his cronies. If he loses, he will vent his spleen on you and kill you where you stand. So tell me Chief of MacDonald, is this the King you wish to back?" Paul Sigardsson never lost his smile as he spoke.

"It may be exactly what you say, my Lord of Rodel, but it changes nothing; the Isles will remain neutral in this for as long as I can manage and that is the end of it!"

"Bah! Fools and folly!" Sigardsson roared as he threw his tankard into the fireplace with tremendous force. He charged out of the hall and into the rain back to his ship. Both Drostan and Coll grumbled and were more like to follow but stayed with their cousin.

"Forgive my Lord of Rodel my friend. He has much to hate Haakon for and it has festered long within him," Cailean calmly said.

"There is nothing to forgive, for I take no offence. I know what Sigardsson says is true; I will just have to hope that I can stay out of this war for as long as I can. I know you cannot Cailean; Haakon has named you for one he wishes to bring down. I truly hope you can defeat him, my friend," the Chief of MacDonald said. His tone and his eyes reflected the truth in his words as he saw his own hope in Haakon's downfall.

The next morning the weather was a little better. The rain held off, though the skies were still grey, the seas more calm and the winds in their favor. Their goodbyes were short and both Sigardsson and the MacDonald were glad of it. The small fleet headed directly south past Colonsay and Islay, then round the Mull of Kintyre, up northeasterly past the Isle of Arran and into the Firth of the Clyde. Their destination was the Island of Bute, to Rothesay, home of the High Steward of Scotland. Eight dragon-ships caused quite a stir amongst the general population. Haakon's pirates were always hunting along the coasts. No one was immune to their brand of terror.

Cailean, as always, had his piper playing loud as his ships came into ground upon the beachhead. The people seemed to settle and became less fearful when his men merely stood there instead of rushing overboard with fire and sword in hand. Cailean and Sigardsson waited patiently until a small mounted party from the castle came to meet them.

They were a score of armed men, all richly dressed and armored, household Knights of the Steward to seek the purpose of this visit. The leader bravely approached. He was a somber looking fellow, blonde hair and blue eyes; his face was hard and unkind. He was perhaps in his early thirties, a man of action, one who had seen his share of conflict and seemed almost bored at this encounter. That Cailean knew was but a ruse, he knew this type, a dangerous man; the face would lull you in with its projection of boredom while the mind assessed everything quickly.

"I am Sir Pierce Curry. I greet you on behalf of the Lord High Steward of Scotland. You are not Norsemen, Islesmen I reckon?" he said levelly, almost disinterested.

"Close enough Sir Knight. I am Cailean Fitzgerald MacKenzie, Chief of MacKenzie." The Knight's face reacted to Cailean's name immediately.

"My friends here are Paul Sigardsson Lord of Rodel of Harris, also chiefs of MacLeod, Tormund of Harris, Torquil of Lewis, my own cousins Drostan MacKenzie of Applecross and Coll MacKenzie of Toscaig. We come seeking Alexander Stewart, High Steward of Scotland." Cailean gave the introductions as was previously arranged. The Lord of Rodel believed they would be better received if Cailean spoke for them all in Norman French. The Knight bowed his head politely to them all. Those behind him seemed somewhat relieved that they were not here for a fight against such numbers.

Sir Pierce Curry directly addressed Cailean. "My Lord, I do regret that the Steward is with the King at Stirling, his brother Robert Stewart lords at Rothesay in his stead." Cailean cursed. This may well slow them down; they needed the High Steward to pave the way to the King without raising alarm all the way up the Clyde.

"Our purpose is with the King, we were hoping to have the High Steward escort us there." The knight seemed to calculate quickly the situation.

"To what purpose, may I ask, do you have with the King?" Sir Pierce asked.

The impatience of the Lord of Rodel was wearing thin, he got enough out of the conversation and jumped in full Gaelic. "War fool, we are at war man!" Sigardsson cursed angrily. The Knight's expression did not change, only his eyes narrowed slightly as he indeed understood Gael.

Cailean then spoke on. "Haakon comes and he comes to take all. We need to get to the King quickly; the High Steward could have paved the way for us."

The Knight actually smiled. "My Lords if you will give me but a moment. Myself, and a few more Knights will accompany you up the Clyde. We will see to all your needs and get you to the King," he said as he turned to his men and after a short discussion sent a few men off back into the castle. While they waited, five of their party dismounted to remove saddlebags and weapons from their mounts and fastened them to their persons.

"How much time do we have?" the Knight asked casually as he strapped on his broadsword over his shoulders.

"Weeks yet we believe, he needs time to assemble his fleet," Cailean said as the Knight nodded.

"How many ships?" he asked quickly.

"Perhaps 300, maybe more, maybe less." It was then the Knight truly showed expression.

"That would mean 30 to 40 thousand men!"

"Aye and if he adds Orkney, the Hebrides, Iceland and Ireland into it you will see eighty thousand," Paul Sigardsson added for good measure. The rest of the Knights stopped what they were doing, as they suddenly understood the magnitude of what they were up against.

Sir Pierce simply nodded. The numbers were significant; he knew that the ships could land anywhere on the coasts, mobility was one of their greatest weapons. Landings, however, at the right place and with enough men could be fought off; Cailean himself was testimony to that. It was not long before his men returned from the castle. A large purse passed to Sir Pierce.

"To cover any expenses we may need to get us to Stirling quickly," the Knight explained as he passed his horse to one of his men. "My Lords, we are as ready as can be."

Cailean nodded with a smile. "Then let us depart," he said holding out his hand towards his ship. They all jumped onto Cailean's ship, feeling more at ease with him than the Lord of Rodel. Sir Pierce marveled at the speed, as the oarsmen showed their prowess and the strong winds sped them up the Firth of the Clyde.

All the way they saw the frightened reaction of the common folk at the sight of eight dragon ships. Panic-stricken, they fled inland but the ships kept up their speed and soon they saw Dumbarton Rock in the distance. The ancient fortress was the capital of the kingdom of Strathclyde, long before King MacAlpine united the kingdoms into the nation of Scotland; it even predated the Romans. It was an impressive twin peak mountain, 240 feet high of volcanic rock with the river Clyde to one side and the river Leven on the other.

Sir Pierce directed Cailean where to dock his ships amongst the hundreds of fishing and merchant vessels while the townsfolk fled and soldiers arrived to replace them believing this newly arriving fleet as hostile. A score or more knights approached at the head of about a hundred pike-men. They relaxed as Sir Pierce spoke with them, but the discussion became heated while Sir Pierce was making his demands clear. The Dumbarton group eventually gave way while a few men turned and went into town with purpose. Sir Pierce returned to Cailean's ship.

"I have secured a safe place for your ships and your men; I will leave a few of my Knights here to see to their needs. I will accompany you to Stirling. Mounts are being acquired for us as we speak. I hope you can ride, my Lord?" Sir Pierce asked.

Cailean laughed. "We can, perhaps not as well as you Sir Knight," he said as he turned to Drostan, Coll and Tynan. "Gather your things, for here we ride on to Stirling, tell the others. Sir Pierce will leave a few of his knights behind with our men to keep the peace and see to their needs," he said as Drostan went to advise his foster father and the sons of Leod.

Cailean and Tynan grabbed their belongings and spoke with the crew. "Here we must leave you; it shall not be more than a few days, a week at best. Sir Pierce will leave a few of his knights to see that there is no trouble with the good folk here. Anything you need you can ask of them," he said knowing his men would be on their best behavior. His men he trusted, the town folk he did not.

He rejoined Sir Pierce and the others. Sigardsson brought with him two of his captains, the sons of Leod had also two sub-chiefs each, Cailean only brought his cousins Drostan and Coll, and Tynan. Those sent in town returned with mounts for them, saddled and ready. Sir Pierce and one other knight, Sir Robert Graham, accompanied them. Their party of fifteen took the quickest road out of Dumbarton, eastwards to Stirling.

Sir Pierce may have initially been slightly worried about his charges riding abilities yet he soon realized there was no need of concern. The Highlanders and Islesmen proved adept riders. They traveled at a fast trot to ensure the maximum distance from their mounts. Sir Pierce guided them through the Campsie Fells, a brace of rolling hills and gentle glens, thickly forested in some areas and open in others. It was a peaceful place of small Lochs and water falls.

Nightfall was upon them as they made it to the village of Balfron, just past Endrick water. There they made their way to the manor house of Sir Adam Montgomery and confirmed that King Alexander was indeed at Stirling and not in Edinburg. For that, Cailean was glad; he had no wish to travel across the country and be even farther away from his ships. Grooms took their mounts to be cared for, their belongings they took with them, Sir Adam saw to all his guests needs. He was a gracious host who was a long-time friend of Sir Pierce. Cailean liked him straight away. He had a roguish and somewhat charming smile, his short blonde hair and blue eyes accentuated his good looks; he was of moderate height with a stocky muscular build of a fighter. Sir Adam it seemed was also in some awe of his guests; Cailean's heroic deeds were still talked about in these parts. This town of Balfron had also the misfortune of being a target of the Shape-shifters evil. The Knight was not long in telling the dark tale.

"A pack of them, the Black Dogs stalked our village for an entire summer. Bairns taken from their from their very beds by what seemed like their own parents, only to change into those terrible Black dogs just outside of the town. The wee ones screaming all the way into the forests to be devoured by those awful beasts. We could only find what was left of them come morning and only a few scattered bones did we ever find."

Sir Adam's face paled at the memory of it. "We did manage to kill three of them, a terrible fight it was. Thirty armed men went out, skilled hunters and trackers, along with experienced soldiers. Only half of us came back, and two more died later of their wounds. The bite of a Black Dog can be deadly; it's like a poison spreading through the body affecting the mind of the victim. They go crazy mad, like a rabid dog, we had no choice but to put them out of their misery."

Cailean nodded, but was still curious. "You killed three you said, I am not sure that constitutes a pack?"

"Ach aye, the others escaped westwards, four or five more we believe. They led us into a trap, it was chaos. The beasts were so fast, attacking horses and men; the terrible screams, the fear and confusion in the darkness, we did not pursue them. I am ashamed that we had not your courage, My Lord Cailean."

"Tush man, what you did was courageous, find no fault in that. When we fought them we outnumbered them greatly and because of our continual confrontations we grew less and less in awe of them," Cailean said to tone down his hero status.

"Perhaps my Lord, yet you fought Dulachan, Fachan, Bogils and such. You followed them to their world after your lady, our courage but pales in comparison," Sir Adam pursued. Sir Pierce and Sir Robert said nothing but listened closely while Coll jumped in.

"If your Lady was as beautiful as Cailean's you would have surely followed after, heroes and fools both."

"Ach aye, fools more be-like," Tynan added as Drostan and Sigardsson both laughed.

"Fools eh? Then who is a bigger fool, the fool who went into yon portal or the fools who followed on after?" Cailean asked as Drostan laughed even harder, slapping both Coll and Tynan upon their shoulders. Coll and Tynan's face both darkened noticeably.

"You, Lord Coll and friend Tynan, went to that dark world as well?" Sir Adam inquired on.

"Aye we did. From the chaos of battle through those blasted portals we went to a world black as night. The place reeked of death and decay, the air so thick and heavy we could barely breathe. Everywhere we turned those demons were about us. If nae for the Elf, we would have been surely lost in those dank tunnels. He led us straight to Kerry; surrounded she was and about to be fed upon by the vile Dulachan," Coll said as he turned to pat Cailean on the shoulder that he continued his tale.

"Cailean fought to rescue her like a man possessed. We had a glimpse of hope, then suddenly the Elf fell dazed like he was ill and without him we could nae get home. Cailean took the lead through that hellish maze of tunnels until we arrived at the very heart of it. By then the Elf had recovered enough to open a portal back to the Highlands, if not for him we would have all surely perished."

Coll said on. "Aye, but it was out of the frying pan and into the fire, for the battle we left behind was still about us. The demons had encircled all those who remained, picking the survivors off one by one. Tamlyn kept the portal open so Cailean, who stayed behind, could destroy the device which kept their world alive." Coll had everyone's attention. Even the servants stared in awe, straining to hear each word. Cailean felt uncomfortable, noticing all eyes upon him.

"Enough already. Too many good friends died that day, the memory of that foul place is far better to be forgotten. I have nae wish to rekindle nightmares that have finally fled nor stir up anxieties of these good folk," Cailean said as his kin and friends nodded in acceptance.

"You are right in that my Lord Cailean, for the days and weeks that followed that terrible summer, fear and suspicion ran wild, mobs and beatings and a few deaths all stemmed from the paranoia of the Black Dog shape-shifters being anywhere or anybody. It was far worse in Stirling and the larger towns," Sir Adam put forth. They all could indeed understand the fear and its unfortunate side effects in such circumstances.

"I will give you a piece of advice concerning the shape-shifters; they all have cold grey eyes, when taking human form they would be timid and shy so as not to draw attention; they do not speak our tongue. They hunt in packs and will normally flee if outnumbered. They only attack when they have no choice or have the advantage of surprise. This much I know, so use it to save those accused if it ever becomes a problem again," Cailean said. He wanted no more innocents to fall prey to hysteria and panic driven mobs.

"It will be as you say my Lord Cailean. Knowledge of your enemy is a great advantage," Sir Adam said and the other knights nodded in agreement. Out of the group, it was surprisingly Paul Sigardsson who remained quiet throughout. Normally boisterous and the center of attention, he remained unnaturally and placidly silent. He watched, listened and smiled. For this is what he wanted, the fame of the Chief of MacKenzie to carry them directly to the King's door. From what he witnessed here amongst Knights and common folk both, Cailean could take him a great deal further than Sigardsson himself ever could. For in the morning he would see the King.

CHAPTER TWELVE

The King

THE MORNING CAME all too early for them, the vast quantities of wine and ale may have had something to do with it. The only one actually eager to get going was the Lord of Rodel. After a quick meal they all headed down to the stables, Sir Adam would accompany them along with ten men; they felt the extra number of armed men would better suit their station.

Tynan grumbled that they had left behind over a thousand men at Dumbarton if representation was that important. "Speed here is of more importance, friend Tynan. Your clansmen would have only slowed us down," Sir Pierce replied levelly. Cailean nodded in agreement, and they spurred on eastwards, passing through the town of Kippen following the Forth River on their left all the way to Stirling.

The land was flat and moor like all around. Out of the flatness, Stirling Rock jutted upwards 250 feet with an almost impregnable castle situated on top. The town itself sprawled along the base of the rock except for the Kings Park, which was set aside for tournaments and the like. Sir Pierce made his way through the warren of streets and alleyways on the quickest route straight to the castle. The gates of the outer bailey were shut to them as throngs of folk waited patiently for entry. With Sir Adam's help, they bypassed the queue. Sir Pierce and Sir Robert dismounted quickly, shouting for the captain of the guards and were not long in waiting. Ten armored men and their captain came out of a small postern door to question them. They had only to wait a few moments before the captain had issued orders for the gates to be opened.

The knights mounted up as Sir Pierce after conversing with the captain turned in his saddle. "My Lords, if you will follow me we are to enter the castle, grooms will take our mounts. We will be allowed rooms to clean and refresh ourselves. Court is in session, a Privy Council, and the major discussion it appears is Haakon of Norway. I will get word to the King that you are here," he said as the massively thick gates opened in front of them. A great portcullis raised beyond the gates, with murder holes lining the sides and roof. Into the outer bailey they rode, where grooms indeed were waiting. Sir Pierce directed his charges upwards into the inner bailey and into the castle.

Armed guards were everywhere, as most of the country's nobles were present, sitting in session in the great hall. Cailean's party was provided rooms to wash off the dust and dirt from their journey. After a quick face wash and a change of clothes, the very best they had, even Drostan and Coll looked quite presentable. It was not long before Sir Robert Graham returned and had brought along a familiar face.

"Cailean! I can scarce believe mine eyes!"

"Andrew, God's blood it has been far too long," Cailean returned as he embraced his old friend and brother in law, Sir Andrew Fraser. There were tears in the Knight's sea-blue eyes while his handsome face smiled intensely as he released his friend and he then noticed the others. "Drostan, Coll and Tynan!" he said embracing them all as well.

"I could scarce believe when Sir Pierce apprised me of your presence here. You could not have come in a more desperate time. The nobles are petitioning against the King in this Norway matter, wanting more discussions and negotiations believing to buy the Hebrides will actually sway Haakon," Sir Andrew said, his face reflecting the disdain he felt at this course of action.

"Nothing will sway Haakon!" bellowed Sigardsson, and Sir Andrew finally noticed the man.

"My Lord Sheriff of Stirling, may I introduce you to Paul Sigardsson, Lord of Rodel of Harris; Tormund Chief of MacLeod of Harris and his brother Torquil, Chief of MacLeod of Lewis. All here to appraise and advise in this of Norway," Cailean said as the men each bowed in turn as they were named to the Sherriff of Stirling.

"My Lords you are most welcome, for your presence here will bear weight in this delicate issue."

"Then let us proceed, my Lord Sherriff, for we have come a long way," Paul Sigardsson said gruffly. Sir Andrew gave a smile and a slight bow of his blonde head.

"If you will follow me then, my Lords, I shall present you to the Privy Council," Sir Andrew replied with a wink to Cailean as he took them to the great hall. Guards almost two score stood before the doors and only after the recognition of the Sherriff of Stirling were they granted entry. Sir Andrew led the way and the main hall opened before them like a great cathedral; benches like pews lined both sides, a path in the center led straight to the throne. Massive timber beams held up the great roof and scores of flags and banners hung down from the ceiling. A man who was speaking suddenly stopped midsentence, and those who filled the benches turned to see who had been allowed entrance to a sealed Privy Council.

Sir Pierce, who had gone in before, moved in beside a richly dressed older gentleman holding a staff in his hands and whispered into his ear. The man's expression changed quickly and he, the High Seneschal of Scotland, banged his staff loudly upon the wooden floor.

"My Lords, it is with great honor that our King, Alexander the third of his name, by Gods' Grace King of Scots may present to you the sons of Leod. Tormund, Chief of MacLeod of Harris. Torquil, Chief of MacLeod of Lewis and My Lord Paul Sigardsson, Lord of Rodel of Harris." The aforementioned men moved towards the dais with Sir Pierce as escort. Each man kneeled before the throne then took to their feet to stand at the right hand side of the King.

The High Seneschal banged his staff again. "My Lords, the King extends his most warmest of welcomes to Drostan MacKenzie, Lord of Applecross; Coll MacKenzie, Lord of Toscaig, and to the illustrious Cailean Fitzgerald MacKenzie, High Chief of MacKenzie and savior of the realm. All Hail," the Seneschal shouted out the last as he banged his staff. The King himself took to his feet, thus the rest of the Privy Council immediately followed.

Cailean, with Drostan and Coll on each side with Tynan and Sir Andrew following stoically behind, walking the path straight to the throne, heads held high and proud. At the base of the dais, they knelt before the King, and Alexander himself stepped forward to greet them. A knight behind the King moved fluidly forward as if to intercept, but the King held out his hand.

"It is quite alright Sandy, we need fear nothing from this paladin," he said softly as Cailean bowed his head deeply to his King. Sir Alexander Fitzalan, Lord High Constable was in charge of the safety of the King, stepped slowly back to where he once stood behind the throne.

Cailean smiled warmly to his monarch. "My Lord King, I am your most humble servant," he said, and he reached forth to take the King's hand to pay homage as vassal to kiss the royal hand.

"Humble is scarce a trait that I would expect of you, Cailean MacKenzie, for we all here owe you an eternal debt of gratitude," the King said with a warm smile and a careful wink. Alexander had a contagious smile, sharp and good-looking features, sandy brown hair and eyes that shone with command despite his youth. He wore a thin but well-groomed mustache that trailed to the base of his chin. He was tall if not slightly less tall than the Highlanders before him. His youthful lean frame sparked of boundless energy.

"Come rise my friends and join us here. Your experience in this matter far exceeds that of my Lord Earl of Dunbar and Lord of the Western March, who was just telling us how to deal with the situation of Haakon's latest proposal," the King said. He returned to the throne and beckoned Cailean and his party to the benches beside him. Alexander again motioned to the nobleman to start where he left off.

"My King, as I was saying we need do nothing; Norway is no threat to your crown. Negotiate if you must, but sooner or later they will concede the Hebrides to Scotland as they should, without confrontation," the noble said as he returned to his seat, another taking his place.

"My King, perhaps a better offer of silver would so sway Haakon? It is said Norway is impoverished; silver will speak loudly to his council, the Hebrides mean little to them. An honest amount would surely entice them better than the meagerly sums we have been offering."

"Yes, my Lord Earl of Lennox, we have heard this argument before. I would not wish to impoverish my realm further, so Haakon can use that money to invest in an expedition against us," the King countered and there were nods from several council members, yet another man took to his feet.

"My King, let us hear then from our new friends. They perhaps, are far more acquainted with Norway's ambitions. I for one would like to know why they are here now!"

The King nodded. "My Lord Robert Bruce, Lord of Annandale has the same question as I. My Lord Chief of Mackenzie, my good friend, if you will?" Alexander asked confidently.

Cailean stood and addressed the council. "My King, my good Lords of Scotland, it is of Norway that has brought us here this day. Haakon comes and he comes for war!" The confident look quickly faded from the King's face as the Lords took to their feet in chaotic display, all trying to speak at once. Alexander let them shout for a few moments more before he raised his hand for silence. The High Seneschal banged his staff to get the councils attention.

"Let him speak. Say on my friend," the King requested, all eyes turned upon the MacKenzie chief.

"My Lord of Rodel did come to me days ago with this news. His family and his agents in both Norway and Orkney have all reported the same thing. Haakon feigns negotiations while he has secretly put the call out to all he holds sway over. Some say two hundred and fifty ships, yet more to be like three hundred. He comes my King, Haakon himself will lead this fleet!"

The Lord of Annandale looked questioningly towards Cailean. "Three hundred ships could mean up to fifty thousand men," he said in disbelief.

"Possibly more, for he will pull in Orkney and the Islesmen and Magnus King of Man. With the Manx fleet he could also sway the Irish; combined you could be looking at eighty to one hundred thousand men," Cailean said coldly, sparing the King and the nobles nothing in his assessment.

"All of this just for the Hebrides, I think not." that was again the Lord of Annandale.

Cailean turned to the noble. "You are right my lord, not just the Hebrides, but for Alexander's crown and Ireland, for that country resides without a King. If he takes Scotland and Ireland, he will set his eyes upon England while its King fights an internal war. Haakon wants it all." The nobles mulled this over, quickly assessing the worst possible scenario yet it was the King who posed the right question.

"How much time do we have?"

"Weeks yet I believe. His forces from Iceland have the farthest to come, they will rendezvous in Orkney then sweep south. We know not where they will land; I only know that Haakon will secure the Hebrides then attack," Cailean said.

"What of our own shipping, my King? Our own fleet and surely these good lords along with the Islesmen can fight off this Norse invasion," another Lord asked. He moved up towards the Highlanders and offered his hand in greeting to Cailean. His was a strong grip, and he had rugged handsome features, dark yet with a kind face; he had the look of a fighter or an experienced soldier.

"My Lord of Douglasdale has posed a valid question. My Lord High Admiral, what say you?" the King asked. Cailean expected it to be another of these Lords yet it was the Earl of Dunbar that took to his feet and spoke.

"I know not my King. My ships are trading vessels, merchant ships, scarce the same quality of the Norse Dragon-ships. As to the Islesmen, I do not think they can match that of Norway."

"My King if I may?" Cailean asked and the King waved his hand to proceed. "Good Lords, I can field twenty ships, my Lord Earl of Ross thirty, the MacLeod's twenty along with my Lord of Rodel. The Isles and other coastal lords perhaps one hundred, still not enough to take on Norway. Besides, the Islesmen will not stand with us; they will remain neutral in this. We have come straight from Angus MacDonald Chief of MacDonald, he will not help nor will the MacDougalls and they who hold the Isles between them. They cannot face Haakon alone and they cannot match the Norway fleet, as they are cut off from the rest of Scotland. Any aid we could possibly send them would be ripped to shreds by those dragon ships."

The Lords of the Privy Council turned quiet at this news. The Islesmen of the Hebrides were a buffer in the past to Norway's ambitions, now that buffer was gone and it seemed turned against them. Haakon's fleet could launch attacks from the safety of the Isles to anywhere along the Scottish seaboard and that deeply frightened these Scots-Norman nobles.

"My King, I believe that this Lord of MacKenzie is our best chance at keeping Scotland safe. Let us hear from him what our strategy should be," the Lord of Douglasdale proposed.

"Yes, Cailean please advise us how to best deal with this threat," the King requested.

"Surprise is now on our side, assemble the nation, for we will need every fighting man we have. Haakon will likely land off our coasts, Arran most probably so he can protect his feet and launch their attacks. If he comes for battle, fight him upon every landing. Draw him in; we know the land better, use it against them; use everything against them. They come late in the season, perhaps even the storms can be used to some advantage. We know not where the main attack will be so I suggest having our forces split up to cover the greatest amount of territory. Their strategy is mostly hit and run but if they get a foothold anywhere, it will be hard to drive them out. Send word to your father-in-law, the King of England, apprize him of Norway's ambitions. For Haakon eyes his throne as well," Cailean said. Paul Sigardsson nodded in approval, the Lord of Rodel was indeed happy with what transpired today. Cailean had accomplished what he had failed to do. Scotland was with him in his fight against Haakon; he could see it on the faces of those Lords of the Privy Council and on King Alexander.

The King took to his feet. "We all here greatly appreciate your words my Lord Chief of Mackenzie. It shall be as you say, for we have the time and surprise is on our side thanks to you. My battle commanders shall draw up further plans and establish where best to place our forces to counter Norway. My Lords, this meeting is adjourned," he announced with a confident tone.

††††

It was late that afternoon when Cailean and his party had been summoned to dine with the King and Queen. Several Lords from the Privy Council attended as well. Alexander Fitzalan, the High Constable never left the King's side. Other high ranking lords, Alexander Stewart of Dundonald the High Steward, also Robert Bruce Lord of Annandale and James Douglas Lord of Douglasdale all were present with their wives. Several other Lords and Knights with their Ladies were present, all those who were closer to the King than most. Cailean and his party were introduced; each in turn knelt to the thrones, all taking the hand of the Queen to kiss in greeting.

Cailean himself was last to do so. The Queen was thrilled to have the Chief of Mackenzie, the great hero at her dinner table. Queen Margaret was pretty, not beautiful; her smile was her best feature. She was of the same age as Alexander and their child, Princess Margaret, was of the same age as Cailean's son Conner.

"My Lord Cailean, my husband is so happy to have you with us. I too am so very pleased, for the stories of your exploits have been a favorite here amongst us at court. Sir Andrew Fraser has spoiled us of your adventures; it is too bad that your Lady wife did not come with you or that of the Elven Lord Tamlyn."

"My Queen I thank you, but perhaps my friend Sir Andrew makes over-much of my deeds," Cailean said. He glared at his brother-in-law the Sherriff of Stirling who just arrived but caught enough of the conversation; he bowed his head as he along with his wife, Lady Isabel, approached the throne. Isabel did not look towards her brother but towards the Queen.

"You are indeed modest Chief of MacKenzie. My friend, your sister, though with much coaxing confirms all of what Sir Andrew has told us," the Queen said as she smiled towards Isabel.

"My deeds are only a result of my love for my wife, my family and my people. Yet I could not have done so without the stalwart champions such as those that I have brought with me, for their deeds have certainly rivaled mine own," Cailean said. His eyes never left his sister's face who, would still not look towards him.

The rest of the meal Cailean joined in long conversation with the King and his closest advisors. Sigardsson remained aloof, and spoke only when asked to comment. All of this was a waste of time for him; he had already achieved what he came for and was eager to be off. Cailean himself was not spared attentions in the slightest; once the Ladies of court lost their timidity they surrounded him with questions. When he tried to downplay his answers, Coll was more than happy to fill them in on the juicy details.

It was hard to endure so when an opportunity for escape came, he took it wholeheartedly. He quickly sought after his sister and brother in law. They had been married only a year; Isabel and Sir Andrew had held a small and private wedding. Neither Cailean nor any of his family had been invited to attend. It was only learned through a letter from Sir Andrew apologizing that he and Isabel had wed and kept the event private, with a small ceremony, all at Isabel's insistence. Sir Andrew felt awful about it but had felt honor-bound to abide by his wife's wishes.

Sir Andrew's face enlightened at Cailean's approach, for he so wished that the tension between his wife and Cailean could somehow be mended.

"Cailean, I will leave the two of you to get caught up on certain matters and such," he said as bowed to his wife and took his leave. Cailean wanted nothing more than to hug his sister, to hold her in his arms, yet her aloof look held him in place. Her beautiful face still held a sharp coldness towards him. They shared the same dark brown eyes and brown wavy hair, but her pert nose and chin was all her own.

"Isa, sister, it has been way to long. Please let this be an end to the tension between us."

"You have not changed, my brother. You bring war with you yet again it seems," she said, her eyes shone with an icy hue.

"This is not my war, I canna be blamed for this. I only came to warn and offer my services to the King."

"You will have my husband at your side in this war. He remembers his vow to you at Lochcarron, to stand at your side should Haakon come in war," she said as tears welled within her eyes. "You bring death to all those around you, my brother. So much death, the sight of you brings back those memories that I have tried so hard to bury. The blood, the screams and those terrible creatures it was like Hell itself opened before our very eyes. I saw my death that day, all hope I had fled. I had made my peace with God. I was ready to be with Anselan, with Jean. When I saw you go through the portal after Kerry, I felt that you too would surely die to save her. I could do nothing but wait and watch as those creatures took us one by one to be torn apart, eaten alive.

"I could not take it anymore; I was about to throw myself at them to end it all. When I saw you and the other's return hope sprang within me then, but with it came such a terrible fear, that we would nae survive. Every time I see you, that fear returns Cailean. I stayed apart from you my brother so I could find peace in my soul, now you come back into my life and War follows on your heels. War that will have my husband in the heart of it, I cannot lose Andrew on top of everything else," she said with tears rolling down her cheeks.

Cailean felt his own tears well up inside. "I am so sorry Isa, I dinna want this, never have. I do what I must, my heart near bursts that I cause this pain within you. I love you with all my heart and I promise that whatever happens I will do all I can to keep Andrew safe," he said as he turned away to leave her alone, the lump in his throat barely letting him get the words out.

He made his way to the King and Queen. "Forgive me, my King, Queen, for it has been a long journey. I pray your leave to retire," he said and the King nodded. "Rest well my Lord, for I shall see thee in the morn," Alexander said as Cailean bowed to his monarch and left the room.

Isabel watched him leave, her heart breaking. She longed to tell him she was sorry. She knew that Cailean was not at fault for any of it, yet it was her heart that would not let it go. Cailean and Andrew had spoken of Haakon for years, now this war was on their doorstep. Her lip trembled, as she now feared she would lose them both in the months ahead.

CHAPTER THIRTEEN

The Death of A Stag

EARLY THE NEXT morning Cailean and his entourage were once again summoned to the King and his small council. Sir Pierce was there with them, Sir Andrew and several other knights, for men such as these, battle tested veterans were trusted by the King more than his nobles of the Privy council when it came to war. The Lords of Annandale and Douglasdale and as always Alexander Fitzalan the Constable, these were men the King valued most in their honest and unbiased opinions. Sigardsson always keen to point out failings in any strategy the southern lords came up with, left the planning mostly to Cailean, as the Chief of MacKenzie was the foremost expert in fighting the Norsemen. Pouring over maps the stratagems were hammered out to the liking of all and with it several contingency plans just in case. Now it all depended on Haakon and where he would land his vast fleet.

When it was to the satisfaction of all, Paul Sigardsson and the sons of Leod begged leave to depart. Alexander granted their request but wished for Cailean and his kin to stay longer for at least a few days and to this Cailean agreed. Sir Pierce had sequestered a suitable escort for the Lord of Rodel and the sons of Leod back to their ships in Dumbarton. Sigardsson hugged Cailean along with his foster sons, but pulled Cailean aside. "Thank you Chief of MacKenzie. What you have done here has most assuredly helped our cause. Scotland has hope now and with it you and I may live a little while longer," he said with a wink and friendly punch on Cailean's shoulder. "Stay not overlong, I head to my friends in Orkney and see what can be learned," he said and with a final bow to the King, he took his leave.

The King was indeed glad Cailean and the others stayed, for he craved a new friendship with the Highland Chief. It was hard for some nobles to accept, as traditionally the Kings of the Canmore line were not so well received in the North. For long generations Scotland had been divided north and south. Now a promising friendship was shaping up between the two men, for Cailean was the King's constant companion. To some this did not sit well, but it bothered neither Cailean nor those that were secure in their own position and friendship with the King. The crown had always its group of sycophants, yet Alexander while still young was smart enough to see through the best of them.

In the days that followed Cailean, Drostan, Coll and Tynan had become so immersed in the life at court they could barely keep up. There was always something going on or their presence was required at an event or function. When the King suggested a hunt in the Royal Forest they were all happy for the break.

A royal hunt was just the sort of thing to get away from court and provide enough sport for thrill seekers old and young alike. On this foray, some fifty hunters in total accompanied the King along with scores of squires, huntsmen and drivers. The morning had looked so promising, soon became overcast, as misty grey clouds blew in from the west threatening rain. The weather however did not dampen the Kings spirits in the slightest, he rode upon a splendid white charger, a handsome beast that was Alexander's favorite as it had always proved surefooted, fearless and loved the chase.

Over one hundred guards escorted the royal party and the nobles to the Royal Park. Massive tents were set up in an open staging area where food and refreshments were offered while drivers were sent out on ahead into the forest to flush out game and direct it towards the hunters. Once the King was ready, he commanded the hounds to be let loose as the hunters took to their mounts and split off into four groups. Cailean, Tynan, Drostan and Coll accompanied the King and his party of Fitzalan, Stewart, Bruce, Douglas and his young son William and Sir Andrew Fraser.

The King was unable to restrain himself from beginning his favorite sport and immediately spurred off after the dogs. Fitzalan followed right behind, charging through the forest at breakneck speeds. King Alexander was especially excited, for the drivers had mentioned rumors of a particularly large stag haunting these woods of late and the King was all for being the one to bring it down. Deeper and deeper they rode into the forest with no sign of game. It was early in the afternoon when they decided to take a short rest. Squires attended the King and huntsmen attended to their dogs. In the distance, they could hear others, their dogs all baying after their prey. Alexander was an impatient hunter so after a quick meal he was calling for his mount and his spear, not wanting to have other hunting parties be the first to make a kill.

The King, impatient with the others, spurred his mount headed onto game trails that crisscrossed the forest with the others scrambling to keep up. The Highlanders were all enjoying themselves in the hunt for they rarely did this in the North. Normally they hunted on foot with bow and arrow but this was an exhilarating adrenalin rush, then at last the King shouted that he had seen the huge Stag ahead. Now the chase was on, Fitzalan pressed on after the King as did Cailean and Tynan. The others broke away, taking a path on each flank hoping to cut it off. The dogs at their heels bounded past them, picking up the scent of the beast.

The King was laughing as he chased after the beast. The thrill of the hunt had totally taken him. Suddenly the forest grew denser, more restricted and overgrown. Cailean noticed an almost eerie silence that he recognized from before, the only sound in the forest was the hunters and the hounds ahead. Nature had somehow gone silent in fear. The baying of the hounds turned to barking, then to growls then to yelping in pain.

Cailean and Tynan spurred on to a ghastly, horrific scene. The stag was massive. Dogs were trying to tear into its flesh but the stag simply ignored them. It had Alexander with his back to a rocky outcrop and nowhere to turn; the great stag lowered its impressive rack charging at the King. Fitzalan hurled his spear at the beast yet it was too fast. The Stag smoothly ducking under the throw with those deadly antlers aiming low to gore the Kings mount.

The enraged beast drove those insanely sharp antlers deep into the horse's side. The horse screamed in agony as the Stag pushed in deeper tearing into vital organs. It then pulled out to attack one of the dogs mauling its haunches. The Kings horse, mortally wounded, collapsed to the ground, trapping the King's leg underneath. Fitzalan drove in his mount between the King and the Stag, drawing out his sword. It was then that the stag reared upwards, transforming fluidly into half beast half man. It roared in fury at the High Constable as it viciously wrenched back the head of his mount with its left hand then with its right it backhanded Fitzalan, who sailed off his mount and into the brush yards away. The Stags jaws bore gleaming white razor sharp teeth that tore out the horse's throat. The beast knew instinctively that on horseback his prey had a chance to escape; alone in the wild on foot they would be easy meat.

The beast was lightning quick; with one deadly swipe, another of the annoying hounds perished. As Cailean drew closer he tossed his spear, it caught the Shape-shifter just below the shoulder blade. It bellowed out in pain as it turned upon Cailean. Those gore dripping antlers took Cailean's mount full on in the face and throat. With an upwards thrust, it drove an antler in under the horse's jaw and into its brain, killing Cailean's mount instantly. Expertly he leapt off his mount to avoid being pinned like the King. His dead horse blocked Tynan from coming into the small clearing, for the beast and the bodies of three horses left little room to maneuver.

The King called for help pinned under his mount he could not get out his sword. The creature then returned his attention to the trapped Monarch. Fitzalan was still dazed but rushed towards the King, almost in a state of shock as his eyes took in the carnage around him. His King lay helpless at the very feet of this terrible creature. Its hate-filled eyes and flesh rendering jaws were ready to strike. With an amazing feat of strength and speed, Cailean darted in grabbing hold of the beast's right antler and wrenching back the head of this terrible monster. With a single slash of his dirk, he slit the beast's throat sending arterial spray out in jets of hot blood that showered both the King and Fitzalan.

"Cailean!" Tynan shouted as he leapt off his mount towards his Chief, caring nothing for the others. The King could only stare incredulously at the Chief of MacKenzie who stood with a bloody dirk in his right hand, the left still held onto the antlers of the beast. He let it drop to the ground as the others poured into the clearing.

Sir Andrew was the first there. "My King?" he cried out fearfully, as Fitzalan bent down to his liege Lord.

"I am well. Trapped I am under my horse but fine, thanks to Cailean."

"I never truly believed, never imagined that this could be real. I am sorry I ever doubted you Andrew," Alexander Fitzalan said, still in shock.

"It is alright Sandy, I scarce believe it myself sometimes," the Fraser returned with a forced grin patted the High Constable upon his shoulder. The others, who had seen what transpired yet were too far away to offer aid, had finally arrived and hurriedly dismounted.

Coll and Drostan, along with the Douglas' came in close and stood in awe as the half-man half-beast slowly reverted to its natural form.

"I will never get used to that," Coll said to his brother.

"Nae myself either. Blasted creatures!" Drostan agreed as he punched his brother to get his attention to the struggling King.

"Come, Coll. Let us free our King before he takes root," he said. The two giant Highlanders lifted the dead bulk enough for Cailean and Fitzalan to drag their monarch out and help him to his feet.

"How is the leg your Grace, not broken?" Fitzalan asked.

"Nae. Sore I say, but not broken. I think I can put weight on it," the King said with a smile. His face was covered in blood and dirt, his clothes were torn and he was clearly shaken but he laughed and embraced Cailean heartily.

"My good friend, you saved my life this day and that I shall never forget. Wait til the court hears of this; Cailean Fitzgerald MacKenzie saved his King from the terrible Shape-shifter," the King said, patting Cailean on the shoulder with pride. Yet Cailean looked to Sir Andrew shaking his head, for he saw several squires and dog handlers, some of which caught site of what was done here in that clearing. Cailean remembered Sir Adam's words of the panic driven mobs. If the word got out that the Shape-shifters were still among them, the fear would spread again.

"My Lord King perhaps that may not be wise," Cailean suggested. The King looked at him questionably.

"What do you mean my friend?"

Sir Andrew came to his brother-in-laws aid. "My King, remember a few years ago, the fear the Shape-shifters caused, the panic and terror filled mobs that hung ten innocent people? If we let this tale spread, who knows what it may do? Superstition runs high within the common folk. They may even claim that you my King are a Shape-shifter in disguise."

"Hardly my Lord Sherriff. I do understand, but we need not suppress this entirely, for rumors will spread of this day which we have no control over," the King glanced towards the nervous squires and dog handlers. "Let us say that a Stag caused this. It gored my mount and trapped me beneath, that it would have killed me if not for my friend here who slew the beast," the King suggested to all, but more directly to Cailean. "Will that step too hard upon your modesty my friend?" the King asked Cailean jovially.

"I think I can live with it my King," Cailean replied as Tynan laughed and the rest followed.

"We have but one problem; we lack a Stag, for we can scarce drag that corpse home in triumph," Fitzalan reminded them.

"We will commandeer one, hopefully the others were more successful in their hunt than ourselves," the King said as they brought up a horse for the King to ride. The squires had to double up on their mounts after offering up their horses to their King, Cailean and the Constable as they journeyed through the forest.

They returned to the tents just before dark for a much needed wash and a change of clothes. The dilemma of the stag was rendered mute, for other hunters had taken two in the hunt and the largest was procured as the beast Cailean killed to protect the King. The noble Sir Duncan Murray who slew the magnificent beast was more than happy to accommodate the King in this and won a large purse of silver for his trouble. Wine poured freely that night as the King and his friends shared in plenty around a great bonfire, laughing and joking to hide the fear of what had truly happened that day.

Deep in the forest, pairs of red eyes peered through the darkness. Massive Black dogs sniffed the air; six of them came warily into the bloody clearing as each one came in to sniff upon the tall human like form lying naked upon the ground. Its grey lifeless eyes stared into the night sky. They all in turn gave a gentle lick upon the face of their dead brother then they tore into the still warm corpses of the three dead horses.

††††

The next day when the King returned to court the rumors were spreading, the truth and the more plausible cover up story were running side by side. The King informed the Queen in private of the real story and the need for the false tale of events. She was shocked at first but understood the need to cover it up. She was scared that her husband had been so close to death and insisted that Cailean should be honored in some way. Alexander stated that he had tried yet the Highland Chief would accept nothing but his eternal friendship, that it was his feudal duty to protect the King at all times as a subject should. The King, after much thought, felt he had something Cailean would accept so he discussed it with the Queen. She was ecstatic in her husband's suggestion and backed him whole-heartedly.

Sir Andrew Fraser had a much harder audience to convince. "Cailean brings these things with him I swear, death follows where he goes! You could have been killed Andrew, you and the King both. I canna take any more loss my love, yours is the death I could never bear," Isabel said as the tears welled in her eyes. She bit her lip to keep them from trembling.

Sir Andrew took her in his arms. "Tush my love. Death comes to us all eventually and when it comes I shall meet it with honor, but that is not for us, not yet. I believe God has plans for us; I dinna believe he saw us through that terrible day only to snatch it away so soon after," he said as he pulled away to hold her at arm's length.

"Do ye think so?"

"Aye I do. Come now you mustn't blame Cailean, if not for him the King would have died; no one else could have got to him in time. Death took no one that day. Besides, if not for your brother we would not be here and our world would be such a different place," he said as he bent his head forward to touch hers.

"Aye I know, I just canna see him. Every time I do, I see Anselan and it tears me apart. I know he is hurting still but I need more time Andrew, when I saw him again everything came back, Anselan and Jean, that dreadful day. I need more time, more time to heal," she said. Her eyes reflected the truth of the matter and Sir Andrew relented.

"Then that's the way it will be. Just do not be overlong about it for we have neglected our nephew and niece for far too long."

"Yes we have, I am sorry," Isabel said. The thought of her niece and nephew brought new feelings of warmth into her soul. She longed to see them. Perhaps the sounds of young children, the laughter and the life would be enough to welcome the Highlands once again. And hopefully it will heal the pain between herself and her brother.

Late in the afternoon on the following day, King Alexander held a small court, summoning as many Lords and Ladies as he could that lived in short proximity to Stirling. Besides the Constable, the High Steward was still at court, Lords of Annandale and Douglasdale, the Earls of Lennox, Fife and Mentieth as well as the Bishops of Glasgow and Fothrif along with scores of Knights all attended this hurried court. The High Seneschal banged his staff, announcing Cailean Fitzgerald High Chief of Clan MacKenzie to approach the King and Queen. Cailean bowed to the Seneschal and gazed straight ahead to his graces as he walked proudly down the aisle.

At the base of the throne, he knelt as King Alexander took to his feet. "My good Lords and Ladies of this realm of Scotland, I Alexander, King of Scots, do approve and appoint Cailean Fitzgerald MacKenzie, Chief of that clan to now amongst his own lands and possessions, to become also Lord of Kintail, with all the rights and privileges therein. This is but a small token of my extreme gratitude for his heroic deeds. I owe this man my life and the realm and I shall be eternally grateful." Cailean still kneeling bowed his head low, then lifting up his head to look the King straight in the eye.

"My King, I am honored to be your true and loyal subject. I will support your laws and goodwill to all within my lands. I thank you for the Lordship of Kintail with all my heart," Cailean said as Alexander smiled warmly upon him.

"Rise my good friend!" Alexander commanded and then embraced him as a brother. Cailean and the rest of the court were shocked at this royal display, they were even more so when Fitzalan the Constable embraced him as well.

"Congratulations my Lord of Kintail. Well and truly deserved my friend," he said. Sir Andrew then congratulated Cailean warmly and Sir Pierce followed, then by a long line of Lords and Ladies. After a celebratory dinner in Cailean's honor, everyone wanted to hear from the new Lord of Kintail about his heroic act. Cailean gave the shortest and almost boring account of events until Coll saved him. Coll made the tale a thrilling epic.

The Stag in his version was a mad brute bent upon killing any who crossed its path. He kept the tale as close to the truth with some minor embellishments. He kept out the fact that the beast was a shape-shifter but the rest was pure Coll. Both the King and Queen were clapping at the end of the story.

"Well done Lord Coll, a magnificent bard you would make," Queen Margaret said with a laugh.

"Your grace is too kind. I am grateful to my cousin who can always provide ample material for many a fine bard," Coll said with his most charming grin aimed towards Cailean. The new lord of Kintail could only roll his eyes and hope that no one wished to hear any more, yet it was not the case. For after a great gulp of wine and with shouts of encouragement, Coll unleashed even more of Cailean's exploits to the applause of everyone. All Cailean could do was sit and listen while dreaming up nasty ways to get back at his cousin for doing this to him.

The night did not seem to end. Wine was in ample supply for the thirsty storytellers and for Cailean to toast to his heroic deeds at the constant urgings of others, so much so that he soon became fully drunk himself. Towards the end of night, he found Sir Pierce beside him.

"Your cousin truly has an art for story telling my Lord of Kintail. I would have given anything to be on the field beside you."

"You will get your chance I believe, Norway will see to it," Cailean returned and the Knight shook his head.

"That will be against men; that I have done many a time. You know what I mean my lord. To fight against these demons, now that would be glorious."

It was Cailean's turn to shake his head while trying to point a finger at one of the two blurry images of the Knight. "I knew a Knight once…that thought as you do. Sir Patrick Comyn, he too wanted to fight these Demons, to seek such glory. He got his wish and a Dulachan killed him," Cailean said. He downed the last of his wine and staggered out of the hall with Tynan helping him along the way.

††††

The bright sunlight seemed to burn out his eyes, so he tried to keep them closed but shutting them only made the room spin. His mouth felt like the insides of a dead whale. His head pounded like a massive drum, yet the drum seemed to have a strange sort of rhythm and a source. Cailean, dizzy with eyes partially closed found the drum. Coll's snoring was that damnable drum. Wanting to silence it hopefully forever, he searched for anything to aid him and found a bucket of wash-water. He then emptied it on his cousin's head, which immediately stopped the insufferable snoring.

"What? What's to do? Is the roof leaking?"

"No damn you I just took a piss," Cailean snarled at his cousin.

"Ach way, you would nae do that, now me on the other hand…" Coll left it there as he rolled over looking around the room trying to focus. "Where are we…Ach now I remember, we are at Stirling castle, with the King and that nasty woman," Coll said through the fog in his head.

Cailean was only half listening. "What woman are ye talking about?"

"The Queen, that little minx kept filling my drink and her own, God's mercy she can out drink the best of us I vow," Coll said as Cailean merely grunted. He then searched for the rest of his entourage.

Drostan was easy to find. He was in the adjoining room on the floor, snoring away like his brother. He woke to the not so gentle kicks from his Chief.

"What in the Seven Hells? Ach Cailean, go away cousin, let the dead rest in peace," he said rolling over and putting his back to Cailean.

"The dead can, yet you however are not. It's almost mid-day."

"Ach wake me tomorrow then," Drostan said earning him an even harder kick in the ass.

"Blast you Cailean, if I dinna love you with all my heart I'd truly kill you were you stand!" Drostan roared as he rolled to his knees then to unsteady feet.

"Good, then help me find Tynan." The wiry fighter was harder to find as he never snored, like a predator never giving himself away.

"Where in God's name is he?" Cailean said as he came back into the room and found Coll sleeping again, so he kicked him too. "No ye don't!"

"Ach let me be. Go bother the King now that you are a Lord. Go off and do some 'Lordy' duties," Coll said which only earned him another kick.

"I am, we must be on the road this day, back to Dumbarton and home," Cailean all but shouted at his cousin.

"Here he is, lying in the bed," Drostan called. Cailean turned and went over to the bed to the sleeping Tynan.

"How did he get the bed?"

"Well do you remember much of last night, cause I surely don't," Drostan said, looking around the room as if expecting to see others from the night's revelry to have camped out in their rooms. They stood watching Tynan peacefully sleeping.

"Wake him, I shall look into getting us some food," Cailean said. Drostan grabbed Tynan by the ankle and yanked him out of the bed, hitting Tynan's head on the floor in the process. Drostan commenced to walk around the room dragging the now fully awake and screaming Tynan.

"Let me go you dunderheid, you misbegotten ape!" Tynan shouted. He grabbed at a stool and managed to throw it at Drostan's back trying to get the big man to release him.

"Dunderheid am I?"

"Aye and a misbegotten ape, lest you forgot!" Tynan yelled back at him as Drostan finally let him go, noticing Coll had fallen back to sleep.

"Come, let's piss on my brother's sleeping head"

Cailean had wandered down the wrong hall. He got turned about then headed back the way he came, heard Coll screaming in rage, then what sounded like the smashing of furniture while passing his rooms. He scarce believed that they would be under attack within the castle so he decided to keep going. Eventually he found the kitchens and politely requested a platter of food and a pitcher of water to wash it down.

For the new lord of Kintail the servants were more than happy to accommodate and even helped him carry the several steaming platters and pitchers. It was a good thing because they took the quickest path back to his rooms for truthfully Cailean was indeed lost. Upon entering his rooms with two servants in tow, he looked upon a war scene.

"Emm, place them… on the floor I guess." For Cailean could not find an unbroken table or bench where to place them. Coll, Drostan and Tynan looked like they had certainly been through war. Drostan and Coll both had an eye swelled almost shut, and Tynan had blood running from his nose, which appeared to be broken yet again. The smell of urine was strong.

"For God you dinna break the chamber pots?" The three of them looked at each other.

"Possibly," Drostan said at the same time Coll said, "Maybe."

"Like travelling with bairns! Eat and then get this and yourselves cleaned up. We must visit with the King and then be on our way back to Lochcarron."

The King and Queen received them kindly at the gardens just outside the palace. Alexander seemed to be nursing a bad head but was still quite happy to see them. Queen Margaret seemed in finer spirits than all the men, laughing at the sight of Drostan and Coll.

"What happened to you both?" she asked with a devilish grin.

"An unfortunate mishap with some stairs my Queen," Coll lied. The Queen laughed yet seemed unconvinced.

"Surely such a storyteller could have invented a finer tale than that?"

"Perhaps given more time…and a clearer head, your grace," Coll said, forcing a smile. Cailean, wanting to get moving and to escape anyone noticing the damage in his rooms, stepped to his cousin's aid.

"My King, my Queen, if we could have your permission to depart, I must return home with all speed gather my men and meet up with Lord of Rodel," Cailean stated evenly. Alexander nodded in agreement with his new Lord of Kintail.

"Yes, my friend. When next we meet we shall be at the head of armies. Godspeed to you and yours and when this war is won we shall look forward to your company again here at court. Hopefully you can bring your Lady wife too. I am sure the queen will look forward to that day."

"When peace claims our shores again I will make every effort to bring her to court," Cailean said and the King embraced him.

"Good luck my friend," Alexander said as he gave the Highlanders leave to go. Sir Pierce, Sir Robert Graham and Sir Adam were waiting for them with their horses.

"I will accompany you to Rothesay if I may? My Lord High Steward requests that I have his brother prepared for possibly a long siege," Sir Pierce asked. Cailean nodded in approval, while he looked to Sir Adam Montgomery.

"Myself as well my lord of Kintail, at least to Balfron. There I must assemble my men to join Sir Andrew's command."

Cailean nodded to him too. "Then, good sirs, let us be off!" he said as he kicked his mount's flanks taking the road westwards home and his to wife.

CHAPTER FOURTEEN

The Trigger

Present day, North America:

I N A REMOTE area in the back hills of Tennessee, Tamlyn opened his portal. Its power trace was disguised as best he could to keep the enemy blinded to his presence. Tamlyn stepped through completely unobserved. The mine entrance was on a hillside half a kilometer away completely grown over with vegetation; however, he would not be using the front door. That way would be blocked to allow the Azael to hide without fear of discovery. They like him would use portals to move in and out of their dark abode. Directly below Tamlyn about two kilometers down lay a thousand or more Azael.

His senses penetrated the depths of the earth and found the Azael, all in hibernation mode. Like him, they needed a Restoration cycle to draw in their power; opening portals for them drew much of their strength. The Azael would be making several jumps all to get to their targets. They needed to strike simultaneously for their plan to work; if they attacked at random then those power plants still operating would be on high alert. Governments and their military would do everything to protect them, making the attacks that much more difficult for the Azael.

Taking out one of the explosives, he set the timer to three seconds. He used his power to mask his presence there, cloaking himself in ghostlike transparency as he opened the portal into the lion's den. His eyes easily penetrated the blackness; all throughout Azael lay quietly and unsuspecting as they drew in their energy. All around them was the vast amount of explosive weaponry that they had stolen. Silently he placed his C4 on top of a cache of explosives and set the timer. He jumped through the portal and closed it behind him. Seconds later with his feet upon the open ground, he felt the first chain of explosions then the great BOOM! The earth beneath his feet trembled and groaned, as the great stockpile of explosives underneath obliterated everything within that mine. The Azael would have no time to flee.

Veins of coal still untouched would ignite and burn underground for years until the fires eventually burned up the fuel source. It was unfortunate that he must cause so much damage but to achieve his goal he had no other choice. The Azael chose these abandoned mines deep in the earth to hide from the eyes of men; now it would be their tomb and the fires would destroy all evidence of their presence there.

Tamlyn opened a new portal, stepped through and once more concealed his presence from the enemy. He stepped upon British soil; from here the Azael would destroy power plants all over Europe. Azael in Ukraine would target Russia and the Middle East. Their base in Japan would attack all of Asia and India, as well as Australia and New Zealand. Their coordinated attacks all over the world would give humanity no chance to prepare.

The enemy had spent years planning this massive assault, and in a three second countdown on a timer set with C4, on four corners of the world, their plans all came to ruin. At the last mine on a small island off the coast of Japan, the last of the hives met their destruction. Tamlyn, as before in Tennessee, Britain and Ukraine set off the C4 explosives destroying the enemy. The Blood-hunt oath surged with satisfaction within in him, feeling no remorse, only a deep desire to seek out the Demons that still lived. For now, the massive threat to humankind was averted. Tamlyn felt relieved that his plan was so easily achieved. He knew that the majority of Azael were dead and he would locate and eradicate those few that may still survive. The Azael and Shape-shifters that had personally attacked him must have been part of a splinter group or groups, separate from their forces in the mines.

Now he could focus all his energy upon those smaller groups, perhaps to find a way to help Morgan as well. He needed to work fast; the drugs had not done what he had hoped. Zhi's warning that the conflict of the two souls would grow worse was a dire foretelling. Tamlyn was in a hard place with hard decisions to make.

The Blood-hunt oath he had taken now forced him down a different road than the one his heart wanted him to take. He was torn between the final eradication of the enemy and helping Morgan and Cameron. All these centuries, his oath coincided with his tracking Cailean's soul from death to rebirth while he waited for Cameron to re-emerge once again. The Blood-hunt oath now was diverting him away from finding salvation for both Morgan and Cameron. He needed to forge a link within his own mind to do both, that in saving his friend would coincide in the destruction of his enemies. Within his mind, he had always believed that the re-emergence of Cameron would be pivotal in the fulfillment of the oath; so as long as he believed that, the oath had allowed him to wait and watch it unfold.

Once his enemy was gone forever, the Blood-hunt oath would exact its final price. He would not survive long, perhaps a year at best. The incredible focus and the drive that fueled the oath would be gone; the will to live would vanish despite everything to keep him alive. He felt ashamed in a way, for if Cameron simply faded as he thought and not jumped into Morgan, Tamlyn's duty would be done.

He would have been ready to return to his home, even knowing the enemy still lived and preyed upon humankind in this world. It was a way to cheat the oath, knowing that the enemy remained a threat even if on a different world. Tamlyn did not know how long the oath would allow him any peace on his Home-world for the pull on his heart for his home was as strong as the Blood-hunt oath. He truly had no idea of the devastation the Azael had in store for the human race until it was revealed to him from the Dark Elemental. Even now, after stopping their plans and killing thousands of the enemy, the thought that he had almost left humankind to a terrible fate still shamed him. This strike against the enemy only fueled his oath to complete the task, diverting him from trying to save Morgan.

Tamlyn had to find a link to accomplish both or Morgan and Cameron would be on their own. He could already feel the pull of the oath; soon it would consume him to where he would abandon his friend, it was imperative that he discovered that link soon. Back in the comfort of his home, he poured himself a glass of wine. Sitting upon his sofa, his mind sought for a plan. A few hours passed when the ringing of his phone snapped him back.

†††††

Morgan woke up; his eyes felt glued shut with sleep. His dreams seemed strange, almost like a memory, but of an unfamiliar childhood. Some with familiar faces that called him by another name, people that were his parents but they were strangers to him. It was all so odd; he remembered being on an alien world being hunted by monsters. He was trying to save Marina, but every time he got close to her something kept blocking him, a wall or doorway would suddenly appear, going through or going around seemed to put him farther away from her. He saw a young boy, his son, though he could not recall his name. Somehow he had to make a choice to be with him or with Marina; it was heart wrenching. The choice was impossible for him to make, he did not know what to do and he fell to the ground with the world falling to ruin all around him. Two separate roads and he had to choose, only one could live, the other would surely die. It was then he awoke, it was all too real. His heart was beating terribly fast and his throat seemed raw. He reached to Marina; he felt reassured by her presence beside him. He rubbed her back massaging it gently.

His love for her consumed him; he could truly not live without her. Morgan knew if anything were to happen to her he would die, he did not want to live in a world without her at his side. He was still afraid that somehow, somewhere he would have to make that choice from his dream and it frightened him. He kissed her head as she turned to him.

She reached up and caressed his face. "Good morning babe. Did you sleep well?" she asked as she smiled lovingly at him.

"No not really hon. I had some crazy dreams, maybe leftover crap from those pills. I dreamt that I had a son Marina, a son. Can you believe it? Me, a father?" he asked incredulously.

Marina pulled herself up on her elbows and looked into his face; his eyes looked haunted, distant and worried all at the same time. "Morgan I don't know how to tell you, I mean I wanted to tell you but I have been so worried about you," she started, but Morgan butted in.

"Tell me what?"

"I have wanted to tell you for a while now that I am pregnant. I am about ten weeks along. Morgan, you are going to be a father." Marina's face did not reflect the happiness this news should represent; she had been so terribly worried about him these last few weeks and unsure as to how this would affect him. Morgan stared at her as if frozen in place, but finally he recovered. He buried his private fears and his eyes took on a healthier pallor, his smile returned.

"Are you freaking kidding me! You...we... are gonna bring into the world a little tiny Hamilton?" he said laughing and kissing her with great enthusiasm.

"I'm sorry Morgan, I should have told you sooner. It's just with you going through all this I thought it would be too much for you to take on right now."

"It's not like you could hide it, I mean eventually there is gonna be a baby belly going on. I know I can be a little slow but I think I would have figured it out," he laughed. "Don't worry about me, I will be ok, I mean better than ok. This is the second greatest day in my life."

"You mean our wedding day was the first?" she said, the joy returned fully in her face.

Morgan paused. "Ok my third greatest day in my life. Our baby is third, our wedding was second and the first is that day I saw you at college, I knew then I could only be with you and no one else," he said as he kissed her passionately. Marina's fears fell to the wayside, and a wave of joy flooded through her. The apprehension she felt at telling him was finally over and warmth and relief filled her soul. They made love that morning, a slower pace, yet still with passion and elation. This was a new chapter in their lives, a turn for the better and together they would overcome anything.

††††

After they showered together, Marina was drying her hair and watching her husband closely. She could see a change in him—no longer did he seem preoccupied with his seizures. It was replaced with an excitement and pride that he was going to be a father.

"Hey, remember you have an appointment this morning to get your hair cut with Anna," she reminded him and Morgan nodded.

"Yes I remember," he replied, running his hand through his hair and scratching his head. A memory of sorts flashed in his mind. It was at a funeral, Anna his hairdresser, was there beside him, holding his hand.

"Morgan? Morgan! Are you alright? You have been sitting there staring into space for five minutes," Marina asked, her face showing immediate signs of worry as she kneeled down beside him.

"Hmm? What? Oh no... no I'm fine was just thinking about something," he answered almost like coming out of a trance.

"You seemed like you were miles away there, babe." she touched his cheek with concern.

"Hey, were we ever at a funeral and ran into Anna there?" he asked. The memory seemed too real to be part of a drug-induced fantasy.

"I don't think so Morgan. We have not been to a funeral in years, and I don't recall her being there."

"Ok then, chalk that up to the drugs too. It's like they have created a batch of new memories. Sometimes I just have to think them through to figure out if they are real or not. It's so messed up." Marina smiled and kissed him. "They will pass Morgan as time goes by and the drug is totally out of your system."

He smiled back. "I hope so. I'm too young to have dementia."

They ate their breakfast with the TV on in the background playing the news. Morgan was listening with half an ear to a report on some tremors felt in Tennessee, which caused a massive coal fire down in an abandoned mine. The reporter stood in a forested area down near the mine, interviewing a local resident.

"You can never tell what's still down in those mines. The tremor probably caused a cave in on some nitro-glycerin, that stuff becomes terribly unstable as it ages. Miners from the forties and fifties probably just left it there when the mines were shut down. It's was an accident just waiting to happen," he said to the reporter, who seemed to agree with the resident.

"So far there have been no deaths or injuries reported and no property damage due to the mine being located miles from any town or farms," the reporter commented. Morgan's attention wavered and turned off the TV and resumed his meal eating in silence. He still was not able to shake the image of the funeral and Anna from his mind. It seemed surreal, like it was a traumatic point in his life, but trying to piece it together in his mind seemed like trying to put a giant square peg into a round hole. The more he tried, the hole became smaller and smaller.

"Hey Morgan, you ready to go?"

"Go?" Morgan looked confused. Marina grabbed him by the chin.

"Fiore's. Anna. Haircut. Ring a bell?" she replied and Morgan nodded.

"Is it time already? Wow. Ok, let me brush my teeth," he said as he jumped up and went to the master-bath upstairs to brush his teeth. He returned shortly, zipping up his hoodie and putting his shoes on then followed Marina to the car. She clicked open the doors as they both piled in and buckled up. The drive to Fiore's went by quickly and it didn't appear to be very busy inside.

Anna waved at them as they came in and sat in the chairs in the waiting area. Anna was doing some last trimming on her client and picked up the mirror so he could view the back of his head. He nodded and smiled that his haircut was more than satisfactory. Anna smiled happily as she removed the apron and brushed away some of the cut hair. The client got up out of the chair, leaving her a tip then he proceeded to the cashier. Anna said her thanks to the man and came smiling up to Morgan and Marina.

"Hi Marina, how have you been? Morgan, you ready?" she asked as she motioned them to come up.

"Things with me are ok, Morgan on the other hand is another topic altogether," Marina replied as Morgan hopped into the chair.

Anna draped the apron over him and secured it behind his neck. Anna's beautiful smile vanished as she turned to Marina.

"What's been going on with Morgan?"

"Morgan's not been well. It may be epilepsy, but we are not sure yet. The doctors can't quite figure it out; they still want to do more tests to determine what's going on inside that brain of his."

"Oh Morgan, I'm so sorry. I have a cousin who had seizures for some time when he was young, then they just went away," she said and her smile came back to encourage him. Anna ran her fingers through his hair; the action seemed to trigger a deep sense of familiarity to him for more than just cutting his hair. It felt like a distant echo of memory within his mind, but it was like tapping into to someone else' memories.

"Yep well I hope mine just go away too," he replied, not really wanting to talk about it as he was getting his hair washed and the scalp massage felt wonderful. Anna and Marina kept on talking like he wasn't even there, which was normal. He focused on Anna's workstation, where there were several photos of her and her son. He smiled at them.

"Hey Anna, how is your son Conner?" This immediately caused the conversation going on between the two women to stop.

"Conner? You mean Carson? He is doing awesome. We were at the park on the weekend and we had a blast. He is almost four and never stops from the time he wakes up til he conks out at night."

"Night...night?" Morgan repeated then he sang. "Not last night, but the night before three little monkeys came to my door. One had a trumpet, one had a drum, one had a panny-cake stuck to his bum." Both Marina and Anna stared at him.

Marina looked pale yet Anna laughed. "Wow that is the same song Carson sang a few weekends ago. It drove me and Pete crazy, he just never stopped singing it. I remember the both of us could not sleep with that silly song stuck in our heads; funny how that is," Anna said as she continued on with the haircut. Marina recalled some of what Morgan had said when he was in the hospital delirious.

"*My… my son, Conner is gone.*" She remembered Tom saying he was confused, now this is the second time the name '*Conner*' came up. Why was Morgan looking so lost right now? She prayed he would not have another seizure. She was getting frustrated; she wanted to help Morgan so much but she did not know how. Marina watched on as Morgan sat staring again. Anna kept on talking, and finally Morgan came back when she asked him how it looked.

"Umm, fine. Awesome…actually as always Anna…thanks," he said. His smile came back but his eyes looked a million miles away.

The car ride home Morgan said nothing, still just staring at the road–he was still staring at nothing as she pulled into their driveway. Turning off the car and looking at him as he sat motionless, Marina grew more and more worried.

"Morgan…Morgan we are home now."

"Yep I know, I'm just thinking," he replied, still staring as Marina turned to him.

"What are you thinking about babe?" she asked as she took his hand and squeezed it.

"Oh I don't know just random stuff. Like how the hell did I know that stupid song?" Morgan said and looked at her with a haunted expression. He felt helpless and so confused. He wanted so desperately to hold it together for her, especially now when she needed him the most. But all he could feel was a darkness ahead that would somehow consume him.

"Marina, if…if things for me go wrong, like if I die or something I want you to find somebody, somebody that will make you happy. Will you promise me that?" he said to her with such terrible fear in his voice.

She looked at him as tears welled up in her eyes. "Morgan, you jerk. You're not going to die, do you understand? Don't say things like that, we will get through this, we will."

He nodded. "OK, I won't," he said, but his face suddenly lined with intense pain.

"Morgan?"

He immediately grabbed his head. "Ohhhh man! The headache is back, like a freaking avalanche!" he said as his face changed to a deathly white and his eyes relayed the horror of his agony. Marina grew instantly frightened and she tried to comfort him. He suddenly opened the car door, jumping out and violently threw up his breakfast. He leaned against the car, his hands on his knees, and was dizzily swaying. Marina launched herself out of the car to his side as he collapsed to the ground in convulsions. She cradled his head in her lap as tears ran down her face. She was almost at her breaking point, but she fought it off, knowing he needed her now and she would not fail him.

The seizure wound down, yet Morgan didn't come too, his breathing was all she could hear. Then the second seizure came upon him more violent than the first. Her neighbor who was getting his mail saw them and knew something was wrong and he rushed over.

"Marina. Marina! I will call 911, ok?" he said as he pulled out his cell phone and put in the emergency call. "They're on their way Marina, hold on Morgan, hold on," he said. Marina could only nod with tears streaming down her face, her world crumbling apart.

†††††

The ambulance ride was a blur for Marina. She was just barely aware of them putting Morgan on oxygen and starting an IV. She knew they were trying to get information from her but she could only shake her head no or nod for yes. Morgan was having his fourth seizure in a row and the EMTs were showing in their faces and in their voices that the situation was very bad. At the hospital, a nurse pulled her along with them as they took Morgan straight in. Incredibly, the same doctor that first saw him was assigned to his case. He fortunately had taken an interest in Morgan and followed up with Dr. Brennan so he was fully up to speed on Morgan.

Somehow, Marina managed to pull out her cell phone and called Tom's number. She dialed it without thinking, not knowing why she chose him and not Morgan's brother or mother. It was like a post hypnotic suggestion. She got Tom on the second ring.

"Hello…hello is any one there?" She could hear Tom ask, but the words just would not come out. She started to panic that he would hang up, believing it was a prank call.

"Marina? Is it you? Is Morgan ok?" Tom somehow knew, yet she could only dumbly nod, as the words were still not there. The silence on the line seemed remarkably long, yet his voice had a strangely calming effect on her.

"It's alright Marina, I will be at the hospital as quick as I can," he said.

Finally, her tear strained voice came back to her. "Ok," she replied then she heard the line click. Marina felt a wave of comfort hit her like a warm reassuring hug and pulled herself together, for her husband and their unborn child.

It was not long before Tom showed up. Saying nothing, he hugged her tightly and she felt a slight tingle through her body. It was comforting and like a boost of positive energy. Marina felt so much better; hope had returned to her, as if Tom's presence somehow would make everything right.

"What happened, Marina?" Tom asked. His words seemed to carry energy that helped her get through the events of that morning. Tom absorbed everything she said about the morning; his appointment with Anna, her son and the song Morgan sang.

All Tom said was "Anna? Conner?" he mulled it over, then said quietly, almost a whisper, "Triggers." Marina did not understand, but couldn't ask because the doctor came up to them.

"Mrs. Hamilton, I'm sorry but we still don't understand what is going on. CAT scans are showing confusing results. We see that the brain is simply over-active; almost double what it should be in a normal brain. We will have to induce a coma to keep him safe until this runs its course. This may be some sort of virus or bacterial infection. We are starting him on antibiotics in the hopes that he will show signs of improvement. We have his brain on monitors so we can watch what's going on inside. I can tell you this is not epilepsy, this is something that I have never seen or heard of before. I have put in some calls to the best neurologists and specialists in the business. With any luck, we can nail this thing and get Morgan on the road to recovery," his tone was encouraging, but knowing her husband was in a coma was far from settling.

Tom's presence continued to reinforce positive energy, feeding hope into her soul. Morgan was moved into intensive care later that evening. Tom always made sure Marina had enough food and something to drink, as if he knew she was pregnant and had to care for more than just herself. Alex showed up a few minutes after Morgan was placed in his room. He hugged Marina for some time before going to his brother's side. He took hold of Morgan's hand and he kissed him on his forehead. Tears welled up in his eyes as he whispered prayers for his brother. Alex was too young to remember his father; for him Morgan had always been both. Marina did her best to comfort Alex, while Tom somehow remained aloof; he seemed to be fighting with some internal decision that he was not quite ready to make.

As the night droned on to the early hours of the morning, Alex moved out to the waiting room to get some coffee. Marina rubbed her eyes and stretched her legs, walking around the room pacing to get the feeling back in her legs. She was watching Tom, who suddenly went odd, as if he heard something no one else did. He took to his feet so fast she could barely believe it. Something else about him changed: he grew taller by six inches and his eyes gave off an amber glow. His cheekbones became more prominent, but the face still resembled Tom's. She believed she was dreaming this; the man she knew for years suddenly changed before her eyes. Fear welled up from somewhere deep inside of her.

"Marina do not move. Stay here with Morgan. Stay quiet and stay low," he whispered sharply. He left her with Morgan, then out of the silence she heard a deafening scream and all hell broke loose.

CHAPTER FIFTEEN

A New Road

TAMLYN FELT THEM. He could scarce believe it but the unmistakable feeling of the enemy saturated his senses. He knew they were very close and now he had no choice. He took his true form and he stood up.

"Marina do not move. Stay here with Morgan. Stay quiet and stay low," he whispered and left her to engage the enemy. He scanned the hallway outside Morgan's room. The nurse's station two doors down on his left was staffed by three nurses, one was talking to two police officers. There were two EMT's standing beside a patient and the waiting room had five people all sitting, except for Alex who was digging out change in his pocket for the coffee machine. Further down the hall, past the nurse's station, he saw two tall men walking towards him. About twenty yards behind him to his right was the stairwell. The lights inside the stairwell suddenly blew out and the door slammed open with a terrible force. A black mist came out from the stairwell, entering the hallway. Immediately the mist moved faster towards him, lights exploding along the way. A terrible ear-piercing scream erupted from the mist.

"Banshee!" he screamed in his mind and his defenses immediately shot up as the mist sped towards him. Some poor unfortunate came out of the room adjacent to Morgan's to see what was going on and came between Tamlyn and the Banshee. The mist solidified into a horrid creature of savage teeth and razor claws that slashed the man to ribbons before he even hit the ground, spraying blood all over the hallway. Screams erupted from all around, one of the police officers was yelling for people to move out of the way as they both drew their weapons.

Tamlyn drew forth his power, creating a brilliant glowing orb similar to what he conjured for Ahmed's children, but this one was a hundred times more deadly. He launched it at the horrid creature and it swallowed the form of the Banshee. Its screams were deafening and people covered their ears in pain as the orb's unrelenting attack continued. The Banshee fled back towards the stairwell, returning to its black mist form with Tamlyn's orb still trying to absorb it. Tamlyn knew the orb would eventually kill the Banshee, but he had no time to worry about it. The people were starting to recover; the EMT's rushed over towards the hapless victim of the Banshee, as Tamlyn bent down to Alex.

"Are you alright?" Alex could barely hear him; the ringing in the ears was still blocking full hearing. Tamlyn quickly scanned the chaos of the waiting room. He observed that the two men down the hallway did not seem affected at all by the Banshee's screams. They seemed only intent on him, closing the distance quickly then fluidly they changed into Werewolves.

"Stay down!" he shouted and drew forth his swords. The people screamed in terror as one Werewolf grabbed the nearest person to it and lifted him right off his feet. It wrenched back the man's head as horrible jaws ripped out his throat. The police officers turned and fired their weapons, emptying their clips into both Werewolves. The beasts screamed in pain and fury but still came on. Tamlyn knew the police officers were dead if he did not act fast. With great speed, he engaged the nearest beast. He ducked low under the beast's deadly reach avoiding razor sharp claws, his one sword drove deep into its belly. Coming up around and behind with fluid super speed, his overhead swing took the creature full in the head, splitting the skull and burying his blade deep through the neck and into its chest. With both his blades buried into the body of the first Werewolf, the second came in for attack. Tamlyn kicked high, catching the beast full in the face and knocking it off its feet. Tamlyn pulled forth his sword from the dead beast and as its partner regained its feet, Tamlyn's sword sliced its throat, almost decapitating its head. It had happened so quickly people were either in shock, or screaming, or running for cover.

The police stared incredulously, as they almost mechanically reloaded their weapons. Tamlyn's senses screamed in warning, he was tackled off his feet, crashing through waiting room chairs, and coffee tables as his sword went flying from his hand. An Azael straddled above him, its armored fist landed a powerful blow to his face with immense strength. This Azael seemed bigger and stronger than other Azael. One hand grabbed Tamlyn's head, lifted him up and smashed him down hard upon the floor. Two glowing orbs appeared as the Azael brought forth its own head. Its insect-like features sickened him, bulbous compound eyes glowed intensely and he felt a searing sensation in his brain. It was delving him—a vicious form of Sharing that normally left the victim in a vegetative state.

Tamlyn heard gunshots. The police had recovered enough to realize he was on their side and unloaded their weapons into the Azael. It released Tamlyn and drew its scimitar, leaving Tamlyn dazed upon the floor as it stalked towards the police officers. They hurriedly reloaded and fired upon the Azael again; the bullets caused it great pain but barely slowed it down. When they were finally out of bullets, they drew forth their nightsticks and stood their ground. The Azael suddenly fell to the floor. Alex was standing behind it and had felled it with a chair, but the beast was quick and lashed out with its foot, catching Alex in his mid-section and knocking him across the floor. The police and the EMTs jumped on the Azael; the police officers were wailing upon it with their nightsticks as one EMT jabbed the Azael with a syringe injecting a massive dose of tranquilizer. The Azael ran one officer through the shoulder and took a swing at the other, tossing him across the room. It kneed one EMT in the face, knocking him out cold and the other was still holding the syringe as the creature raised its bloodied scimitar.

The Azael suddenly staggered from the drug's affect. Tamlyn now stood with both swords in his hands, protecting the EMT. The Azael considered its options and stepped back. It opened a dark void and jumped through, leaving the waiting room in confused chaos. Tamlyn moved towards the fallen police officer; he was alive. The blade caught him high on the chest, missing the lung.

"That creature is the one you seek for the murders with the missing heads," he said and the officer nodded that he understood.

"Thank you," he said with a quivered voice. Tamlyn called to the EMT to attend the wounded officer.

"Did you see that thing? I injected enough midazolam to knock out a freaking rhino and it still was able to get away," the EMT said to Tamlyn and the wounded officer. Nurses who were not on the phone calling for help rushed to the wounded. Tamlyn saw security running down the hall and coming out of the stairwell.

He bent over Alex. "Are you ok?" he asked and Alex nodded.

"What the hell Tom! You're like a freaking *Jedi* or something?"

Tamlyn smiled encouragingly. "Something like that yes. I need you to do something for me. Get Marina home safe, I have to take Morgan. It's him that I am trying to save. I hope not to be long, but you must see that she's safe," he said and Alex nodded that he understood.

"I will, I will. Can you heal him, make him like he was?"

Tamlyn looked hard into Alex's eyes; a great and terrible fear shone back at him. "I promise Alex I will try, but I must go now."

Alex nodded. "May the force be with you," he said with a quirky smile that was so like his brother.

Tamlyn took off towards Morgan's room. The link he sought after to connect the Blood-hunt oath into salvation for his friend was now forged. He could almost feel it clicking together in his mind. Rushing back towards Morgan's room, he saw Marina in the doorway with a look of complete shock on her face.

"You saw?" he asked quickly, moving her into the room. She looked at him and nodded as Tamlyn started to remove the IV, oxygen and all of the monitoring equipment hooked up to Morgan.

"Tom?" was all she could get out.

"My true name is Tamlyn. I am a friend, as I have always been. I am here to protect Morgan, but he needs help. Help that he cannot get here! I must take him away to a safe place where he can be healed. Trust me Marina," he said.

Alex came in behind her and placed comforting hands upon her shoulders. Her lips trembled in fear, yet somehow despite the chaos that had just unfolded around her she felt some comfort in his words and the sincerity in his eyes. Tamlyn scooped up Morgan effortlessly and opened a portal behind him.

"Go with Alex, say nothing of this. I will return as quickly as I can," he said reassuringly as he carried through and shut the portal behind him.

Tamlyn stepped out of the portal and into his apartment. He sensed nothing out of the ordinary within his home; he knew he was safe at least for the moment. He placed Morgan upon the sofa and went down on one knee beside him. He gently placed his hand upon Morgan's head, sending forth his power into Morgan to pull him from the comatose state and to tune down the brains activity, enough to at least put the seizures and the headaches at bay. He knew this was only going to hold a short while.

Morgan started to stir. "Tom … Tom what …? Your eyes are yellowy and your hair is silver and long … Oh man, is this another freaking hallucination?"

"No Morgan, no more hallucinations. What you see is real."

"Ok, then why do you look like you stepped out of the *World of War-Craft*? You look like an Elf."

Tamlyn smiled, standing to his full height. "Essentially you are correct; my people have been called Elfin by your ancestor's once long ago, but that right now is unimportant. What is important is that your condition cannot be cured with the medical practices of this world. Your only choice is to come with me to be restored or stay here living out the rest of your life in a coma."

Morgan looked at him with that quirky smile of his. "This is kinda like the *Matrix*, where I chose either the red or the blue pill. Gee that's not really much of a choice, is it?"

Tamlyn nodded comfortingly. "I'm afraid not," he replied.

Morgan bobbed his head, indicating he was ready. "Ok, my friend the Elf, let's go to Rivendell then. Umm this isn't going to hurt is it?" Morgan worriedly asked.

Tamlyn laughed at him. "It will hurt you more than it hurt will me."

"Great, just great," Morgan answered. Tamlyn sat down with his legs crossed and pulled out the traveling stone.

"What's that?" Morgan asked as he sat down in front of Tamlyn.

"It's a traveling stone, I need it to open the wormhole I'm about to create."

"Wormhole…like in *Star Trek*?" Morgan asked, his curiosity piqued.

"It would be far better if you do not talk," Tamlyn said to him with a level tone and Morgan nodded. Tamlyn summoned his power. The demand was far more than just jumping through gateways across the Earth; traveling across the vastness of space required far more power.

Its effect was instant, forming small then growing into a large circle about nine feet in height. It shimmered with a bright iridescence; Morgan had to divert his eyes from its glow. It had no effect upon Tamlyn, who telekinetically sent the traveling stone to cross over, unlocking the portal and allowing them the ability to step through.

"Come, it will be safe I promise you," he said. He held out his hand to direct Morgan through and for once Morgan didn't hesitate.

†††††

"Holy Crap and kick me in the balls!" Morgan said in awe as he stepped into an alien world. They stood upon a small plateau; the pastel blue sky held a massive red moon that seemed impossibly close. They stood on polished black stone surrounded by carefully manicured grass, watching as strange birds took flight in the air before them. Below were stone steps carved from the mountainside leading downwards into a forested valley. A morning fog hung low in the air and here and there tall stone towers poked above strange treetops. The valley was vast; small lakes and waterfalls could be seen from this majestic vantage point.

"Welcome to my home, Morgan!" Tamlyn said with glistening eyes. It had been a long time since he had last seen this valley.

"Umm, yeah, thanks!" he replied still trying to grasp it all.

"It is still a fair walk to my community," Tamlyn said as he took the steps downward.

"Why not just pop us right into the town square then?" Morgan asked.

"The gateway would kill anyone where it opened; for safety we have this area designated for portals to avoid any accidents," Tamlyn replied. He continued down the steps with Morgan immediately behind him, his eyes wide open taking it all in.

"I see. Well then, I'm up for a little hike I guess. Nothing scary is going to jump out and eat me?" Morgan asked as his voice trembled with both fear and curiosity. Tamlyn laughed at Morgan's apprehension.

"You are quite safe. This valley is quite well protected; in fact, both of us have been under surveillance since the portal closed."

"You mean like security cameras?" Morgan asked.

"Something like that, yes," Tamlyn replied. He chanced a look back at Morgan, who was trying to look everywhere at once, eyes wide in wonderment with an edge of panic lingering on the fringe. They walked on with only the sounds of the forest and the waterfalls in the background, yet the serenity of his surroundings did not put Morgan at ease.

"So is this place where we are going, is it like a hospital for Elves or something?" he asked.

"Not exactly, it is the Guild-home of the Warrior Cast. Those of us who wish to learn the art of combat come here. My race is immortal, and there are hundreds of Guilds on this world. It is common for my people to study here at one point or another before choosing another guild to enrich their lives. Only Guild Masters stay in a Guild for life. There is one here that I believe can help you, she is well versed in the healing arts and spent long years on your world, she knows well the mind of men," Tamlyn replied and he suddenly stopped in his tracks; Morgan almost bumped into him. He saw three tall figures step out of the forest in front of them, so well camouflaged he didn't see them until just now. Quickly, he looked for an escape route, but three more appeared directly behind.

"Be at ease Morgan, you are quite safe," Tamlyn said as he stood his ground before his own kind. One stepped directly in front of Tamlyn and pulled back his hood to reveal long golden hair, eyes of amber and ears that came to a delicate point. His face was expressionless as he and Tamlyn reached and clasped their arms together, heads bowed synchronized, foreheads gently touched. They stood locked in this embrace for what seemed like an eternity to Morgan; the others stood watching in eerie silence making him feel even more uncomfortable. When they at last broke the connection the Elf that touched heads with Tamlyn moved in front of Morgan bearing a welcoming smile. He bowed his head and with his left hand he touched his forehead then brought his hand downwards, palm open.

"He welcomes you Morgan, for you have saved our world from the enemy as you did your own." Morgan stared at him in confusion.

"I did?"

Tamlyn laughed. "Yes, you. But that was long ago, many lives you have lived since then. It is the reason you are here with me now."

"Yeah, well that's real nice and all, but you freaking lost me. I mean, you were my best friend growing up and I find out you are not even human, that you're an alien! And, I apparently saved everybody, but that really wasn't me either, just someone I used to be in a past life? Now I just came through a freaking wormhole to end up on another planet—why? Because I am having seizures? Does everybody with epilepsy get a ticket to crazy land?" Morgan's nerves were fraying apart quickly.

"You do not have epilepsy Morgan; the seizures are only a side-effect of what was done to you. The world that you know was once very different, you traveled upon a different path; your soul in that world was of a different man, Cameron MacLean. He was tricked into going back in time to be with his soul mate. He unwittingly tampered with the timeline and when he returned the world that he knew was gone, replaced with the one you live in. The soul of Cameron resides now within you, the same soul yet of different realities. All the past lives he had lived along with yours are trying to exist within a single mind. I brought you here to restore you, to separate Cameron from your mind before it drives you mad," Tamlyn said. Morgan's legs buckled beneath him, Tamlyn caught him and held him up.

"He came back weeks ago, didn't he? I mean, the night before the seizures first happened, I felt something in my head like my brain was full of static or something. You're not gonna do like brain surgery right, I mean take out my brain or something?" Morgan asked. The whites of his eyes seemed to grow with an inner fear as his imagination took flight.

Tamlyn shook his head. "No, nothing like that I promise you, we will only extract Cameron's soul."

A huge sigh erupted from Morgan. "Thank God, I just had visions of you taking out my brain and that scared the shit out me. So what will happen to Cameron then, will you return him to his life or something?" Morgan asked. He saw Tamlyn's jaw tighten and a single tear trickle down his cheek.

"His world no longer exists; removing him could perhaps destroy his soul. It may be the only way… to save you."

Morgan faltered a step; he had not felt such sadness from anyone as it flooded through his friend.

"I'm sorry, I didn't know, I just thought you could fix us both," Morgan said. As his voice trailed off to a whisper, he caught Tamlyn shaking his head.

"He is a good man, a kind soul and my friend; I believed I could help him but I could not find a way. He deserves life," Tamlyn said. Still his eyes reflected the sorrow and a sense of failure, yet also Morgan noticed there was a slight cast of hope.

"Whatever you need me to do I'll do it," Morgan said with determination and the Elf placed a comforting hand upon his shoulder. Tamlyn quickly turned as a new group showed up. The leader was a beautiful woman, with long and lush silver hair, tall and dressed in similar garb as the others, though her manner did not seem all that friendly to Morgan. Her amber eyes shone with hatred as she moved in front of Tamlyn. Her fist smashed his cheek so quickly Morgan could barely see it as Tamlyn took the blow that wrenched his head sideways with the force of it. Tamlyn did not defend himself as a second and third blow came just as fast that

Morgan could hardly follow it. Tamlyn blocked the next blow with cat-like reflexes, but the woman responded with a front kick that took him full in the jaw, knocking him off his feet. The other warriors merely stepped back to allow the combatants their space.

"Aaaarrr!" The woman spat through clenched jaws. She pulled out her swords from their scabbards on her back and attacked. Tamlyn recovered quick enough to draw his own to block the assault.

"Um, Tom, she looks really pissed at you!" he shouted with some distress in his voice.

"It is a family matter, no need to worry," Tamlyn replied as he defended himself. Deep down on so many layers he knew it was deserved. Centuries of pent up anger and emotional pain reflected in the fury of her eyes. Her temper was always more volatile than his own; several times he saw an opening to disarm her yet he let it play out. He had always been her superior in combat; even with the time away from his world he was still her better.

Her fury fuelled her strength, as the two warriors danced with razor edged and magic honed steel. It was then that the woman's eyes turned from anger to terrible sadness; she could not hold back the tears as she drove her twin swords deep into the earth and enveloped Tamlyn, wrapping her arms around him, her head sobbing into his chest. Tamlyn simply let his swords fall to the ground and hugged her in return; his eyes let forth his own tears. He held her tightly, comforting her. Morgan watched in silence, for the pain that had somehow been inflicted upon them seemed so terribly deep. He sensed their sorrow and was moved to tears because of it.

When she finally released Tamlyn, they looked deeply into each other's eyes. She reached for his arms and he took her in his own, bowing their heads together to make their foreheads touch, the same greeting as before. Morgan figured this was a special greeting of sorts and waited for it to enfold patiently. When they finally broke off, the woman smiled in understanding although the sadness still touched her eyes. She hugged Tamlyn again then kissed him upon each cheek.

They both turned towards Morgan. "Morgan, this is Tamara, my sister-in-law. Her sister was my wife and Tamara was also wife to my brother." Morgan bowed his head. It was all he could think to do; he caught the 'was' in the introduction and knew the pain they had endured came from the loss of both. Tamara approached him with kinder eyes; she was truly a beautiful creature, almost angelic in her perfection. She took his hands and gave them a gentle squeeze.

"Welcome to our Guild-home, Savior. I will do all that I can to help you," she said, looking so deeply within Morgan's eyes that he felt she was there in his head with him. A calmness surrounded him for the first time since he stepped foot upon this world.

"I thank you, thank you very much," was all he could reply as he became more and more confused.

"Tamlyn, you both will follow me to the infirmary so I can better assess the condition," Tamara instructed, her face lightened with a gentle smile. Tamlyn bowed his head in acceptance, picking up his swords he nodded to Morgan and held his hand open for him to follow.

"What is that thing you did back there with the arms and head touching?" Morgan asked, for he could not believe how quickly Tamara went from wanting to kill to wanting to help.

"It is called Sharing; it is a connection of minds, often it is done when one has been apart for some time. It allows us to see and feel all that has transpired during the absence, it is beneficial when there is so much to tell," Tamlyn replied as Morgan nodded to the response.

"Why didn't she just do that first, instead of trying to kill you?"

Tamlyn's face again dimmed with sorrow. "Her loss is very deep: a husband, a sister and two brothers, and it was I that lead them to their doom. Perhaps had I returned those centuries ago I would have let her take my life, but for a debt I owed Cameron I stayed away. I hope now we can mourn and heal together."

Morgan followed on in silence. The sorrow he felt from them both was like something he had never before felt, for to him it would be like losing Marina; she was his soul-mate and maybe he understood something of their pain.

He followed on through a stone path that carved the way through the forest floor. They passed under a great stone arch, which reminded him of the blocks of Stonehenge, but these stones were taller, with straighter edges and intricately carved runes that had a Celtic like design. Two more did he walk under, each larger than the last, becoming more impressive with their height and design. They followed the path as it edged closer to a stream on their left, and then the stream came to a small waterfall. The waterfall fed a square moat ten yards wide that surrounded a walled structure made of a red stone. The path led them to a bridge in front of the structure and its main entrance. It was here Tamara and Tamlyn turned with Morgan, while the rest of the party traveled on.

"Here we are, Morgan," Tamlyn said. Morgan looked upwards, impressed; the structure was immense, about the size of a city block at its base and stood at least six stories high.

"This is the infirmary? You must have a lot of injured people–this place is huge," Morgan said.

"Actually, we can self-heal even the most terrible of injuries, this is a place of contemplation, to restore ourselves from within; also our historical archives are within these walls. It is here we can help you without being disturbed," Tamlyn explained as they crossed the bridge and went into the great hall. A massive staircase opened before them as they ventured upwards to the next floor. Another set of stairs flanked the main staircase, taking them to the third floor.

They proceeded along the main hallway to the end of the structure, turning into a simple room.

Windows ran the length of the room giving more than enough light. The room itself seemed almost sterile with no furniture of any kind. Tamara proceeded to the middle of the room, motioning Morgan to follow. She took his hands in hers. "Do not worry Morgan, this will not hurt. You witnessed this before outside, the Sharing; it will be like dreaming. I will need to probe your mind, or to be more concise, to probe Cameron's mind. It is he that we must bring forth to see what has been done to perhaps save you both," she said. Her smile exuded a confidence that empowered Morgan to believe she could put things right.

"Ok, what do you need me to do?" he asked.

"Take hold of my arms and slowly bow your head until it touches mine, there you will feel a tingle. Do not recoil for it will not hurt."

Morgan did as she asked. He felt the tingle as she described, then oblivion.

CHAPTER SIXTEEN

A Desparate Plan

TAMLYN WATCHED ON as the minutes passed by, growing to hours upon hours. Tamara delved so very deep in the Sharing that her face began showing signs of strain and frustration at the task she had undertaken. He knew she had studied the mind of humankind, thousands of years ago. Ancient man had revered her as a goddess, yet she was only there to observe and learn all that the ancient cultures and the people could provide. In turn, she gave them basic knowledge in craft, crops and healing. It had all come with a price of sorts, for she had grown to love them and could not help see them age and then die. Sometimes they were reborn and the process would start all over again. Once she felt she had learned all that she could, she left Earth and never returned for the pain was all too close to the surface. Tamlyn had never seen a Sharing go on this long. Tamara was more stubborn than anyone he knew, if there was any way to save Cameron she would find it. Then abruptly she broke the connection.

"Tamlyn!" she called. They both aided Morgan to the floor as he collapsed unconscious. "He will be out some time I think. I was quite thorough in my examination," she said, wiping the sweat from her brow in frustration.

"What did you discover? Can you help him?" he asked, his eyes searched hers for some hopeful sign.

"You were correct in believing this was not some sickness of the mind. The creature that sent him on that journey into the past was indeed malicious in her vengeance. Cameron and Morgan are the same yet different, each with their own deep-rooted subconscious filled with separate knowledge and past lives. It is similar to a condition of men called a split personality where one personality shows itself while the other is unaware, but that is where the similarity ends. Right now, Cameron is aware of Morgan; he sees it all as if in a dream state and is constantly fighting to wake. The situation will grow worse and the two minds will try to dominate the brain at the same time. Madness will overcome them both," she said with a sigh then her beautiful face colored with concern.

"That I believe is not the worst of it, for I feel that even in death these two will be locked like two load-stones, reborn from one life to the next in constant struggle, madness from birth to death. How could the soul-mates ever find themselves again through that chaos? My heart cries out for this thing that was done to them," she said. Her voice shivered with compassion for the injustice.

"Then there is no hope? I was so sure that you above all would find a way. Cameron has sacrificed so much; even now he wished to end it, to kill him, to make it right for Morgan," Tamlyn felt sick at the thought of failure again.

"To do that would kill Morgan's soul as well, and that is something I cannot and will not do. There still is hope, something we have not yet tried. When Cailean destroyed the crystal matrix on that evil world, the creature that did this to him psychically latched onto his mind while her planet was heaving in its destruction. She only broke off her assault because she too was caught up in that maelstrom allowing Cailean to escape through the portal you created. It took her centuries to gather her power to exact her vengeance. That psychic latching aided her in seeking the soul of the man who destroyed her world; she traced that soul all the way to Cameron and then invaded his mind. She laid there for weeks, stimulating all the essential areas for her master plan. While using Cameron himself as a map to guide her through the layers of time and set the same triggers for Cailean, so when she made the introduction of Cameron into Cailean it was seamless. In fact, she stayed within his mind after that introduction for days, making sure all the connections were flawless. The trigger was set to separate them only after he went to that dying world. Once Cailean jumped through the portal returning him to Earth they became separated; Cameron was left alone there until she brought him back into the new timeline she helped to create," Tamara said.

Tamlyn nodded, for much of that he knew, what he didn't know was that Cailean's mind was also doctored to allow the connection. "You are thinking of returning Cameron back into Cailean? They lived in peace for a year; you believe that they could do so yet again?" he said and hope flared in Tamlyn's eyes, but he saw the tension in her face.

"That may be the only way to save them, but I do not know how to do it," she replied, hope extinguished from her eyes as it still flared in Tamlyn.

"But I think I know someone who does."

Tamara looked hard upon him, her eyes seeking to understand. "You mean to go back to that world, confront her?" she asked in disbelief.

"Perhaps we can convince her to show mercy."

Tamara shook her head. "I do not think that will be wise. She tenaciously sought this vengeance and made it last for an eternity. You think she will just change her mind and restore him out of the goodness of her heart? You are mad if you think she will help of her own free will."

"Perhaps you can persuade her," Tamlyn said with a smile.

"You overestimate my skills of persuasion then. I cannot think of any reasoning or incentive I can use to change her mind," she returned.

"You always underestimate yourself. I have faith in you and your abilities," he said, again with a smile.

"You are planning something. I see it in your eyes," she said, studying him shrewdly.

"Tamara, you are as sharp as ever," he replied with a laugh of his own. They turned towards the door as a figure stood waiting patiently to enter.

"You may enter," Tamara said with a warm smile as her eyes shone with overweening pride as the figure bowed his head slightly.

"Tamlyn this is one you should meet. A long time he has waited to see you," she stated as she waived the newcomer over.

Tamlyn's eyes lit up in disbelief. "It is not possible," he said, his look was of shock as he turned back at Tamara whose face glowed proudly. The warrior bowed his head and smiled. Tall and lean with long silver hair and piercing amber eyes, a strong chin and crisp cheekbones gave his face an all too familiar look.

"He is his father's son. Jeren, this is your uncle." Tamlyn extended his arm in greeting as Jeren grasped his in welcome.

"Jeren? You are named after my sire and are the very image of your father," Tamlyn said with a wondrous smile.

"He is a far better warrior than Finn ever was, even you Tamlyn he succeeds. Jeren is truly gifted, never have I seen the like," his mother said in pride.

"You have my sincerest apologies; you and Jenna were pregnant together, before the invasion. My quest to destroy the enemy, the Blood-hunt oath kept me apart. My responsibilities tore forever upon my heart. I stood divided between duty towards my family or to the one who sacrificed everything to save us all. Being immortal, I had chosen to stay on the Earth to do what I could to bring solace to Cameron. My regrets Jeren, I sincerely wish to make it up to you one day," Tamlyn's face paled as he reflected back in the loss of his wife Jenna and their child. They had planned to raise their families together, but that had been in a time of peace, never realizing invasion and war was on their doorstep.

"Do not blame yourself uncle, the Guild takes care of its own; the Guild is our family. Mother had felt my father's and her brother's deaths across the stars, she grieved deeply for them all. Yet she knew you still lived and held onto that," Jeren said as his eyes lit up with fire. "My father's brother; the last of the Legion that took up the Blood-hunt, chasing the enemy across the stars," he said in a voice so remarkably like his father's, with the same strength and pride.

"He embraces the old ways. The others regale him with tales of the past and of wars that were better never to have been fought," Tamara said as if this was a discussion long talked through. Jeren bowed his head with a slight redness growing upon his cheeks. His eyes locked on to Morgan sleeping upon the floor.

"You have returned with a creature from the world you have called home after all these years? To what end?" Jeren asked as his curiosity drove him as it always had, his famous uncle had returned with another being to the Warrior's guild. Its implications were dark judging by the mood his mother and uncle shared before he came into the room. The war that had so nearly destroyed them seemed to be still far from over.

His mother stepped forth. "This is no mere creature; within this being is the one we all owe a debt of eternal gratitude. It was he who had destroyed the Invader's home-world and destroyed their means of navigation across the stars. If not for him our world would have eventually fallen."

Jeren's eyes narrowed, scrutinizing Morgan further, weighing his mother's words. "You must Share with me Uncle when you have a moment. I wish to understand more, for I sense you have a task still to fulfill with this one and I will join you in that task to whatever end."

Tamlyn looked hard into his nephew's eyes, knowing he could not be dissuaded. It was a chance to redeem his father's death, to bring this conflict at last to an end, not just for him but also for his family. Tamara's lip trembled in fear for her son but she also knew she had no right to hold him back. Tamlyn watched the exchange in silence, understanding well his mother's trepidations. He turned and faced his nephew fully, placing his hand upon his shoulder.

"We shall see after we have our Sharing, then you can decide for yourself what we face. I owe a great debt to this man, and I will do whatever it takes to save him. Your strength and skill would be tested beyond anything you have encountered and may indeed take our very lives."

††††

Morgan awoke suddenly. It was dark outside, but the entry way gave off an orange glow that produced enough light for him to see. He sat up, looked around and felt right away he was not alone.

The tall figure moved silently towards him. "How do you feel?" it said as the figure came close enough to be recognized.

Morgan rubbed his head with his hands. "Ok I guess Tom, I mean Tamlyn. It is still all a little fuzzy, but no pain, not really. It's like my brain just had a terribly long cold shower," he said with a grin, as his stomach growled loudly.

"Hungry too, how long have I been laying here?"

Tamlyn laughed. "You should be; you have been out for a day and a half."

"No shit. Wow, reminds me of my college days. That explains why I really have to pee," Morgan replied as Tamlyn laughed again and extended out his hand.

"Come, the washroom is across the hall."

Morgan took the helpful hand and tried standing up, only to find out how wobbly he was on his feet. "I'm ok… just a little woozy that's all," he said with a reassuring smile while Tamlyn stood ready to catch him if he fell. Tamlyn escorted him across the massive hallway and into a washroom unlike anything Morgan had ever seen. It was illuminated with the same orange glow that was in his room yet became brighter once he crossed the threshold. There was cascade of cool water pouring out of the wall into a large waist high basin. The basin tapered at the far end allowing the water to drain in a trough along the wall. Morgan quickly figured out that the trough was the urinal. After doing his business Morgan went to the basin and washed his hands and face, then ran cool water through his hair. After toweling himself dry he noticed clothing on the bench, similar to the clothing the others wore, though smaller in size. It seemed custom made for him, shirt, pants, socks, boots and cloak; it was great to get out of the hospital garb.

He rejoined Tamlyn and immediately the Elf noticed Morgan looked much better, less pale and exhausted.

"Thanks for all of this," Morgan said holding his hands out almost for inspection, while Tamlyn nodded in his approval.

"Umm Tamlyn, the time here, is like back home right? Like spending a couple of days here is not like a hundred years back home is it?" Morgan asked.

"Rip Van Winkle, is that what you fear?" Tamlyn chuckled. "Do not worry, time is essentially the same here, my world is slightly bigger than yours; our days here are twenty eight hours long. You need not be afraid, we will get you back to your world soon enough. Once Tamara and the others go through a Restoration cycle we will be ready."

Morgan nodded at that, not really knowing what a Restoration cycle was, but if it had to be done to help him he was all for it. "So do you know how to help me?" he asked almost nonchalantly. Tamlyn looked at him with hard eyes.

"I have a plan, but it will not be easy. We must go back to the world you once destroyed and ask the creature that did this to you for aid."

Morgan looked at him with a disbelieving face. "You think that is a good idea? I mean really, that's all you got?"

Tamlyn's face softened. "Tamara can be quite persuasive when she wants to be. Come, let us get some food in you first and we can go over what needs to be done after," he said. They left the room and headed down the stairs to the second level, then again down the massive hallway as the smells of food directed them to the kitchens.

Several others were already in the room and smiled as they entered. They touched their forehead with their fingers upon their left hands then extended the hands downward palm open. Morgan returned the gesture and their faces returned warm smiles and invitations to join them.

"Morgan take their hand one at a time. You will feel a tingle in your mind, it will not hurt, this will enable them to speak and understand your language," Tamlyn instructed. Morgan did so to each of the three at the table, and felt the slight tingle Tamlyn described.

The Elf who Morgan first took the hand of smiled warmly. "Greetings Morgan, welcome to our home. I am Mikka, this is Renn and Ronan," he said. Renn passed two plates and two long spoons to them both, along with several steaming bowls of food. One bowl contained a couscous like dish with chopped vegetables; another looked like a mixed greens salad, the other what appeared to be ravioli in a pink sauce. Morgan was so hungry his normally fussy nature was shoved aside as he dug in. Renn filled two mugs for them both.

"It's like a mild red wine, a little sweeter too," Tamlyn provided as Morgan took a giant swig. Morgan savored every bite. The three companions politely let them eat until they had their fill.

"I take it you three have been through a recent restoration?" Tamlyn asked them.

"On the last high moon. We are ready to go as soon as the others are done their cycle," Mikka quickly answered with enthusiasm in his voice.

"Ten full Guild-masters will accompany you on this task," Renn added, his tone exerting a cool calmness.

"Hopefully that will be enough," Tamlyn replied, equally calm.

"Guild-masters …they kinda like the Navy Seals?" Morgan asked, wanting to be part of the conversation.

Tamlyn placed a comforting hand upon his shoulder. "Yes very much so. Do not worry Morgan, I believe you are quite safe from this creature we are about to confront. If she wanted to kill you she would have done so already," Tamlyn said to ease his friend's anxiety.

"She can always change her mind," Morgan replied nervously.

"I suppose she could, but that is a chance we will have to take."

"Hey, how are we going to confront her on her world? I mean I thought you said I destroyed it?"

Tamlyn smiled at him. "Enough of it remains. Cailean destroyed the force field that kept the world alive, and their ability to travel across the stars. When we journey there, it will be in a corporeal form: our bodies will remain here; our minds shall journey to that haunted world. We will be nothing but ghost like images of ourselves, like a hologram," Tamlyn answered him and Morgan nodded in understanding, thinking it through.

"Ok then why the muscle? What do we need ten Guild-masters for?"

Tamlyn's face turned to stone, dark and cold. "They are for when we return you home to confront the enemy entrenched upon your world. I took you from your hospital bed after an attack upon you there."

Morgan's face paled. "Marina?"

"She is safe, she is with Alex, safer than if she was still with you at home. The creatures of that hellish world would not hesitate to kill you given the chance; some would quite enjoy it," Tamlyn said to reassure him of Marina's safety. Tamlyn then revealed more. "Recently I had eradicated thousands of them hidden deep in abandoned mines. They were getting ready to strike against the human race. They had a tremendous stockpile of weapons that I was able to explode to annihilate them. However not all were killed, that is why we are going back with you. Not only to restore you but to cleanse your world of these demons. Given enough of a chance these creatures will restore their numbers, enough to plunge your world into an eternal nightmare," Tamlyn said. The others silently nodded as strong hands gripped their weapons in an eager anticipation.

††††

Three days passed while Tamlyn showed Morgan the warrior's Guild home, including all the different buildings and much of the valley that surrounded them. Morgan watched as Guild Masters drilled hundreds of students amongst the training grounds.

"Wow this is really like *Jedi*-school isn't it?" Morgan said jokingly and Tamlyn laughed at him. "Tell me about him. Cailean … err … Cameron," Morgan asked.

Tamlyn moved in beside him. "They were one in the same for a while but I know what you mean. Cailean was strong and determined, stubborn too much like you. He was a Highland Chief in a turbulent time, a great tactician and a deadly swordsman. He saved a woman of surpassing beauty from certain death. Her name was Kerry and she was identical to Marina in every way, right down to the soul they shared. Cailean and Kerry were soul mates. That is why you were pulled to Marina so strongly here in the present, as was Cameron," Tamlyn said as his eyes drifted through time, recalling that memory. Morgan watched him closely.

"How did Cameron end up in me?" he asked, wanting to get finally to the bottom of the matter.

"Your world, your time was not the true timeline. All of it changed but a short while ago, yet the change took place 750 years in the past. Cameron was you, in his time he met Marina as you did in college. He felt the same attraction as you, yet he didn't annoy her until she finally agreed to go out with him," Tamlyn laughed as he went on.

"He could not let her go from his thoughts but she stayed with the man she was living with and then got married. Cameron himself met someone and he too married. It was not long until Cameron had a child from that marriage, although the marriage did not last. He could never let Marina go and that was his weakness that was carefully exploited. The Goddess of that hellish world manipulated his thoughts and stimulated madness within. At his almost certain breaking point, she offered to send him back in time to be with his soul mate for an entire year and that all that would transpire in the present would be but a single day. As you know Cameron took the offer and was sent back in time, to relive that life again as Cailean. The creature stayed with him, altering his path in history ever so slightly. Originally Cailean had saved Kerry's life during a Viking raid but Kerry had been raped just before Cailean saved her. With Cameron, the Goddess had altered history by getting Cailean to Kerry before the rape, thus the child of that rape was never born. That child was the progenitor of the line that ended with Cameron and his son. Saving Kerry, he wiped out his own family line, creating a different path for your soul to take to the world you know as Morgan Hamilton.

"That night you said felt so odd, that was Cameron returning to the present. He gradually discovered what he had done; he had erased himself, his family and his son from existence. In the end, all he could do was follow my summons to your office where he too used to work. That morning he ran into Marina, he saw in her eyes only a fleeting recognition buried deep inside her. Then you called to her and he saw the happiness in her eyes. Cameron knew that somehow her life had changed as well and her happiness was all that mattered to him. He then came to me to the alleyway alongside your building, devastated and lost. I confirmed to him all that he had discovered and comforted him as best I could until he slowly faded away as the timeline he created finally cemented within the fabric of time and space.

"As old world of Cameron faded, so did his material form, yet his spirit was still present and like two magnets Cameron's spirit merged with yours. Two minds, two spirits the same, now fighting inside your brain causing the seizures and it will only grow worse. And even when you die your souls shall forever be entangled; every time you are reborn again you will suffer the same madness, the same seizures for an eternity," Tamlyn said, the pain lined his face as he unfolded the events. Morgan grew paler by the moment and looked like he was going to be sick.

"Well that really sucks!" Morgan shouted. "And you think going back to that place–to the creature that set all this up, that she is just going to fix it…to somehow make it all better? That is the biggest dumbass plan I have ever heard of. Look, I know you are doing everything you can to help but there has got to be a better way," Morgan said, the defeat in his voice flushed away the hope he once had. Tamlyn closely watched him; the sympathy he felt for his friend was so very deep. He had been caught up in this saga from the beginning, and almost eight centuries later he was still unsure what the outcome would be.

"It is my hope that from confronting this creature we may learn more of your condition, whether directly or indirectly," Tamlyn said, trying to give Morgan some small glimmer of hope.

"Whatever you think is right. I have nothing to lose at this point so the sooner we do this the sooner I can get home," Morgan said trying to be strong yet Tamlyn saw the fear engraved in his eyes.

"There is one more thing; when we go it is Cameron that must be conscious within you. You, my friend, we will have to bury within your subconscious; it will be similar to dreaming although you will have no control of the dream. Cameron was on that haunted world only a short time ago, the markers within his mind will allow us to navigate there," Tamlyn explained and Morgan simply nodded.

"Like I said, whatever you think is right," he still looked like he was going to be sick. Morgan always liked to control his surroundings, now he would not even be in control of himself.

††††

The next day Morgan had time to think upon what Tamlyn had said and for what he had done all these years for him. Tamlyn could have left him all those years ago, abandoning him to his fate. Now he was doing all this for him and he felt ashamed that he lashed out in anger. After the morning meal, he caught up with Tamlyn.

"Hey Tam, I just wanted to say I'm sorry for what I said yesterday. I was a little freaked out, still am but I can't blame you at all. Thank you for trying to help," Morgan said as he did his best to put on a good face.

Tamlyn smiled warmly. "No need to apologize Morgan, for what you have gone through I don't blame you one bit. We are still in for a bumpy ride you and I," Tamlyn said with a laugh.

"So this reincarnation thing is what really happens to us then? All the religious stuff, heaven and hell and all the rest of it, it's not all true?" Morgan inquired.

Tamlyn shook his head. "Reincarnation exists but for the rest of it I do not know all the answers. Not everyone is immediately reborn when they die. There were times it took years for your soul to emerge again and in some cases some souls never do. As for heaven and hell, I have caught glimpses of them. When one dies there is a veil that opens for a brief moment only; my kind has the ability to see it revealed before the eternal curtain closes once again. I feel that time runs differently there, a single day in your world could be a year there, perhaps more. I know not why or how a soul returns, perhaps that is what you call God's will," Tamlyn said and Morgan shook his head.

"Well I didn't expect it to be that easy, I guess it remains just a leap of faith for us mere mortals," he said with a laugh.

Two days later Tamara emerged from her Restoration. She sought out Tamlyn in the early hours of the morning. "You watch over him even as he sleeps, even though he could not be any safer within these walls," she said to him, her face bore a curious smile.

"He has gone through much; the seizures are still highly active within him. We owe them both so very much, for what Cameron had sacrificed to save our world as well as his own," Tamlyn replied, reinforcing not just for himself and for her, but also his decision to have stayed away on Earth all those centuries.

"You need not explain to me for we have Shared. I see that you do this not just for his sake but for Jenna as well. You want to see those that took her from you eradicated, vengeance still fuels the Blood-hunt within you. You have killed thousands of these fiends yet the oath still drives you on; it's single-minded determination that will not let you have any peace until that goal is achieved," she said softly, her hand caressed his cheek in compassion.

At her touch the fires within him soared; she was truly beautiful, so much the mirror of her sister. Feelings of guilt touched his eyes and she saw it. "Jenna would not have wished for you to be celibate, in fact she would have insisted that you find another..." That was as far as she got before he swept her up in his arms. Passions quickly took them, centuries of absence within them both released in a torrential avalanche of emotions that overtook them as only passions in an immortal race could.

That morning Morgan awoke to an empty room. Tamlyn was absent—it was strange as he was usually there when Morgan woke up. He showered, dressed and went into the kitchen for his morning meal where he found Ronan waiting for him.

"Good morning Morgan. Come have some nourishment, for the others have finished their Restoration and we will be embarking on our journey soon." Morgan nodded as he saw the fire light up in Ronan's eyes, the intense anticipation of their journey and the confrontation of the enemy stoking that fire.

"Tell me Ronan, have you fought these creatures before?" Morgan asked, hoping to learn a little more of the enemy that threatened his world.

"I have, I was here in those darkest of our times. I fought at Ashenfold with my brothers, we did not know then that we were at war. Dark was that battle, we failed and the city was overrun. It was not until Sansi Falls did we first come against the wickedest of weapons, the Reavers." Morgan saw the Elf's face change—radiating a terrible sadness. Morgan's curiosity was hard to contain as he noticed hesitation in Ronan's voice.

"What are Reavers?" he asked seeking more yet not wanting to upset his new friend.

"They are our dead and totally under control of the Azael. They fight as though alive, yet do not feel pain or tire; it takes much to bring one down. When they first came against us it was terrible—we could scarce believe what we saw, our own kind fighting for the enemy. We nearly lost, our lines were overrun and our spirits shattered as hundreds of us fell in the first moments of that battle. It was then that we bore witness to the evil of the transformation of our own kind being re-animated into these Reavers. We saw firsthand this evil spell they cast upon our brothers and sisters. They are an abomination and it causes us great emotional pain in destroying them. It enraged us and in our fury we turned the tide of that battle. At Sansi Falls we defeated them, but it had been at a terrible cost." There was dreadful sorrow in Ronan's eyes as he unfolded his tale.

Morgan swallowed hard. "Kinda like Zombies, oh man they creep me out; I mean I'm a big fan of '*The Walking Dead*,' but that's TV and video games. To have to actually experience it, I don't think I would ever sleep again," Morgan said. He saw confusion on Ronan's face. "Ahh hard to explain, don't worry about it," he added as Tamlyn and Tamara came in together. Ronan bowed his head, touching his forehead with his fingers then brought his palm down open in greeting. Tamlyn and Tamara did the same in return.

Morgan sensed a difference in them both; the slight lines of tension seemed to have vanished and a more comfortable mood embraced each of them. Morgan and Ronan looked to each other and were quick to establish in their own minds the reason behind it. Morgan smiled at Ronan but all he got was a brief nod from the warrior. Quickly the hall filled up as the others of their company joined them.

They all ate vast quantities of food; after a Restoration it requires great amounts to fully recover. He sat in silence as they all said very little. When they *did* speak, it was said in their own tongue. For the first time in his life, Morgan sat feeling out of place. They were immortal beings, thousands of years old, exceptionally skilled warriors that could kill him in less than a heartbeat. Yet somehow they all treated him like a hero, which in itself was very weird as it was not him that did anything. It was Cailean who was the hero, and Cameron who was now within him who had experienced it all. Sometimes he wondered if he was still in a coma and this was some bizarre nightmare playing itself out in his head. He decided to pinch himself just in case. Tamlyn watched him, a smile seeped into his face at Morgan's slight grimace in pain.

"Morgan, are you ready? You recall what you must do?" he asked knowing that Morgan was truly afraid of this next step.

"You can bring me back right? I mean, it's not permanent or anything?"

Tamlyn winked at him. "It will be like dreaming, I promise."

"Then why do I feel like I'm going to throw up?" Morgan replied as his pallor turned almost ashen.

Tamara took to her feet. "Come Morgan. It is time to bring forth Cameron MacLean," she gently placed her hand upon his head and he felt a tingle like ice water down his neck. Then there was a surge in his head almost like when a limb falls asleep; the vertigo overwhelmed him, and suddenly oblivion.

Tamara released her grip as the others in the hall watched the transformation.

"Tamlyn? This is real, not a dream?"

The Elf took a step closer. "Cameron? Are you with us?"

"I think so…it is all kinda surreal, like waking up and not knowing who or where you are. Is this your world… am I on an alien planet? Wow, I guess this is my second alien planet, if we are taking score. Why am I here? Is this your solution—I mean is this how I am to live out my life—here with you?" Cameron asked.

Tamlyn's face was anxious; his eyes hinted that there was much more to this situation than he cared to admit. "Cameron, the situation is more complicated, my world here is only a brief stop; we are, to coin a human phrase 'not out of the woods yet.'"

Cameron looked at Tamlyn and the others gathered around him. He saw their faces were confident, eager and determined. To Cameron it was far better than fear and panic, which was more akin to what he was feeling. "Just tell me we are not going to *Mordor*?" Cameron replied with a less-than-confident smirk as Tamlyn patted him on this shoulder with a laugh.

"In a way—yes we are; back to that dead world," Tamlyn answered. His lips still smiled but his eyes mirrored traces of uncertainty that caused the panic in Cameron to swell like the rising tide within. Cameron took a few deep breaths to regain a bit of self-control.

Tamara felt for him and placed her hands upon his shoulders, looking him deep in the eyes. "We will let no harm come to you. Even if this creature refuses to help, we may still learn enough to figure out how to make this right," she said confident in her claims, enough to give Cameron some comfort. He nodded he was ready.

Tamlyn smiled. "Then let us make our way to the portal." As one, they took to their feet, fluid in form and grace.

CHAPTER SEVENTEEN

Back To Hell

THE HIKE TO the portal plateau was a new one for Cameron, the memory of it was originally Morgan's. For Cameron it was like walking a path you had just dreamed about, overpoweringly familiar. Like a surreal form of deja vu.

Once they arrived, Tamara asked them to form a circle and guided Cameron to sit inside the circle facing her. "Sit, right in front of me," she instructed. Cameron followed her lead. The rest all sat with their legs crossed under them; each one placed their hands upon the shoulder of the one beside them. Tamlyn sat on Tamara's right, his left hand upon her right shoulder. Jeren on her left placed his right hand upon her left shoulder to complete the circle.

Tamara placed both her hands upon Cameron's head. "Think of that Dead world Cameron. Recall in your mind that moment; isolate that in your thoughts. I will do the rest," she instructed. Cameron put all his thoughts on that horrid place and closed his eyes. He felt a surge of energy and when he reopened his eyes gone was the lush green world. At the speed of thought he was now once again upon that hellish world. It was a cold grey and lifeless place with ruins all about; ancient and haunted.

Cameron noticed quickly he was in a corporeal state; he was there yet not entirely, more ghost-like. They all took to their feet, looking about to view their surroundings. Tamlyn stood at his side.

"We are actually here!" Cameron said as he looked down at his almost translucent hands. "Well sort of, I guess."

"Come, we are at the base of the amphitheater, ahead lies our path," Tamlyn said as they followed silently behind him. These ruins were almost eight hundred years old yet to Cameron his magical journey on this dark world was only some weeks ago. Memories flooded his mind of that terrible battle in Scotland and the pursuit through the portal to rescue Kerry. Fleeing on a nightmare trek through the maze like corridors to this open aired amphitheater and the crystal matrix that kept this world alive. To say it was all massively surreal was a gross understatement. Now here he was back on this hellish world again, the last place in the universe he wanted to be.

Tamlyn led them through the ruins seemingly he knew what path to take, for soon Cameron saw a figure standing alone in the distance peering into the starlit sky. The view was miraculous; with the atmosphere gone, there was nothing to hinder the universe in all its majesty. They approached the figure with ghost like steps, yet she somehow sensed their presence and turned to face them, lavender eyes burning with malice.

"I can smell your fear, even in your corporeal state you reek of it," her smile twisted cruelly as she laughed. She looked upon Tamlyn and the others with no hint of worry.

Then she turned her gaze towards Cameron. "The Ljosalfar brought you to me obviously but to what end? To restore the timeline? That I will never do," those lavender eyes scrutinized his face with a terrible intensity. "No…no that is not why…you are here seeking my help!" she laughed again, looking hard at the one who had destroyed her world.

"So you have discovered the full weight of my vengeance? Two souls inexorably tied together until the end of the universe. Both trying to control, yet chaos will run its course through you every time you are reborn. Madness will consume you and the struggle for dominance will never allow you to live long. The soul-mates will never be together again," she outlined his dark future with a mocking sympathetic pout. Her words stung him deeply and she knew it, so smug in her plan as her vengeance had indeed been met. Cameron trembled at the thought of an eternity in perpetual madness. This was not going well. He looked to Tamara for guidance for Tamlyn said she would be the one to negotiate with this creature, but Tamara was not there.

Tamlyn moved protectively beside him. "You have already caused enough suffering; he has lost everything, his family, his son, isn't that enough? Can you not help him, show mercy to a defeated foe?" he asked passionately.

"Mercy? Mercy to one such as this? Surely you jest? This is a just punishment for a terrible crime. You speak of the loss of one child? He has killed millions of mine! You ask for mercy, you must be insane to even suggest such a thing."

Tamlyn would not give up so easily. "Your children murdered innocents, millions of them. We did not cause the calamity that touched your world, nor did we ask you to invade ours. Your children could have gone to a world with no sentient life and rebuilt your society, to start again. The choice was theirs to make, yet they chose to attack inhabited worlds. They brought their own destruction when they made that choice," he said in wrath, fueled in remembrance of the devastation wrought in those dark times.

Those lavender eyes turned upon him now in full fury. "I would not deny my children their need to hunt, to feed. It is what they are, their nature. The strong survive and the weak perish, it is the way of the cosmos," she spat as she turned her back upon them and returned to stare into the heavens. "Go home Ljosalfar, make ready for what is to come and take the human with you so he can bear witness to what will soon happen upon his world," smiling again, she relished in the plans she had long set in motion.

Cameron moved towards her. "What will happen, what is she talking about?" his voice carried echoes of fear.

"I believe she is talking about the Azael, their plans to plunge your world into darkness so her children can then walk the earth openly, feeding and multiplying in great numbers. But I am afraid that plan will never come to fruition. For the great hordes of Azael are no more, I destroyed them in their secret lairs across your world with the very weapons they were going to use against the human race," Tamlyn said confidently. Yet the reaction he obtained was not what he expected.

Still smiling she turned upon him. "You may have intercepted one attack, but there are many more, I have set into play contingency plans, my children are masters of survival and even far more devious than I. Go Ljosalfar, leave my world for there is nothing you can do," she said and once again turned her back to them in contempt.

"Perhaps there is something I can!" Tamara said appearing out of nowhere. Her corporeal form enveloped the woman and the two became one, a purple glow grew and surged. The creature screamed in fury as she fought a psychic duel against Tamara with everything she had. The glow intensified as the battle continued. Cameron could do nothing but watch in horror, not knowing what was happening but knew that his very soul hung in the balance.

Cameron felt a surge of panic swell inside watching this epic battle of wills. If Tamara failed, he was certainly doomed. The lavender-eyed Goddess let out one more long devastating scream that seemed to cause the ground to shake; then she was gone. Only Tamara existed in her place.

"You were right Tamlyn, although she hid it well, she had not much life force left within her. Her schemes with Cameron had left her with almost nothing. When I attacked, she used all her remaining power trying to keep me from delving her mind yet she lacked the strength to stop me from getting what I needed. She could no longer hold her form; she is now truly dead like her world," Tamara said with a trace of sorrow. She cast her gaze towards Cameron as she saw the hope reflecting in his eyes. Cameron could not ask, could not form the words. It was Tamlyn who spoke first.

"Did you get what you needed? Can you help him?" he asked as every frazzled nerve left in Cameron strained to hear the next precious word.

"Yes," she replied. "I think I can, it will not be easy for I will need the power of all of us to make it happen," she answered as she regained some of her strength. Cameron once again felt hope rise within.

"We will give our lives if necessary," Jeren put in and the others nodded in their own willingness to do whatever it takes.

"That will not be required my son, but the power will drain us greatly, it was very wise of you to recommend the Restoration before we attempted this journey Tamlyn." she smiled warmly to Tamlyn taking his hand. "The only way to save them is to retrace Cameron's path. The conduits forged through the layers of time are still present. To save Morgan and Cameron we have to take them back into the past. We will re-insert Cameron back into Cailean then Morgan will be cured," Tamara said.

Cameron shivered deeply, this was he had truly wanted, were he felt he sincerely belonged. Here in the present, there was nothing for him but in the past, he can be again with Kerry.

"What about Cailean what will happen to him? Will not we be exchanging one madness for another? Will not the turmoil that affects Morgan transfer to Cailean?" Tamlyn asked worriedly. The logic of it now hit Cameron; he had just found new hope only for it to be possibly shattered apart.

"After I delved into Morgan's mind I told you that I discovered the creature spent a long time within both Cameron's and Cailean's mind, setting all the right triggers to hold both minds. When Cameron saved Kerry from the rape, altering the timeline, the girl child Meaghan was not born. In Cameron's timeline it was from her womb did the soul of Cailean eventually pass into, reborn anew upon his death. When this did not happen, a new timeline evolved to finally end here in the present with Morgan. When Cameron was ripped out of Cailean, he was thrust back into the future intact, inserted into the new timeline where his soul already existed in Morgan.

"It is the soul and the subconscious containing all those memories of Cameron's past lives that are conflicting within Morgan and the past lives from Cailean forward. We need to re-insert Cameron into Cailean before his death, before his soul takes that first change in time, the transition will not be smooth," Tamara explained. She touched Cameron's face with her nearly transparent hand and strangely enough he felt it as she peered deeply into his eyes. Her smile showed him that salvation was possible, but Tamlyn still knew that the solution was not that easy.

"This will not harm Cailean? There was a time close to the end of Cameron's year that the memories of Cameron himself caused something similar to what was happening to Morgan." Tamara nodded as she followed Tamlyn's line of thought and of his concerns.

"That was only because the essence of Cameron was the dominant one—here it will be Cailean so there will be no conflict. It all started with Cailean, and changed with his death. Once Cameron is re-inserted, those past lives will dissipate one after another as each new one is reborn. By the time he is to become Morgan those two souls will have merged into one." It was the only option left for Cameron, but it was a leap of faith and there were no assurances that this would truly work.

Tamlyn watched his friend gaze out into the heavens in the very footsteps the lavender-eyed Goddess had stood in, Tamlyn moved beside him, and took up the gaze. Cameron searched hard for what it was the woman was staring at but only the billions upon billions of stars twinkled back at him.

"What was she staring at I wonder, what is that part of space?" Tamlyn looked hard upon the stars casting out his gaze, calculating in his mind and he shivered.

"That part of space is where your world lies."

Cameron looked like he was going to throw up. "That is not very comforting. I have had enough of this place can we go now?"

Tamlyn nodded to his friend. "Tamara, you must now choose our path," he said deferring to her direction.

Tamara smiled. "We must join hands. We will return to our world, back to our bodies then we must journey to where this all began."

Once they joined hands, Cameron felt the surge of power and again at the speed of thought he was back upon Tamlyn's world and in Morgan's body once more. Tamlyn brought forth his power, summoning the portal back to Earth.

"It is back to your old apartment once more Cameron–that is where the journey started for you," he said as he peered into the portal yet all Cameron could see was a bright iridescent light.

"Come, it is safe," Tamlyn said. He stepped into the portal to enter into what once was Cameron's old living room. Cameron stepped into his old home once more, the walls were the same yet the furniture was different, a part of the carpet had been removed–after seeing blood splatter upon the walls, Cameron could figure out why.

"What happened here?" he asked curiously. Tamlyn placed a comforting hand upon his shoulder.

"The Azael that took the photo and your tartan tie was from the future. When it left your apartment it was still your timeline but when he returned it was changed and unfortunately for the current occupant, it did not wish to leave any witnesses. I am very sorry."

Cameron nodded. "Just one more death to lay upon the enemy's feet, another death for them to answer to."

"They will pay for this, I promise," Tamlyn said as Cameron again looked around the once familiar apartment.

"Well you have never broken a promise to me before," Cameron replied, as Tamara confronted Tamlyn.

"Going back in time will be difficult, we will need a time and place after Cailean came back from that world. It would have to be when you were not at his side, preferably when he was alone, can you recall a time such as this?" she asked Tamlyn who took some time to search his memory for what she needed.

"Largs!" he answered.

Jeren approached them. "What is a Larg?"

Cameron whose grandfather had drilled him in Scottish history as a boy, replied. "It is not a what, it is a place, and if I am not mistaken it was a battlefield too."

Tamlyn smiled at him. "Yes, that is when and where we must go."

Tamara moved into the Sharing with Tamlyn, obtaining the necessary details, the exact timing in history; she only had one chance at this and knew it.

"Going through time is a delicate journey, like flipping through the pages of a very large book. Once we start, it will gain momentum, the pages will flip fast and we have to stop at precisely the exact page. The conduit in the hallway will guide us but we have to stop three years after your original arrival, all of you must tune your minds to me, I will borrow much and you will feel the drain, be prepared," she looked to them all, gaging their resolve. None flinched nor wavered; all there knew what was required of them. Tamara would drain them both mentally and physically, like opening a major artery; the flow of energy would energize the conduit, forcing an opening into the past.

Tamara's eyes glowed with the power she summoned from her companions. She took Cameron by the hand and entered into the hallway, the hairs on the back of his neck stood up remembering the last time he was here. The darkness that surrounded them went into a midnight shade of black as the void enveloped the hallway. Cameron could still feel Tamara's grip on him even though he could not see her. Now just like before a doorway opened for him, he could see the morning mists tumble through familiar glens.

"Go through now!" He heard Tamara shout and he ran through the doorway, his feet landing upon the Highland's dew soaked grass. He turned to see a black doorway behind him, Tamara and the rest charging through it. Although they were weakened from the journey they came through with swords drawn, ready to face the enemy.

Cameron recognized this place: the glen of Loch Monar, it was here where he had first arrived hunting the Munro raiders over 750 years in the past. He took in a deep breath of air, the feeling hit him again, just like before, goose bumps covered his body. The deep warm feeling of 'coming home' enveloped him.

CHAPTER EIGHTEEN

Dark Omens

Scotland 1263…

THE RIDE WESTWARDS for Cailean seemed to take less time than their initial journey to Stirling. Leaving Sir Adam with his small escort behind at Balfron, Sir Pierce led them on through Kippen and into Dumbarton itself until almost the supper hour. Cailean shouted out to his crews to be ready to disembark as soon as possible. This proved a little hectic, for many of his men were in the town in its taverns and brothels. The word had quickly spread that Cailean had returned and was eager to be off and any who did not get back to their ships would be left behind.

Sir Pierce, with his own small group reunited, climbed into Cailean's dragon-ship for the journey to Bute to Rothesay castle. Fortunately, all of Cailean's men were accounted for; the last few came running down the beaches and onto the decks of the last ship to pull out. Under oar-power they made it to Rothesay on Bute before nightfall. Sir Pierce and his party left them there in the small harbor, Cailean politely refused to spend the night in the castle preferring to spend it out under the stars with his men. The Knight then said his good-byes and hoped they would engage the enemy in the weeks ahead together.

It was early the next morning, almost at first light with a quick breakfast that the four dragon-ships were on their way on a southwest course. Once around the Mull of Kintyre they made good speed on a northerly route past Islay and stopped in the harbor of Calgary on the Isle of Mull for the night.

Wary fishermen kept their distance and a watchful eye during the night, but the MacKenzie fleet were only concerned about a good night's rest. The morning came peacefully, with the wary fishermen offering some of their catch at a fair price. Cailean accepted warmly, asking them of any news that may have come their way.

"Not much in news my lord, are you part of Magnus's fleet?"

"You mean Magnus of Man?" Cailean quickly asked.

"Aye him, are you part of that fleet?"

"No we are not, has Magnus assembled his ships?"

The old man was confused then seemed to understand. "Aye my Lord he has, then I do have some news for you. He sailed by two days ago in the afternoon, some 60 war ships like yours my lord, heading straight north to meet the Norway King," the man said. Cailean paid him handsomely and thanked him kindly. He allowed his men to take up the fish he just bought and ordered that they have it quickly prepared for the breakfast meal as he was in a hurry to be off. Returning to Drostan and Coll, he let them know what he had just heard from the fisherman.

"Well I'd say that was perfect timing," Cailean said to his cousins.

Coll nodded in agreement. "Four against sixty, not the best of odds," he said.

"They are only Manxmen," Drostan said in jest.

"Regardless we are lucky. We must proceed carefully northwards and let us hope Sigardsson has enough sense to watch his back," Cailean said sharply.

"Good advice for us all," Tynan warned and the others nodded in agreement.

The four dragon-ships warily ventured northwards from Calgary bay, always with sharp eyes straining ahead watching for Magnus of Man's fleet. They saw nothing and by late afternoon they sailed into the Sound of Sleat passing a few Matheson fishermen that had not seen any great fleet of ships come this way. With that Cailean breathed a little easier: Magnus must have ventured past the Isle of Skye into Little Minch, hopefully not to pay any type of punitive visit to either Lewis or Harris on his way to Haakon.

Cailean had his men pull in to the Kyle of Lochalsh. There he allowed them a rest or to stretch their legs and get in a good hot meal. He sought out Kenneth Matheson, his father-in-law and found that the man had already assembled his clan in two divisions. He was intently worried that Haakon would be paying them all a visit.

"I doubt he will take the time for personal vendettas. I believe he will head straight south," Cailean said to keep Matheson's fears at bay, but his father-in-law was not so easily convinced.

"Haakon may head straight south, but what of the others? God's blood, Magnus sits now in Duntulm bay on Skye. He took back the castle you took last summer from the Norsemen. The MacLeod's who held it against them now all hang in chains over the walls by their ankles and not one of them still has their heads. If Haakon gives Magnus and the Icelander's free reign settling old scores, then we are undone."

Cailean had not known Magnus was in Skye. He quickly surmised the situation, noting perhaps that it was merely a stopover for Magnus's fleet before they headed up further North. Taking back the castle may have been coincidental or by design, he knew not, however Matheson had a point.

"If they take this course, do what you think is best. Fall back inland if you must, the MacRae's and the Grants will take you in, for in Kintail, it seems I am its new Lord," Cailean said discreetly almost as an afterthought.

Yet Kenneth Matheson was as sharp as ever. "Lord of Kintail? That is no small thing. What did you do lad?" he asked fearfully, knowing Cailean's inadvertent ability to find trouble.

"Emm, perhaps I may have saved the King's life from a shape-shifter while we were out hunting stags."

"Ach laddie you do have a pension for danger it seems. Saving the King's life… were they after you or him?"

Cailean simply shrugged. "I know not, perhaps neither. Just in the wrong place at the wrong time," Cailean said and his father-in-law shook him by the shoulder.

"Laddie, that should be engraved upon a cairn over yer grave someday. You are always at the wrong place at the wrong time," he laughed.

"Aye you have the right of it. But at Stirling I dinna think it was me or the King. A town we went through had a problem with a pack of Black Dogs, some were killed some got away. It was only one that we slew, in the form of a great stag that drew us deeper and deeper into the forest. I think it was luring us into a trap, yet it got itself surrounded by our hunting party so it had no choice but to turn and fight. We thought it far better to downplay the entire thing for the common folk as the Shape-shifters cause too much fear and distrust. Better for them to hear a rogue stag tried to gore the King than that of the shape-shifters still being amongst them," Cailean said as Matheson nodded.

"Who knows, the truth may serve better than to be buried. Yet for the now we have bigger concerns."

"Well to that I will have all of MacKenzie assembled, we but wait for the Lord of Rodel to inform us of the Norwegian's plans. Once I know Haakon's fleet has bypassed my territories I will sail south after them and join up with the King's forces," Cailean gave his account of what his plans were going forward in this war.

Kenneth Matheson nodded. "Well Haakon seems to be coming late in the season, my old bones say there are storms coming, perhaps our weather will aid us," he said jokingly.

"We can only hope. Do not put too much into our gales for we are up against the best seafarers the world has ever seen, storms mean little to them," Cailean returned as the more he thought of it, perhaps the Matheson was on to something. They shared the evening meal and a fatherly embrace at their depature for Cailean was yearning to be home, to his wife and children now that he was close he took up a turn on the oars himself.

With good winds and in just little over an hour later, he beached his ship upon the shores of Lochcarron and fell straight to the waiting arms of his beautiful wife. Both Tamlyn and Kyle stood waiting for their friend.

Kerry kissed him hungrily. "Oh my love, my love I have missed you so!" she cried out as she returned to her kissing, with no care as to the disembarkment of all the crews around her.

"Come lass, let me at least say hello to the others," Cailean said as Kerry smiled.

"If you must then. Tamlyn and Kyle await yonder. I did nae think you would be here this eve. Tamlyn said you were coming, he convinced us to come wait for you, though I thought it be too late in the day for your return."

"You think that sailing in the night would keep me from you, in these familiar waters? Come, let us greet the others," he said wrapping his arm around her. They headed up to Kyle his steward and to Tamlyn who was showing some concern in his tightening brow. Cailean released his wife to embrace Kyle and then to Tamlyn.

The tall Elf seemed to know something was not quite right with their trip south. "What happened with the King? Did all go well?" Tamlyn asked curiously.

"Emm you can say that, they are warned and are readying their forces. We wait for Haakon to make the first move," Cailean answered then turned to Kyle. "Is everything ready here?"

"Aye my Chief. All is ready, four thousand assembled, two for you and two for me," Kyle said with a grin.

"Good then hopefully it will not be long," Cailean returned. Yet Kyle and the rest became just as curious and wanted to know more, for when Cailean makes so little of a trip it usually means something happened.

Kerry was also quick to notice that same fact. She turned and punched him on the shoulder. "Out with it! What did you do Cailean?" Her husband's cheeks grew instantly red and she knew she was right.

Coll could not hold back. "You do realize you are addressing the new Lord of Kintail!" he said with a huge grin upon his face.

"Thank you," Cailean said sharply as Coll just laughed.

"Aye well you canna hide it for too long," Coll said as he patted his cousin on the back. "Our Chief saved the King's life while out hunting, yet we dinna know we were the ones being hunted. A Shape-shifter lured us deep in the woods. It gored the King's mount and woulda killed the King if not for Cailean's timely arrival," Coll continued to relate Cailean's heroic deeds and then on to the ceremony that made him Lord of Kintail.

"You canna stay out of trouble, can you?" Kerry asked almost scornfully.

"It's not like I go lookin for it!" Cailean said in his defense as they all laughed at him, even Kerry could not help herself.

"At least you are safe, you all are." she in turn hugged Coll, Drostan and Tynan.

"By the Mass I could certainly use some ale," Coll all but shouted as they all laughed and headed back up to the keep. Both went in separate directions, Coll and the others to find some ale, and for Cailean and Kerry it was to see their children.

Kerry took him by the hand and they crept quietly into the children's room right next to their own. Both Conner and Matilda were fast asleep. Cailean squatted down beside the bed and kissed his son upon his head. Conner never stirred as Cailean gently brushed the hair out of the boy's face. Kerry squatted down beside him, leaning her head upon her husband's shoulder, and took his hand within her own.

"So small, so precious," Cailean whispered as he watched his son and was tenderly mesmerized by the boy's gentle breathing. He patted his wife's arm and they rose together and went over to the crib where baby Matilda slept soundly.

"As beautiful as her mother," he whispered and laid a gentle kiss upon his daughter's tiny forehead.

"Come my love let them sleep, for I too wish for your gentle kisses," Kerry whispered seductively.

"If I must," he replied with a teasing wink and headed quietly to their room.

††††

The days seemed to run into each other as one storm after another struck the Highlands. The storms did not break fully until near the end of July. It was an intensely bright sunny day when Cailean found himself working away with Kyle at the stockpile of supplies and weapons, concerned mostly for the logistics of this military expedition. He had commandeered every fletcher and bow maker in the area.

His brother Anselan years ago had the right idea; bowmen could be the key in this warfare. The odds were too strong against him, and archers; if used properly, could make Norse landings anywhere too costly. Cailean silently wished for 500 Welsh long-bowmen to add to his ranks. Those deadly archers, massed together would be a tremendous advantage yet the Welsh had their own problems and not

212

likely to come to the aid of their fellow Celts. Cailean had to make do with the shorter-range Scot's bow but believed it would be enough for his purposes.

He was distracted when some shouting coming from the beach suddenly brought him to full attention; Cailean could see a ship approaching fast. It was clearly on the horizon, a single dragon-ship. He could see as it approached that it was one of the MacLeod's.

Torquil MacLeod jumped into the sea and came up the beach towards them.

"You come from Sigardsson? Where is he?" Cailean asked hurriedly.

"Aye I do. We were at Skara Brae, on Orkney's Mainland. Haakon sits in Kirkwall with his fleet," Torquil said as Cailean cursed at their audacity.

"Skara Brae, you cut dangerously close my lord."

Torquil smiled. "Thank my Lord of Rodel, the cove he found was quite secluded and the people there friendly to his cause." Cailean only shook his head, knowing how big a risk Sigardsson was taking but allowed the MacLeod to go on. "Magnus of Man still sits on Skye but sent a score of his ships north to Orkney, and news is a host of chiefs from Iceland are only days away. Sigardsson informants say they will move on Scotland on August 5, whether Iceland is there or not."

"What else did his informants say? What of Haakon's plans?" Cailean asked sharply.

"He will come straight south, no delays, with no diversions. Haakon wants to surprise Scotland so he will not be diverted nor give away his advantage. There is talk of either Bute or Arran, that way he can disembark easily and safely. From there he can launch attacks deep into the rich south of Scotland," Torquil explained. Cailean sighed in relief, as he had no wish to be penned up in the north against part of Haakon's fleet while the real battle was happening in the south.

"Then our original plan stands. We follow on behind them and join up with the King's forces in western Argyll. From there we cover Loch Fyne, the Firth of Clyde and basically to be ready wherever they need us," Cailean said levelly. Both men knew it was not the best plan but dealing with too many unknowns, he could scarce think of anything better.

He had handpicked his men for their fighting abilities and their endurance for they would most likely need to travel good distances and expect to fight once they got there. If they only knew ahead of time where the Norsemen would attack, then that would move the odds more in Scotland's favor. For now, they had to make do and hope they had sufficient countermeasures in place to keep the Norsemen from gaining any foothold on Scottish soil.

The MacLeod chief did not stay long for his brother Tormund, dispatched to Harris to raise fighting men there, now Torquil had to do the same on Lewis. Sigardsson would provide them their next move, Cailean was as ready as he could be had only to wait patiently. The days simply trickled by, the only news coming in was from the Isle of Skye. Magnus King of Man was undoing all that Cailean had done with the MacLeod's on Skye. All the Norse held strongpoints cleared of Norsemen only a year ago, were now again under Norse control.

This did not bode well for the Scots or for Cailean as Isle of Skye was so very close to his lands. The days seemed to have them all on edge. Cailean spent his time divided between drilling his men for battle and spending time with his wife. He would be away from her for who knew how long; the very thought of it made him pine for her even more. They spent every moment they could together intimately and passionately. It seemed almost impossible for him to get enough of her and her of him. There was always a longing so powerful when they were apart. He knew this war would have to be fought and knew he had to be there, though his heart would ache at their parting, it would have to endure to ensure their future.

It was on August 5 when the first omen appeared, whether good or bad it was too early to say. A solar eclipse had everyone out staring in awe and in wonder, perhaps foretelling dark times ahead. Yet Cailean smiled and knew that Haakon was sailing against Scotland this day and the superstitious Norsemen would indeed see it as a bad sign.

Four days later ten dragon-ships came into Lochcarron, yet only one drove into the beachhead. Paul Sigardsson jumped off its decks and into the surf. Cailean, Coll and Drostan quickly joined him.

"It's time my Lord of Kintail," he said coolly as Cailean nodded to the Norseman, acknowledging the anticipation in the old warrior's face.

Cailean turned to Drostan and Coll. "Assemble our men we leave within the hour," Cailean ordered and left them to do it. For himself it was a quick good-bye to his wife and children and some last minute commands to Tamlyn and Kyle. Upon his return to the beach Sigardsson informed Cailean that Haakon's fleet met up with the King of Man on Skye, their combined fleets, some three hundred and more dragon ships left just yesterday heading due south.

"Haakon is to be meeting Ewan MacDougall and Angus MacDonald on Islay in a few days. Haakon expects to add the Islesmen to his fleet. If he is successful, that would be bad for Scotland," Sigardsson said ominously. Cailean nodded in agreement, for one advantage the Scots had was that they knew the land and in battle that can be pivotal in any victory. With the MacDougalls and MacDonalds combined, they too knew the land so using it against them as an advantage would be lost.

It played heavily on Cailean's mind as he boarded his ship and gave the order to be off. Twenty ships sped westwards out of Loch Carron as Kerry wiped her tears; her eyes were solely set on just one of them. She gave a silent prayer to God to protect her husband and see him home safe.

The twenty dragon-ships skirted the Scottish coast through the Sound of Sleat and pulled into the sheltered bay of Arisaig. Again the wariness of the townsfolk, the fear of their ships being Norse or any other raider kept them far away, retreating deep into the hills and glens for safety. For too long these people had been terrible victims, so much so that the sight of a dragon-ship, let alone twenty, had them all melt quickly away.

Regardless, sentries still posted, for a sleeping army was at its most vulnerable. The morning came upon them with sullen red skies. Sigardsson looked upon them with disdain, noting that bad weather was about to roll in. The Norseman did not fear the foul weather this close to the coast, as they would be traveling. He smiled at the thought of Norway's fleet taking up the 150 mile journey from Skye to Islay in such stormy conditions. For Cailean and his small fleet a ragged journey took them into Mingary for the night.

Early the next morning they slipped past Tobermory and into the Sound of Mull. They sailed carefully, taking a southwards turn in the Firth of Lorn and skirting past the Isle of Kerra. This was where King Alexander II was bound for when he passed away years ago; his own attempt to reclaim the Hebrides, which his son was now about to go to war over. They kept a wary eye out for Ewan MacDougall, for the Chief of MacDougall could take offense; these were his waters and he was far touchier than Angus MacDonald and had more ships.

They beached their ships on the Isle of Luing. Night was approaching, and they did not want to venture into the treacherous waters of the Gulf of Corryvreckan amongst its shallows, skerries and deadly whirlpools. The cloudy grey skies did nothing to welcome them as they pressed on in the morning through a high tide in the Gulf of Corryvreckan. With Sigardsson leading the way, the expert seafarer knew what he was about as the ships went single file, all a ropes throwing distance to each other should they need the strength of extra vessels if caught in a whirlpool.

Making their delicate way, they soon pulled into Loch Crinan in Argyll. A group of young men awaited them there. They were all mounted and sat patiently for the newcomers to disembark and sort out their supplies. These men all bore welcoming smiles as Cailean, Tynan, Drostan, Coll and Sigardsson approached.

"Are you my lord of Kintail?" the dark haired youth asked. To Cailean he could not be more than twenty years old, with roguish good looks, his companions were all fair haired and slightly older in age. They were all lightly armored, each carrying spear and shield as well as long swords strapped across their backs.

"I am Cailean Chief of MacKenzie, and Lord of Kintail," Cailean replied to the young man's inquiry.

"Greetings then my Lord for I am Cailean Mor Campbell of Clackmannanshire. These are my cousin's Niall, Ian and Robert Campbell," the young man said, introducing the men at his side.

"Well met Cailean Mor, you are far from Clackmannanshire are you not?" Cailean returned, smiling warmly at another of his namesake.

"Aye my Lord, as are you, yet both here for the same thing I believe: Scotland's very survival. However, I am here simply because these are my mother's lands here and up to Loch Awe and I know them well. I can get you through to Sir Andrew the Fraser and his host at Cairndow," the Campbell explained. Cailean then introduced his men while his captains made sure the ships were securely anchored and all supplies divvied out equally.

"What news have you of Haakon? Has he landed yet?" Cailean asked the young man.

"Not that I know of; the last I had heard the Norwegian fleet sits still on Islay and Jura. Both MacDougall and MacDonald are staying neutral despite Haakon being there in person. It is said, however, that they play the waiting game to see which side appears to be winning and they will quickly join them."

Cailean nodded at the lad's assessment as Sigardsson growled in disdain and eagerness to be on the move. It was beautiful country, with rolling hills and wide glens. The Campbell's had joined them on foot releasing their mounts to find their way home. The terrain was easier traveled on foot, the thirty miles to Cairndow they covered just after nightfall, which greatly surprised the Fraser when he was told of a host approaching his right flank.

"By the Mass Cailean, 30 miles in a single day, and on foot, an amazing feat. Come, you and yours can do with a good rest, food we have aplenty," the Fraser said and delivered for Cailean and his were well and truly spent.

It had seemed the rush to get there was in vain. Cailean's host of some three thousand men did nothing for the next few days except rest and wait for word on Haakon. Sir Andrew's own cavalry host numbered at 1500, all light horse, for they needed speed and to be light footed for the terrain just could not support heavy cavalry. It was August 18 when a rider came; Haakon had taken both Arran and Bute.

CHAPTER NINETEEN

Loch Lomond

HAAKON HAD INDEED come for war. His massive fleet took over the islands of Arran and Bute. The Lord High Steward of Scotland was not in Rothesay castle but his brother was, trapped and currently under siege. Sir Pierce and Sir Robert Graham stood at ready directly across the Clyde at the town of Largs with a Knightly host of some two thousand cavalry. Sir Pierce, suited up in his best armor, sat waiting impatiently for the Norsemen to make their move.

He had with him two Dominican friars, King Alexander's shrewdest negotiators. They were a little fearful of what they were asked to do, yet understood that their efforts could perhaps save many lives. Negotiating with Haakon was like walking into the lion's den. They were assured that Haakon was a godly man and would not have any man of faith killed outright as that would not look good for his cause if the Pope in Rome heard of such. However, Haakon's cronies were not so God fearing and this is what caused some trepidation amongst the good friars. Their only task was to stall for time and hopefully allow the rest of Scotland to rally behind the King. On a small boat, they rowed over to Arran while Sir Pierce watched them go. Now the knight could do nothing but wait.

He had a long wait. Haakon did not seem in too much of a hurry and seemed content sitting safely on Arran. Magnus of Man however was not; after sitting a week he grew bored, took about 50 ships and raided up Loch Fyne. Two days of hit and run raids, of burnings and slaughter, never staying long enough for Cailean and his men to engage them. It only added to the Scot's frustrations as Magnus returned with his booty while the Dominican monks still went back and forth in their negotiations.

King Alexander was south of Dumbarton with some fifteen thousand men, and more apparently coming in from the north. Most of the Scottish nobles called for patience, to delay for time and for the autumn gales that could work in their favor. In the weeks that followed, a few storms came and went, perhaps keeping the Norsemen from moving yet the tensions were still building on both sides.

Magnus went out again in mid-September, this time with 60 dragon ships he slipped out of Bute heading up the Clyde and into Loch Long. Magnus bypassed a Scottish army sitting north of Kilmacolm patrolling the Clyde. He sailed up to Arrochar and from there he ingeniously pulled his ships out of the water, rolling them out on rounded logs. He had his ships dragged through the narrow isthmus to Tarbet and entered Scotland's largest freshwater loch, Loch Lomond unopposed. Magnus had left Arrochar and Tarbet a blazing ruin as Cailean and his men led by a group of MacGregor's arrived too late.

The Norsemen had just left Tarbet. Some sailed north yet most went southwards. Cailean didn't like it, but convinced Sir Andrew to take his cavalry to the other side of Loch Lomond while Cailean would take his force and proceed southwards after the raiders. This way, both sides of the Loch could be defended. Sir Andrew reluctantly agreed and his mounted host took off into the night. Cailean and his MacGregor guides warily headed southwards.

Magnus of Man had unleashed hell in Loch Lomond. The unsuspecting people, mostly MacGregor, MacFarlane, Buchanan and Colquhoun populated this serene Loch. They always believed they were safe from the Norse marauders and the raiders took full advantage of this. Families and neighbor's awoke to screams and slaughter, none were spared. Fathers and sons either slain out of hand or were made to watch as wives, mothers, sisters and daughters were all brutally and repeatedly raped before they too were cruelly put to death. Everything they owned was rooted through and loaded into waiting dragon-ships. Once again Cailean's men made it too late to save Inverberg, catching only a single ship of stragglers still enjoying their sport of gouging out the eyes and loping off feet at the ankles while laughing at their victim's feeble efforts to escape. Ninety of the raiders died savagely upon the Highlander's and the Islesmen steel. They showed mercy to those unfortunate souls, victims of the Norsemen's wicked sport, comforting them as best they could before the end.

It was the same for Sir Andrew's command upon Inversnaid, arriving too late as the small town was a burning ruin. They caught only two small groups of about forty raiders each, laden with booty. They were all dead within minutes as Sir Andrew's cavalry sliced them to pieces, his force then circled the town as the last dragon-ship pulled away from its shores. A few bowmen fired arrows at the Scots but they were as ineffectual as their taunting insults. Four stragglers came out of hiding in a vain attempt to make it back to the safety of their ships–all four were savagely skewered upon steel tipped lances silencing the taunts of the fleeing Norsemen.

The small village of Luss suffered much the same. Cailean's host could not keep up with the speed of the Dragon-ships and Luss too went up in flames. As with Inverberg, they fought raiders on the outskirts of Luss, hunting in groups of thirty to fifty. These all easily dispatched yet it provided no comfort to the few survivors. They could only watch as the Norsemen slipped away in their ships out into the morning mists.

On the east side of the Loch, the villages of Rowardennan and Balmaha were attacked almost simultaneously. Sir Andrew's host had to navigate around Ben Lomond for better ground and engaged a suitable force of raiders at Rowardennan. It was mostly chaos as Scots cavalry appeared out of nowhere, surprising the Norsemen who dropped their bounty and ran for the safety of their ships. Only a few raiders held their ground against a scattered Scots cavalry, selling their lives dearly. Sir Andrew, frustrated at this type of warfare had not realized Balmaha just five miles away was already up in flames. Refugees with only the clothes on their backs made their way to Rowardennan to find it also destroyed. The Scottish cavalry despondently headed south.

Magnus continued his raiding through the day. His ships surrounded the larger inhabited islands in the loch. Completely protected from any reprisals from Scottish forces they leisurely slaughtered everyone they found. Neither Cailean nor Sir Andrew could do anything about it; they had not the shipping or the numbers to move against Magnus. The horror and the slaughter were almost unimaginable and not a single island inhabitant escaped their cruelty. It was well into the night when the last of the screams where suddenly silenced, as great fires went up all over the islands easily seen from the mainland.

In the early morning hours Magnus' fleet was again on the move. Most struck hard and fast into the tiny channel of the river Leven, oarsmen jumping out of their ships and pulling on scores of ropes to drag their ships through tall reeds and eventually into the open waters of the Clyde. Others raided the surrounding shores, waiting for their turn down the river Leven. Loch Lomond was a smoldering ruin with very few devastated and sorrow filled survivors.

This brought the Scot's morale to a terrible low. Magnus of Man returned triumphantly to Bute, his ships fully laden with booty that only fuelled the Norsemen's desire for more. Some further raiding took place and all with the same results as in Loch Lomond, the Norsemen in and out before any Scottish forces could arrive to engage them. Ewan MacDougall did some raids of his own, mostly against neighboring clans whether endorsed by Haakon or not it was all very demoralizing for the Scots.

Several storms had come in, limiting the raids yet it seemed the Norsemen were in no hurry. Cailean had again joined up with Sir Andrew and they were constantly on the move always trying to anticipate the enemy's next plan of attack. The King's Dominican monks were still going back and forth while woeful rumors were spreading all over Scotland. The one rumor that made King Alexander almost sick to his stomach was that Haakon was waiting for an Irish army. With an Irish host they would launch a massive assault with multiple attacks that would cover the entire southwest of Scotland in flames.

It was on the 28th of September when Cailean suddenly and dramatically took ill collapsing on the southeastern side of Loch Fyne in the Cowal district. It was the exact moment Cameron MacLean had stepped once again into the Highlands around Loch Monar in Morgan Hamilton's body.

CHAPTER TWENTY

Largs

"I'M FINE, ACH I am, really I'm fine. It was just a slight mishap, no doubt brought on from a lack of sleep!" Cailean said, trying to sit up from his cot. His head pounded viciously while Tynan and Sir Andrew watched on with worried faces. He was at least dry and warm in his tent situated in the middle of their camp with coal burning braziers keeping them sufficiently warm. The camp was quickly erected when Cailean suddenly fell ill. Sir Andrew ordered his squires to set up his tent right there and then.

They had been constantly on the move these past weeks, everyone was tired, wet and in need of a good rest. Cailean had driven himself hard, out at all hours with no sleep eating little or nothing. He was constantly on reconnaissance, seeking out the best spots for ambush and for defense. Their attempts to engage the Norse raiders had been futile. They did however, clash with some MacDougalls raiding in Cowal. It was a brief conflict and once Sir Andrew's forces on horseback appeared on their flank, they quickly escaped back to their ships. Cailean's sudden collapse happened shortly after and being on the east side of Loch Fyne seemed as good a place as any to make camp.

Tynan and Sir Andrew both noticed that after a good meal and a full day's rest that Cailean had appeared recovered, or at least looked like his old self once again, his color had come back and his eyes did not look so haggard. Tynan had privately feared a relapse, a complete shut down within his Chief, as it had happened years ago against the Dulachan. Now with Cailean's quick recovery, Tynan's worries melted away.

They had just received supplies from the King bringing in much needed food and tents to house them all as the storms seemed to be rolling in with more frequency. Good news came along with the supplies, word on the Irish front; they, like the Isles, did not wish to take part in the Scots-Norwegian war, they wanted to remain neutral in the matter at least for now. The Norse found it hard to convince the Irish at this time, being so late in the season for campaigning and with winter only a short time away. The news was good for the Scot's morale. King Alexander was still sitting south of Dumbarton with about 25 thousand men with at least five other holding forces like Cailean's all along the coastal areas. A total host all combined of about forty thousand, now all they needed was a battle.

Cailean now recovered and back on his feet, was feeling as good as ever and eager to confront his enemy. The only thing troubling his mind was a nagging recollection, almost like a strange premonition, something from his memory but it seemed more like a dream. It was stuck in his head and he felt a strong pull, a need to get further south, to Largs. Why Largs he could not say, but every instinct in him said this war would somehow be decided there. The feeling was too hard to ignore, so he called for his men and his captains, telling them they were moving out. He really could not explain this to his brother-in-law but he would at least try.

"My gut tells me we have to move south, towards Largs."

Sir Andrew looked at him questioningly. "We would have to cross the Clyde and in this weather," he said, looking at the building black clouds and wondering if Cailean's wits had fled him entirely.

"Look, Andrew you need not come, I can attach my men to Sir Pierce's cavalry there." Sir Andrew looked hard into Cailean's face, seeing the determined look in his eyes and then shook his head in defeat.

"I trust your gut over anything, I will come with you, and I am sure a few will follow as well," he said with a smile, knowing that young Cailean Mor Campbell and Sir Adam Montgomery would not be left behind. These two and more seemed almost inseparable from the Chief of MacKenzie.

Cailean nodded. "We can leave Sigardsson here with his men, take with us who you wish but we will need to move soon," Cailean said as he too looked to the darkening skies. Drostan and Coll seemed to take it in stride for Cailean's instincts had proved themselves in the past. Sigardsson had wanted to go as well but his age was catching up with him, a few more days rest seemed too much a temptation. Sir Andrew was quick about it issuing orders to break camp quickly. The squires and soldiers broke their camp down, tents and supplies all loaded upon pack horses, as two thousand men made their way southeast ten miles to Dunoon.

The Sherriff of Stirling commandeered every ship and transport vessel to ferry their small host across the Clyde. They waited til nightfall to make their crossing, hoping the darkness would hide them. Cailean knew this was dangerous, if the Norse saw them and attacked, they were doomed. The transport ships and merchant vessels were extremely vulnerable; loaded with men, horses and supplies the Norse dragon-ships would tear them apart.

With bad seas and after several tense hours, Cailean and his small host disembarked at Gourock bay and began making their way up Lyle hill heading south towards Largs in the early morning hours of September 30. It was fifteen miles from Gourock to Largs, with blustering autumn winds at their backs pushing them onwards. The skies threatened to open up on them yet did not. It just seemed to feed itself, building up its power growing bigger and bigger.

"We shall see a mighty storm soon I think," Sir Andrew said on the journey south, his eyes riveted upon the skies. The ominous rumble of thunder was their constant companion.

"Tis doubtful our foes will move in this weather," Sir Adam said, he too scanning the horizon.

"Surely the Norse will not stray from the safety of their harbor in this," the Campbell added to the conversation. Both Drostan and Coll looked at each other and laughed.

"What, did I miss something?" the young man asked Cailean.

"Nae my friend, it is only your lack of experience with our foes. Storm's such as these they dinna fear. They are the best seafarers in the world. You would not think any sane opponent would sail in such storms, yet to these Norsemen, they would use them to their advantage. Strike when you least expect them, that is how they think," Cailean explained to the young man who seemed like a sponge, he absorbed all that was said and applied it well. Throughout this campaign, although confrontations had been limited, he had done what he was told without question and understood his role completely. He was an apt student and Cailean and the others liked him well.

"Then you are expecting them to move out in this storm, to use it as a cover?" he asked yet Cailean said nothing straight away, he simply nodded. The young man thought it through. "Then they would nae waste this chance, when our forces unsuspecting…" he said as Cailean finished it for him.

"A great pincer's attack; two forces to surround and cut off their target, the King at Dumbarton I'd say would be their best move," Cailean said evenly as the young man paled slightly.

"We had best warn the King then, if the Norsemen so move they will be caught totally unawares, with the King captured or dead we are undone," the youth said, pulling up the reins on his horse.

"Nae need we have already done so, Sir Andrew sent off one of his knights with those very instructions when we landed. Fear not," Cailean said.

"Forgive me my Lord, yes you would have, I simply forgot who I was riding with," the Campbell said.

"There is nothing to forgive my friend, you learn fast and that will keep you alive much longer than most," Cailean returned with a wink as Sir Andrew laughed.

"There is hope for him yet," the Fraser added as the Campbell's face reddened slightly.

It was almost evening when one of Sir Pierce's patrols joined them just a mile north of Largs. They pushed on quickly to Sir Pierce's position on the heights overlooking the beaches and the town of Largs. They set up their camp just behind Curry's in a wooded area to help get out of the winds.

Sir Pierce received them kindly. "I hope you are right my lord of Kintail, I would relish a fight with these bastards after what they did in Loch Lomond."

Cailean and the others shared that sentiment wholeheartedly. To those that had followed Cailean, it was still so very fresh in their minds and this had only fueled the fires of vengeance to a fervent intensity.

"If they are looking for a storm to hide their approach then I believe we shall have one fairly soon," Cailean said as the Knight nodded.

"We will have our patrols out all night regardless, if they move we will know soon enough."

"Then I feel we are in for a long night," Cailean returned as the winds increased and the lightning danced across a black sky.

††††

Thunder pounded the heavens as the winds stirred up boiling seas and the waves battered the shores. It was in the late hours of October 1 when a soggy Coll entered Cailean's tent shaking his Chief roughly. "Cousin, cousin awake, you were right. Haakon is moving, I would say at least half his fleet is moving up the Clyde," Coll said with a hungry anticipation in his voice.

Cailean rubbed his eyes and yawed while nodding his head. "Have the storms let up?" Cailean inquired.

"Nae, if anything they have grown worse. Even the Norsemen are having trouble getting up the Clyde, like a great witches cauldron it is," Coll replied eagerly. This was what he and his brother Drostan were waiting for all their lives and now vengeance was within their grasp. Cailean nodded as he strapped on sword, dirk and targe.

"Sir Pierce?" Cailean inquired as to the readiness of the knightly portion of their host.

"He be in his shiniest best, he and the others are all gearing up, and keeping a close watch up here on the heights." Coll answered with great enthusiasm.

Cailean assessed that piece of information and smiled. The Knight was being patient, keeping to the heights and out of site of the Norsemen, hoping to get them to land, to get them out of their ships and fight them head on. Sir Andrew joined Cailean with his group of Knights, Sir Adam and the Campbell with their men, all lightly armored, mail and half-helms; they would fight alongside the Highlanders who wore only their plaids, breeches or kilt. Cailean's force of about three thousand strong with his Highlanders and some 900 joined his host of foot from the surrounding area. Their men formed in behind the mounted Knights, their strategy was to use the cavalry charge to break their ranks then the Highlanders would follow closely behind and destroy those that remained.

Cailean and his commanders joined the front lines to watch the struggling Norse fleet's progress. It was difficult to make out with the driving rains greatly reducing vision. Yet for the sheer mass of the fleet, it was not hard to miss the action. Far too many ships in such turbulent waters was a full on disaster. To the southwest coast of Scotland came the Father of all storms. Giant waves came at them from all sides, oars were ripped asunder as ships collided, splintering shafts and sending oarsmen flying across flooded decks. One massive wave took out four ships, sending them and their crews to the murky depths. Several more tried to make it to shore were smashed upon rocks then pulled back out to sea only to quickly sink.

The Scots cheered on as one ship after another lost its battle with the storm. It was as if God and his angels were on their side while the Norse fleet floundered in the Clyde. They had to abandon their struggle up the Clyde as they were relentlessly driven southwards towards Largs. Those that may have doubted Cailean's instincts now questioned them no more. Cailean had counted at least twenty-three ships that went under those hungry waves, fourteen more were disabled and lisping badly, those that tried to aid were soon themselves destroyed. Damaged ships with their oars sheared off smashed into those still under some control, adding to the deadly flotsam. The storm pummeled the Norse fleet for what seemed like hours as they tried to make it back to Rothesay, a testimony to the skill of the Norsemen.

After scores of ships either sunk or were so badly damaged they were now entirely at the mercy of the waves and the driving winds pushing them into the shores of Largs. The Scots host still waited as storm battered ships emptied their crews upon the shores in two separate groups. The smaller of the two held about two thousand Norsemen, the larger about three or four times that. They were now about four hundred yards apart.

Sir Pierce gave the order; knowing clearly that it was better to keep them apart, attacking the smaller group would only draw on the larger. Some 1500 Scottish cavalry poured down from the heights, a great arrowhead formation charged down through the storm and tore through the smaller first group like a sickle slicing through straw. The tired and demoralized Norsemen tried to form up a shield barrier but the tremendous speed, the sheer weight of horse and man packed tightly in that formation decimated the Norse defenses, leaving a bloody trampled ruin in their wake. Those few that survived the onslaught of cavalry fell to the charging Highlanders.

Sir Pierce's charge had lost its impetus, he shouted commands to reform the arrowhead but had little time and space to assemble a full charge as the larger group of Norsemen surged towards them. The Norse shield wall seemed to swallow up the Scots as it opened to allow the cavalry through only to surround them cutting them off from the supporting Highlanders. The knights fought well and were hard to bring down. Sir Pierce now cut off from his fellow knights was quickly surrounded. His sword flayed left and right, his mount kicked wildly at those trying to press too close. He laughed as those who fell beneath his sword piled high about him. A Norsemen wielding a great axe tried to end him, Sir Pierce took the blow upon his shield. The terrible blow completely numbed his shield arm, so intent he was on the axe wielder that another giant Norseman with a massive sword swung hard, burying the sword deep in Sir Pierce's armored thigh almost severing the leg. Blood burst out from the terrible wound as the knight swayed in his saddle until another blow from the axe wielder sent him crashing to the ground. The giant Norsemen bent down over the dying Knight and removed his jeweled belt, holding it high in triumph. He had no real time to celebrate as the Highlanders finally swarmed in.

Drostan and Coll led the MacKenzie charge for there was no stopping them. They both were in 'Berserker' mode from the onset. Drostan's giant sword and Coll's deadly axe together were like a meat grinder from hell.

Sir Andrew held Cailean back. "You need not be in the front. Hang back, be the commander, not the soldier!" he shouted over the din of battle. Cailean Mor Campbell and his cousins could not be held back for they too needed this battle, needed to be in the heat of it as only young men could. The devastation brought by the Norse in Loch Lomond fed the Scot's frustration and anger that it had to be met with extreme violence. The Campbell's showed their wrath and their worth upon that bloody beach. The Knights found themselves surrounded; their charge ground to a halt as the Highlanders surged in, smashing through the Norse lines to their rescue.

The Norsemen tried to reform their ranks yet were not quick enough. Drostan and Coll saw Sir Pierce go down through the press and they were fighting their way to his side. The large Norseman held up Sir Pierce's gold and gem covered belt waving his trophy proudly as Coll buried his axe in the man's head, the belt fell from his dead hands, forgotten as the battle carried on. Cailean now found himself in the midst of things, he being one of the best swordsmen in the North felled one after another. Tynan, who always covered his back, his axes dealt with any opponents Cailean did not see.

The Knights did their best to eradicate themselves from the battle. The cavalry's greatest strength was their speed and crushing force that nothing could stand against. Here they were vulnerable and had to pull out far enough away and charge again, to finally break the Norse lines. To the embattled Highlanders it looked as if the Knights were abandoning them; confusion led to doubt as the Highlander's looked ahead and saw the Norse were about to be greatly reinforced. Forty dragon-ships were heading towards the battle to rescue their forces fighting on the shore. Both battle lines drew back for the Norsemen looked to the heights and saw the Scots also being reinforced. The vanguard of King Alexander's army had finally arrived. The banners of Sir Alexander Steward of Dundonald, the High Steward of Scotland and the banner of Alexander Fitzalan the High Constable flew proudly in the powerful winds. The new host blew their horns for rally as the two lines of antagonists pulled themselves apart.

What was left of Sir Pierce's command turned and headed up to the heights and joined the King's army. Cailean ordered his men to draw off while the Norsemen did the same. The Scot's archers moved in, sending volley after volley into the enemy. Only half of the newly arrived Norsemen jumped into the surf to join their brothers, mostly to give aid to the wounded. The Steward and the Constable in seeing their chance gave the command to charge as the Scot's cavalry surged down the slopes into the Norsemen with devastating effect. Cailean and his Highlanders stayed back and out of the way as the cavalry ripped right through the Norsemen leaving a mass of carnage and ruin in their wake. It accomplished what it intended to do. The Norsemen smartly kept their backs to the sea as the Scot's cavalry pulled sufficiently away to regroup for another charge, striking the raiders again with the Highlanders swarming through any openings in the Norse lines. After several charges the Scots forces pulled around again for another attack yet it was not necessary, for the Norsemen it seems had had enough, making their way back to their ships as best they could to make for safer landings.

Sir Andrew pounded Cailean upon the shoulder joyfully. "A victory my friend, a Victory!" the Knight said.

Tynan wiped the rain from his face and watched on. "Aye but was it enough? Did we cause enough damage for them to abandon this war?" he asked his Chief.

"We can only hope my friend, between us and Mother Nature perhaps we have proved too tough a nut to crack," Cailean said smiling, as his brother-in-law laughed heartily.

"For God I hope you are right Cailean," Sir Andrew said as their men made their way off the field victoriously watching the Norsemen depart. The Constable had ordered that the Scots wounded and dead be removed from the field, the raiders were to be left there as a reminder to their brothers. The villagers went in amongst the Norsemen's wounded and dead, robbing the corpses of anything of value. The Scot's forces drew back up the heights as five dragon ships came back to Largs late in the day, and under the watchful eyes of the Scot's the Norse took away their dead. The Scots allowed them that simple courtesy.

Two days later a courier came out of Rothesay from the Steward's brother, the siege was lifted as Magnus of Man pulled out of Arran to head for home. Haakon it seemed was heading home to Norway; this war was over. After the battle of Largs, the Islesmen turned on them, when the MacDougall attacked several Norse outposts that appeared to be the final straw for Haakon. The Scots let out a collective sigh of relief and bells all over the land rang long and loud. Though Alexander did not actually take part in the battle, it was still a mighty victory for him and Scotland. He was indeed a gracious King, he had emptied the royal coffers to help rebuild and feed the victims of the Loch Lomond raids. It was a turning point in his young reign, as Scotland could for once say it was untied north and south. For Cailean, it meant life and perhaps a lasting peace in the north, at least against the Norsemen.

Largs was the center of great celebrations, Cailean and his company were nothing but enthusiastic in furthering those celebrations. In the wee hours of the morning Cailean, quite sufficiently drunk, decided that perhaps it was best to find his bed before he passed out. He staggered through the camp to his tent with Drostan and Tynan happily in tow. They were lucky enough to find the right tent and literally fell into it. He managed to plop himself upon his cot, and after several attempts unlaced his brogans to get ready for a good night's sleep. He was just about to doze off as he heard Coll outside talking but paid it no heed.

Coll, staggering towards the tents, saw six cloaked figures approach out of the foggy night. Their path was taking them directly to his and Cailean's tent. He noticed as they walked up to him, five of them were very tall and one was about Cailean's size. The lead one pulled back his hood and Coll instantly relaxed his grip on his axe.

"Greetings my friend. Why are you here?" Coll asked as Tamlyn smiled warmly at him.

"I have a message," the Elf Lord replied, as the others doffed back their hoods. Coll looked on in disbelief.

"More of ye, I dinna know if that is good or bad," he drunkenly said with a grin.

"Good I should say," Tamlyn replied. He reached for Coll's hand in greeting, and as the Highlander took it he felt a tingle shoot up his arm and into his head. He would have collapsed upon the ground had not Jeren caught and held him while Tamlyn and Tamara went into the tent. Drostan was already snoring, yet Cailean sensed a presence in his tent. He pulled out his dirk in reflex, but breathed out a sigh as he saw Tamlyn. He quickly went back into panic mode, for if Tamlyn was here perhaps something bad must have happened back home.

Tamlyn sensed his worry. "Fear not. All is well at home, I but bring a message only," Tamlyn said as he bent down, reaching out to Cailean's hand and sending him into oblivion. Tynan who stirred found himself staring at the most beautiful of Elf maidens then she touched his face and sent him into a deep sleep.

Jeren brought in Coll and eased him comfortably to the floor. Tamlyn moved quickly over to Drostan and sent him into a deeper state so as not to be disturbed Cameron looked upon these men, these who were so close to him, then he gazed upon his own face in Cailean's. It instantly caused shivers to run down his spine.

"Cameron you lay here beside Cailean," Tamara instructed.

"Are you sure this will work? What if you are wrong? What if the same thing happens to Cailean as it did with Morgan?" Cameron said with a verge of panic in his voice.

"Trust me Cameron, everything is already preset in Cailean's mind to accept you. The subconscious works chronologically within the human mind, your Cameron side will align with Cailean as it was before. This time I will subdue your persona, meld it so that you will not know your future self, you will be fully and only Cailean. The madness in the future is due to you being taken from your timeline and thrust into Morgan's, two sets of past lives in your subconscious running simultaneously. The mind could not accept the two diverging patterns. Here in the past there is no conflict, yet as you live and die and are reborn those lives that you lived in Cameron's time will fade as they do not come to be in this new time line. His mind will define them as dreams and when you eventually become Morgan they will have all faded," Tamara explained with confidence in her words that Cameron accepted. In truth he had no choice, he could not exist in the future, his salvation was once again in the past and this is also where he truly wished to be.

"Jeren go outside with the others, set your wards, for we must not be disturbed," Tamlyn said as Jeren nodded and disappeared quickly outside. Jeren and the others wove a ward around the tent to make anyone who approached instantly forget why they came and receive a subliminal message to go back whence they came.

Tamlyn bent close to Cameron. "This in a way is good bye my dear friend. I know this is not what you planned for your life, but it is life. You will be with your soul-mate, and that my good friend is a rare thing," the Elf Lord said his face both sad and hopeful at the same time; he reached for Cameron's hand and took it.

"I'm sorry you all had to do this, this is all my fault. For what you have all gone through I am so very grateful, to be with her again is far more than I could have ever hoped for," Cameron said as he felt a tingle in his head and Tamlyn eased him down.

"The alcohol in Cailean's body will actually aid in the transfer, it will slow his body's defenses to allow me to perform this task without fighting every connection," Tamara said as she took on an eerie glow. Her powerful aura shone so intensely Tamlyn had to turn away. She sat between the two men, her left hand upon Cameron's head–her right upon Cailean. Tamlyn could only wait and hope that the transfer would not kill them all.

CHAPTER TWENTY ONE

Beginning's End

TAMLYN STRESSFULLY WATCHED on as time passed at a frightening pace. The glow around Tamara was fading as sweat saturated her brow. Had she not been through the Restoration she would have burnt out long ago. As it stood now, she was fading fast and he knew it. He had no way to know for sure how far along or how much farther she had to go. He only knew that if he did not help her everything that they had done would have been in vain.

Gently he put his hands upon her head, sending minor flows of energy and gradually increasing the flow as he put forth all he had, even if it meant ending his own life. Her glow renewed, strength returned, Tamara shut off the flow, whether she somehow sensed his weakness or needed no more he could not tell. Her face reflected the concentration in her task. The lavender eyed Goddess had over 750 years to put her plan in motion, she knew exactly what to do and how to go about it. Tamara had only scanned her mind for a brief moment, hoping that she had gleaned enough to put things right. She had been confident in the beginning, but here and now perhaps it was too much to hope that it would all work out. Tamlyn felt a twinge of despair creep into his mind; he had failed too many times with Cameron and this was the last chance. He watched as Tamara opened her eyes and removed her hands from their heads.

"It is done, so complex; every synapse had to be separated then retied. All that was Cameron is now re-installed into Cailean. The link between Cameron and Cailean is more symbiotic, whereas with Cameron and Morgan it was destructive in nature which I believe was by design of that creature," she said bitterly. "Now every future life in the subconscious is set to fade after each new one emerges. What could not work within Morgan has a chance in Cailean thanks to that creature as she had preset all the connection points beforehand to make it work. I doubt she thought of ever resealing them once she threw Cameron back into Morgan's time line," she said, trying to get back to her feet.

"Steady now. Are you well?" Tamlyn asked as he held her, supporting her until she nodded to him and was able to stand on her own. "How soon will we know this worked?" he asked as Tamara looked at him warmly.

"I know you need this to work, for them both. We will see over the next few days, if what I have done will not unravel."

Tamlyn nodded. That was as much as he could hope for now.

"How long before sunrise?" she asked.

"About an hour, maybe a few minutes less," he returned as Tamara looked to her two patients.

"Then let us not wake them just yet. The wards can hold for hours still, then we can shift," she said quietly.

Tamlyn nodded, Morgan and Cailean would need their rest to recover from this nights work. Tamlyn knew that the next few days would be the most important. For Cailean his overtiredness might be due to the excess of the celebrations, masking the true cause, the integration of Cameron. Instead of drowning within Morgan and constantly fighting for air only to be pushed back down time after time, Cameron was now seamlessly integrated within Cailean.

Tamlyn was anxious to see for himself how all of Tamara's efforts proved to be successful in their conscious state. He did not have long to wait, Morgan finally stirred himself to consciousness.

"Easy now Morgan, you have been through much," Tamlyn said bending down low to help his friend sit up.

"Everything is kinda fuzzy, before my brain felt like it was squeezed into a tiny ball, now it feels like it just popped back in place," he said shakily. Tamara bent down in front, she took his head in her hands as Tamlyn grew more concerned for her.

"Are you strong enough for this?"

"Are you? You filled me with your energy, I am sufficiently restored," she said evenly to stop him from worrying too much. Tamara quickly Shared into Morgan's mind, she was thorough enough yet not overly long, just enough to make certain that all traces of Cameron were indeed gone. She confirmed that the neurological pathways had healed, no part of the brain showed any lasting damage that could cause further seizures.

She smiled when she removed her hands. "Well this one at least has come through this ordeal quite well. He should have no further relapses," she said and Tamlyn smiled with relief as he helped Morgan to his feet.

"Now we must release the others and make the shift," Tamara said to Tamlyn. He nodded and bent over Tynan, touching his forehead then doing the same to Coll as Tamara released Drostan. Tamlyn motioned to Morgan.

"Come here to me Morgan, we are going to Shift now," Tamlyn said. Tamara exited the tent out into the foggy morning to inform the others that it was time to drop the ward and make their Shift. Morgan looked to Tamlyn, a little confused.

"The Shift is to step into another dimension within the same plane of existence. We will be part of this world yet they will not see or hear us. We need to monitor Cailean to see if the integration of Cameron has caused them any ill side effects as it did with you," Tamlyn quickly explained as he moved in behind Morgan and placed his hands upon Morgan's shoulders.

"Hold still, this will not hurt," he said. Morgan felt a sudden oddness, strangely lighter; the world around him took on a different hue. Morgan looked to Tamlyn and he appeared the same yet different, it was as if he was on the other side of a hazy mirror looking into the real world. He jumped a little when Tynan, Drostan and Coll suddenly sat up simultaneously, all looking to each other.

"That was a wee bit odd," Coll said as he scratched his beard, while his brother nodded in unconcerned agreement and looked around the tent seeing Cailean still sleeping.

"Anyone have to take a piss?" Drostan said with a smile as Coll burst out laughing. Tynan smirked while Cailean woke up with a groan.

"God's Blood, nae more drinking! Like a swarm of angry bee's in ma' head," Cailean said as he slowly took to his feet and poured a bucket of cold water over his throbbing head.

"Aye drown out the nasty buggers!" Drostan said with a deep laugh then he tossed his Chief a blanket to dry himself with.

"I'm pretty sure I threw up in that bucket," Coll said mischievously and Cailean gave him a sharp look. The others laughed for they could tease their chief as no one else could.

"Are we done here? Can we go home?" Tynan asked.

"Well we should first see to some food, if we can keep it down," Cailean answered then he continued. "We will'nae stay long, much depends on Haakon, we will shadow him north. See to it he does nae harm on his way out." They all nodded, for Sigardsson who joined them just yesterday was also eager to follow the Norwegian King home. Rumors had it that due to the storm they lost over eighty ships, and half as much or possibly more ships damaged. Casualties perhaps exaggerated to be almost 16 thousand men. The Scot's losses were relatively small, only numbering into the hundreds at the battle of Largs. The most notable was Sir Pierce Curry whom they had all befriended. Of Haakon, he had lost heart in this war, his chiefs all urging him to go home, too many misfortunes and his men were no longer eager to fight. Magnus King of Man had already gone home, and Haakon was said to be leaving this very day.

"We will give Haakon a day's travel, then we follow behind. Hopefully he heads straight for home. For us we will pay our respects to our King then we make our way to our ships at Loch Crinan," Cailean said. The others followed him out of their tent and into the camp for some food. Tamlyn and Morgan stepped through the canvas wall behind them.

"Like a freaking ghost," Morgan said out loud.

"How is he?" Jeren asked as he stepped in beside Tamara and his uncle.

Tamlyn, who did not want to sound too hopeful, replied. "Well so far, he seems to be showing no ill effects. I don't know, perhaps it's too early to tell."

Morgan was in awe taking all of this in, walking through a 13th century military camp. "This is incredible, like walking through actual history. I can't believe that this is me, way back in the day," Morgan said while Tamlyn smiled at him. "I'm a full blown Chief, a hero, a freaking hero, I just can't believe it. I am just a regular guy, I'm no hero…"

Tamlyn stopped him right there. "Do not sell yourself short, I have known you all your life. You have it within you, insurmountable courage, when the situation arises you will show your worth." Yet Morgan was not completely convinced, he felt ashamed somehow, that he could in no way show the courage and the valor of those whose lives he once lived. The entire situation was so overwhelming and he felt very pathetic in the grand scale of things.

Morgan watched Cailean closely, followed his every step. Cailean appeared normal while he ate with the others, talking and joking with his men. Morgan could see the pride on their faces, Cailean was a man they all deeply respected and admired. "Geez, even I would follow this guy anywhere," Morgan said to himself. He however noticed that Cailean seemed to be constantly looking over his shoulder towards them, as if sensing them.

"He keeps looking at us, can he see us?" Morgan asked.

"No but perhaps he can sense us, like catching something out of the corner of your eye. Maybe with the integration of Cameron, his senses are somehow, heightened. When I first met him there was something about his aura that stood out from the others," Tamlyn said, yet Morgan kept watching.

"Won't that happen now, I mean when he goes back home, the Tamlyn in the past will see them together again?" Morgan's perceptiveness was encouraging to the Elf who shook his head.

"Do not worry, Tamara has seen to it. The reinstall into Cailean was thorough, made to last. Whereas the creature from that dead world set it loosely in the forefront of Cailean's mind, easily seen by myself. It was purposely done, so that when Cameron's time was up he could be effortlessly yanked out."

Morgan nodded, trying so very hard to believe that Tamara had everything covered, that not a single thing was overlooked.

They followed Cailean as he joined his Viking friend Paul Sigardsson and the MacLeods. The Islesmen were all gearing up to move back to their ships. They joined Cailean and the others making their way to the King's pavilion. The King and his commanders received them with much pomp and ceremony. Cailean and his men proved their worth at Loch Lomond and at Largs. Alexander High King of Scots was especially sad to see them go. Alexander hugged his new friend and promises were made for a return to Stirling. The High Constable did the same, Fitzalan was more than proud to call Cailean his friend. For a popular and powerful Highland Chief like Cailean to support the King carried a strong message to all. The Highlanders had been instrumental in this war proving at last that Scotland, north and south, was united under Alexander.

Again Morgan was in awe. It was surreal that in his past life, on top of everything else, he was a friend to a king. As Cailean and his party took their leave, he turned on his heels, pulling out his broadsword pointing skyward. "All Hail the King!" he shouted as swords everywhere screamed in unison, and took up the hail.

"All Hail the King! All Hail the King! Alexander! Alexander! Long live the King!" Hundreds upon hundreds called out as the King's cheeks reddened and a lump swelled in his throat over the powerful stream of emotion from all those who loved and supported him, all of this started by his true friend. Alexander tried to catch a glimpse of the Lord of Kintail, yet he and his men had disappeared in the friendly mob.

Cailean and his men pulled out of Largs heading north up the coast on foot. The sun was shining warmly upon them all, the storms seemed to have abated; it was to him a good sign. Sir Andrew Fraser, Sir Adam Montgomery and Cailean Mor Campbell accompanied them northwards. Arriving at Gourock late in the afternoon, Sir Andrew made sure that ample shipping was provided in the King's name to ferry Cailean and his men across the Clyde to Dunoon. It took all the shipping available at Gourock to manage it, merchant vessels all, with Sigardsson offering harsh comments and sarcasms all the way.

While they traveled, Cailean unknowingly was under intense scrutiny by an unseen party. Tamara and the others relieved that he seemed to show no signs of distress. Still at times Cailean would look their way, towards Morgan and the rest as if he could somehow see through the veil of dimensions. He frowned when he did so, almost second guessing himself for trying to see something that wasn't really there. Eventually he stopped all together, which eased Morgan's anxiety just a little bit.

Morgan was still afraid that it would all unravel only to be worse off than before. Every fantastic and miraculous step they had taken in this journey was all such an incredible long shot from the very beginning. It seemed almost impossible, yet here they were hundreds of centuries in the past and everything was falling neatly into place. When he looked to Tamara for any sign of worry, she showed nothing. Her beautiful face never wavered from the sureness and confidence it portrayed. She never once took her eyes off her patient, almost daring Cailean to show some sign of distress, yet there was nothing.

Morgan felt the tension of Tamlyn and Tamara ease with each passing hour. Observing this, his own fears faded as he took in this magnificent journey. He had never been to Scotland and seeing it now, albeit 750 years in the past, was impressive. He could not help but see the fabulous beauty of it. Perhaps when all of this was over he would bring Marina here for a vacation. That immediately brought on thoughts of his wife for he missed her terribly. It felt like weeks since he had seen her, maybe longer, she would be worried sick about him. He wanted to get home in a hurry, yet deep inside of him was the need to see Cailean/Cameron reunited with Kerry. It somehow meant everything to him for Cameron had lost so much. Morgan needed to see them together as it would bring peace to his soul, to their soul.

†††††

In the evening, after the last ship dropped off the rest of Cailean's men, Sir Adam and Sir Andrew took their leave of the Highlanders.

"My Lord of Kintail, it has indeed been a pleasure, an honor to meet and fight beside you. May God give you the peace and happiness that you so richly deserve," Sir Adam said as Cailean embraced him.

"And to you as well my friend. We shall see each other again, when we visit south," Cailean said as he then turned to his brother-in-law.

The Sherriff of Stirling placed a friendly hand upon Cailean's shoulder. "I must return to Alexander and join his escort back to Stirling," he said. His face could not hide his emotions, and Cailean could find no fault in it. "I will miss you my good-brother, Lord of Kintail!" he said with a tear in his eye.

Cailean hugged him warmly. "We kept our vow did we not? Together, side-by-side, the Norsemen defeated, a good day for Scotland is it not?" Cailean said and his face shone with pride.

"Aye, with you on her side my friend she will see many a good day. Give my love to Kerry, Conner and Matilda," the Fraser returned proudly as he jumped into the ship.

Cailean smiled and waved good-bye to his brother-in-law. "Tell my sister… tell Isabel I love her, perhaps one day…"

"She knows Cailean, she knows, she will visit you in the north soon, I promise," Sir Andrew shouted as his ship passed on. Cailean watched on as the current carried the Fraser southwards. Cailean found young Campbell and his kin ready to push on towards Loch Crinan. It was fully dark when the Highlanders arrived at the shores of Loch Fyne in Cowal. The night was warm and clear so they camped out under the stars. Come morning they would cross the Loch to Lochgilphead, if the Campbell could secure enough shipping to get them across. Three thousand men would take some time to cross yet take far less than the forty mile round trip around Loch Fyne. It took the greater part of the day to get all his men across, then the few miles to Loch Crinan and to their dragon-ships.

It was there that the rest of Tamlyn's party, Ronan, Mikka and the others were waiting for them. They too had Shifted to avoid any accidental meetings with the locals. Cailean's ships were in reasonably good shape, they made it through the storms unscathed. Rain and seawater had to be bailed out, gear and cordage put in the sun to be dried. Cailean made sure all his men had a good hot meal in them for they would leave come morning and he wanted them ready for the journey. As dawn casted its morning light, Cailean made his good-byes to the Campbell.

"So my good friend Cailean Mor, is it off to Clackmannanshire for you and your kin?" Cailean asked amiably to the young man.

"Well nae, as ta that, I think I am gonna stay in the area, in my lands here. They have a godly beauty to them that I just canna ignore," the young man said.

"Then my friend I thank you for all you have done. Farewell Cailean Mor," Cailean said as he took the young man's arm in friendship.

"Fare you well my Lord of Kintail," Campbell replied as he watched the twenty dragon-ships sail out of Loch Crinan and head for home.

††††

With good winds and strong backs, they sailed past the Isle of Scarba and into the Firth of Lorn. Constantly keeping their eyes peeled to the horizon as they were now in the heart of MacDougall territory. Cailean had no wish to come across Ewan MacDougall. For though that Chief was now fully behind the Scots, he may still wish to settle some scores with the Chief of MacKenzie for the beating the MacDougall's took in Argyll. Luckily the day proved uneventful with no sign of any shipping, friendly or hostile did they see in their journey north.

Their day ended on the Isle of Muck. The crews were exhausted, the winds were changing and Cailean felt better to make for land than to push on. The fishermen upon Muck were more than happy to speak to the Chief of MacKenzie. Cailean, eager for any news gave them a warm welcome.

"Haakon's great fleet came by only yesterday my Lord, heading north to be sure. With the Lord of Lorn Chief Ewan was a chasin' em. There was a sea-battle it was said, just past Rum with stragglers of

Haakon's, that were caught well behind the main body. MacDougall attacked, tearing them all apart. It is said he's being eager to prove himself to the Scot's King," the fisherman relayed to Cailean. He laughed heartily as did Sigardsson. It explained why they had not seen MacDougall, for they knew he had assembled all his ships.

"What of Haakon himself, where is he bound?" Sigardsson asked on. The fisherman scratched his beard and looked at the Norseman.

"He be bound for Skye, then to Orkney, but I canna say fer sure my Lord." The man said as Sigardsson looked to Cailean at that, for Skye could be a mere stopover, nothing more. Yet Skye was too close for the Lord of Rodel and for Cailean. If Haakon stayed on Skye with his fleet then this war was not over yet. Cailean thanked the man kindly and gave him two pieces of silver, which possibly worked out to be a full year's income for the man.

Once the Highlanders turned in for the night, Tamara hovered over her patient. Her unseen hands touched Cailean's face, her mind touching his.

"All seems well within, I can say with confidence that the procedure worked better than we thought," Tamara said encouragingly. With that Tamlyn smiled, relief bathing his face.

"Then we can go. Open a portal to Loch Monar, follow the conduit back to the future and Morgan home safe," Tamlyn said but Morgan stepped in.

"Please can we stay, just until I see them together, I need to see it. I need to know for my own piece of mind that everything Cameron sacrificed was worth it. I need to see him with her," he cast haunted eyes toward Tamlyn then to Tamara, who saw the desire so deep within him.

"Tamlyn, think upon Cailean's return, how close were you to him?"

Tamlyn's brow darkened as he recalled that event centuries in the past then frowned. "I can sense a Shift perhaps as close as fifty yards, however as I recall I did not approach. I stayed back as Cailean came home, allowed them to have a moment together. I had stayed upon the tower; it is far enough away from the beach where they arrived. Yet we cannot stay there long, if my past self catches even the merest scent of anything amiss all we have done will be for nothing," Tamlyn said worriedly, and Morgan thankfully nodded.

"I need just to see them together that's all," he pleaded and Tamara jumped in on Morgan's behalf.

"Perhaps this is the best way for us to make sure the procedure will hold and that it is strong enough for Cailean and Cameron, seeing Kerry will be an emotional surge that may bear watching."

Tamlyn looked to them both; he saw in Tamara's face a slight cast of worry touching her eyes. This would be the final test, the reunion with Kerry would determine if what they had done would hold together. They had all come too far to have it all come apart now. He knew how Morgan was feeling and of Tamara's concerns. He nodded, conceding to their wishes, for a trickle of doubt made its way into his mind. If they were to leave now, and the reunion with Kerry triggered any type of negative reaction or if they missed anything–it was that thought that convinced him the need to stay.

"Then we shall stay and see," Tamlyn said. He placed a gentle hand upon Morgan's shoulder and with that Morgan breathed a huge sigh of relief.

The morning found Cailean up early; he walked through the camp over sleeping bodies with Tynan in tow. He walked to the highest point on the island scanning across the horizon. Tynan searched too, believing to be looking for Haakon's fleet, but the Chief of MacKenzie was simply looking towards home. His thoughts were solely upon his wife and children. Strange dreams came to him in the night, of strange places and events. Mostly they were of Kerry or of someone much like her, they were disturbing, the images were fleeting and fading as moments passed. It all made him pine for his wife that much more. The grey skies shadowed his mood as he prayed she was well. He somehow felt Tamlyn's presence in a way, how or why he knew not. It caused him some anxiety and the need to get home.

The seas were churning yet the currents and wind all sped them along at top speeds. It was as if Mother Nature had felt his desire to get him home. Their journey took them into the Sound of Sleat and into the Kyle of Lochalsh. Cailean was in the lead ship with his banners of the great Stag head flying proudly and his piper playing a hearty tune, making the Matheson's upon the shores ease up on their swords. Kenneth and his brother David greeted him warmly.

"You followed Haakon north son?" Kenneth inquired of his son-in-law.

"Aye well sort of, do ya know where he went?" Cailean asked and his father-in-law huffed.

"His fleet came through here just yesterday. We evacuated the women and children and assembled all our men upon our shores; every one of us carried a bow and full quivers. Yet they just sailed on by, ship upon every damn ship, so many you probably could have walked across to Skye without getting yer feet wet."

"Then we must leave now, for if he heads for my lands!" Cailean said with panic in his voice.

"Easy now lad easy, David followed on with a host of my men, they went past yer lands, past Applecross heading north," his father-in-law said to ease his fears and take the worry immediately out of his face.

"Thanks be to God for that, I have had enough of this Norwegian King!" Cailean said as he hugged his father-in-law. Now Cailean and his men were ready to go home, this late in the harvest they would have to scramble to keep up enough stores to last them through the winter months. Sigardsson took his leave of him there too, as did the sons Leod, they too eager to be home. Drostan and Coll said their farewells to their foster father as the small fleet parted ways in the Inner Sound. Cailean was sad to see the Lord of Rodel go, the gruff and often argumentative individual who ran more hot than cold had been instrumental in this expedition. It had been his determination and creativity that drew in Cailean and ultimately brought his plans to fruition. He had been smart enough to use Cailean in bringing Alexander and the nobles to his side. He was a crafty old bugger, Cailean gave him that.

The sun was almost setting as his ships plowed hard into the beaches at Lochcarron. The sea gulls circling his ship seemed to be following him home and trumpeting their arrival. Cailean had seen Tamlyn upon the tower wave in greeting then he heard his wife shouting his name. There were hundreds of people lining the shores, wives, mothers, sisters and family. This expedition had been expected to carry a terrible cost in lives, yet not even Cailean could have predicted this outcome. As for his losses he had none, not a single man lost, many bore wounds yet this was a toll almost unheard of.

Kerry made her way through the throngs and into his arms. There was an almost overwhelming sense of love surging through Cailean it was like seeing her for the first time all over again. So powerful was the feeling that he would never again leave her side. He twirled her high in the air, her laugh to him was like that of angels and goose bumps covered him in his closeness to her. Cailean was indeed at his happiest of moments. The time away was only weeks yet to him it seemed a lifetime. They kissed and it was like magic, a miracle so desperately sought after. To hold her in his arms was a feeling like no other. Tears came to his eyes that he could not stop; her hands upon his cheeks brushed them away.

"Oh my love my heart, thank God and all his Angels for the sight of ye!" Cailean said. He could barely get his words out.

"My love?" Kerry said questioningly staring deeply into his eyes.

"Ach nae worry, tears of joy surely, nothing more. Joy fills my soul with the very sight of you lass. The war is done, over, peace we have and I shall never again leave thy side," Cailean said and they kissed again.

"You have promised me something like that once before my Lord," she said teasingly.

"Aye but that was different, I am a new man it seems. I know that we live in a turbulent time, to never let my guard down, not even now, but I swear with all my heart no more journeys will I take unless you be at my side," he said as their foreheads touched softly, both seeking to drown in each other's eyes. That glossy eyed look he found there in her eyes spoke wonders to his soul. That love was not just an unseen thing shared upon the soul, here it was a visible sign observed by all. It had moved everyone around them. The seagulls circled above them, filling the air with their calls. To Morgan it was a feeling so profound it was something he would never ever forget. It was a feeling Morgan shared with Marina, like an echo from the past pulling them together to rekindle a love, a connection that bound them throughout the layers of time. Its potency never diminished from here to the future, everlasting until the end of time.

This was what Morgan needed to see and feel for himself, he owed it to Cameron as much as he owed it to himself. He felt the gentle touch upon his shoulder as Tamlyn nodded that it was time to go. Morgan cast one last look upon Cailean and Kerry and then catching the eyes of Cailean, who it seemed could almost see through the Shift and smiled back at them, as if to say 'thank you'. The meeting between Cailean and Kerry had been everything that they hoped for and now it was time to let them be, to go on with their lives and for Morgan, it was time to go home.

CHAPTER TWENTY TWO

Nowhere To Hide

MORGAN AND THE others left the shores of Lochcarron behind them. He felt almost numb and in a way saddened that he had to leave this most beautiful of places, the people and this point in time. He felt tremendously relieved that their task was successful, at least in part. Cameron was now happily restored–for what he had lost in the future, he would find in the past with his soul mate and now Morgan was on his way back to the future to be with his. Still, the warriors around him were a harsh reminder that this was far from finished.

They were here to put an end to the evil of these creatures, as it could not be allowed to continue, eradication was the only option. That in itself was what truly and deeply frightened Morgan. All he could think about now was Marina, hoping that she was safe and sound in the future and anxiously worrying about him. Deep down he was almost frantic, that somehow the timeline had again shifted in some small way–that this nightmare would not end well.

They walked nearly two hours before Tamlyn said that they were far enough away to open a gateway back to Loch Monar that he himself in the past could not sense.

"This should be far enough," Tamlyn said as he opened the gateway back to Loch Monar, back to where they first arrived, where

Cameron first arrived. Tamara then located the trace patterns of the conduit leading back to Morgan's time. She summoned her power. Her eyes glowed, reflecting the tremendous energy flowing within her as the others added their power into her, opening the conduit in reverse. Suddenly the doorway opened out of the nothingness around them. A black void in the shape of a tall door stood before them, it was sliver thin. Morgan could see that the reverse side was like a dulled mirror. They stood before the black side, and Tamlyn motioned to him.

"Follow right behind me, we are returning to your time," he said as he charged through with Morgan right behind. One foot landed upon a hardwood floor in a darkened hallway as the other left behind the green grasses of the past. When he came through, Tamlyn guided him from the hallway and into the living room to allow space for the others who followed immediately behind. Tamara was the last one through, and Morgan finally felt the hairs on the back of his neck come to rest and relax. He had not realized how wired he was until the adrenalin surge finally subsided.

"We made it, we did it!" he said almost too hopefully, waiting for one of them to drop the proverbial bombshell that something went wrong. He was tense when no one responded, then as Tamlyn finished his survey of the room; there was a slight hesitation in his look then he touched Morgan gently upon the shoulder.

"All seems well, nothing seems different," he said tentatively. Morgan breathed somewhat easier, yet still worried about the Elf's uncertainty.

Tamlyn smiled at Morgan. "Come, we should return to my loft. There we can gather our strength and then get you home to Marina." Morgan nodded to that as Tamlyn opened a gateway to his loft. Morgan again had to avert his eyes from the brightness, stepping through blindly and when he opened them, he paled at the sight of the horror around him.

It was a scene from the darkest of nightmares. Tears ran down Tamlyn's face as he took in the terrible evil that had transpired here. Pinned to the wall above his fireplace was a headless corpse, crucified horribly. The body held cruelly to the wall with daggers through the palms and shoulders. The body appeared male, naked and what looked to have had his flesh removed. Tamlyn shook in rage, for no doubt the man had been skinned while still alive.

Morgan did his best not to throw up as his own fears started to take over. "Do you know this guy?" he asked shakily, which broke Tamlyn's gaze upon that poor wretched soul.

"His name was Robert Franklin. He was the building's superintendent. No doubt he came in response to my security alarm," he said sadly as he took in the rest of his home. Everything was torn apart. There were words written in blood on the wall above the body, but was nothing Morgan could understand.

"What does it say?" Morgan softly asked while the others gripped their weapons as if waiting for an attack.

"It is in their language, it says 'Nowhere to hide,'" Tamlyn saw a sword embedded in the wall. It had pinned a newspaper, '*The Telegraph*' to the wall.

"What is it?" Morgan asked as his own fear increased looking at the dismay painted upon Tamlyn's face. The Elf pulled out the sword and he looked hard at the blade, his face paled as he recognized the origin of the sword and of the headlines of the newspaper.

"Tamlyn please I'm flipping out here," Morgan said as his voice shredded with panic.

"The newspaper is a British newspaper; the headlines are of a bombing of Lyon's Corp. A company I founded and currently work for in the antiquities markets. It says it was terrorists; the bomb destroyed the entire office building. Every one that worked there was killed," his voice trembled in shock and disbelief.

He held up the sword. "This sword is a weapon used by Shaolin monks. I fear everyone that has given refuge to me has suffered," Tamlyn said sadly as he went into his study. The bookcases were torn from the walls; the concealed storage room was laid bare. Tamlyn quickly noticed that two things were missing; Cailean's sword and the Azael Spearhead. The one thing he could have used to track the Azael was gone.

Tamlyn now seethed in rage, his fury was frightful to behold. He went back to the others.

"There are those out there that have given me aid, they will be in danger or maybe already dead. We go to them now to save them or to avenge them," Tamlyn said, his jaw clenched tightly as he pulled out his swords. The others remained cool yet that was only on the surface, for rage like that of Tamlyn's mirrored in their eyes.

All of them except for Jeren, who was born after the war, had fought these creatures and suffered at their hands. They still remembered so very clearly the pain and horror inflicted by these demons, they knew that here and now it must finally end.

"Morgan you must come with us, I can't leave you here, not now. You would be much safer with us. I must save those that have sheltered me. I do not know what may happen if I leave you behind. I am sorry," Tamlyn said as Morgan nodded that he understood. He was truly afraid; he was so close to being home safe but just around the corner death could be waiting for him.

He looked to the poor headless victim and swallowed. *What would they do to me if they caught me, the one responsible for destroying their world?* He thought and he felt the bile rise in his throat. "Let's do this," Morgan said trying to hide his fear.

Tamlyn opened a gateway to the Shaolin monastery. Tamlyn and the others charged through, swords ready, Morgan followed right behind them. As he stepped through, he saw Tamlyn scream in pain and anguish, Morgan could not control his stomach this time and vomited repeatedly.

The Elf Lord fell to his knees as he tried to take in what his eyes were showing him. Tears streamed down his face as the once beautiful and serene of places was now so terribly marred. The steps to the temple seemed painted with blood; dozens of sharpened stakes lined the base of the stairs, each with a head of a monk skewered upon it. All had their eyes and their tongues removed. The headless bodies hung from the walls upside down, each one missing their arms and their testicles.

The Azael enjoyed inflicting pain and anguish as if they could almost feed upon it. Tamlyn could not believe what had happened here, it tore his heart to shreds. The suffering these men endured was more than he could bear. Moving through the temple, they found bodies of two Azael, some Shape-shifters, Fachan, and others of their kind. The monks had put up a fight, yet proved no match for these walking nightmares.

The courtyard was more of the same, of terrible torture, headless bodies tied to trees with their own intestines, their hands and feet cut off. They found more monks impaled upon sharpened poles, cruelly driven through their back passage and up along their spine. The poor monks own body weight and gravity slowly impaled them until the sharpened end emerged from either their chest or throat. Long had been their suffering. This was no way for any man or creature to die. Only the most sadistic and depraved of killers could revel in this horror.

The savage killers had piled the tongues, eyeballs, hands and feet by the koi pond, a haunting display covered in flies and maggots. Again they found the words "Nowhere to hide" written in blood, horrifically plastered upon the courtyard walls. A thorough search revealed no one had survived this sadistically cruel event.

Tamlyn found Zhi, sitting serenely in a chair, his head placed in his lap. His hands and feet were brutally hacked off and there, piled in front of him were the testicles of his brother monks.

Tamlyn was beyond numb at this atrocity. He knelt before his old friend. "Oh Zhi, I am so very sorry for this, forgive me if you can. May your soul be truly at peace my friend," Tamlyn said his face damp with tears as he sheathed his swords.

"Burn it, burn this place to the ground, the stench of evil shall only be cleansed by fire!" he numbly said as the others went off to do as he ordered. Within minutes, flames were coming from the upper stories. This ancient structure, beautiful in design, a home and safe haven to him in the past, a place of worship and wisdom was now fully engulfed in flames. The taint would never leave unless removed; the fire would cleanse the miasma of evil that had penetrated it to its very foundations.

"Come we must continue on, for others may have shared their fate," Tamlyn said as he opened another portal, fully accepting that he would be too late once again.

††††

They stepped out of the portal and into the cool air of the early morning hours, the desert sands moved lazily upon strong winds. Warriors poured through the brightness of the portal ready to engage the cruel enemy. Tamlyn already feared the worst. He had been too late to save Zhi and his fellow monks and was expecting no less here. The killings in China had been days old, here in Northern Iraq he prepared himself for the same.

They followed Tamlyn quickly to Ahmed's door as he placed a worried ear upon it to listen for any signs of struggle. It was all too quiet. He could not sense the enemy's presence, which could mean that they had already been and gone. The door was unlocked and as they stealthily entered, any hopes Tamlyn may have had that he was in time vanished as another bloody nightmare tore at his soul.

Morgan again fell to the ground retching terribly. The home was torn apart, headless bodies pinned to every wall. This was fresh, blood still dripped from every crook and crevice. The closest body was that of a woman–Tamlyn rushed towards her.

"Fatima!" he cried as he desperately removed the daggers that pinned her corpse to the wall. He gently lowered her to the floor. He looked around the room finding five heads–all missing their eyes that this time had been casually thrown on the floor. Tamlyn looked to the four other bodies he saw also crucified and pinned to the walls, instantly surmising that these were bodies of men, their flesh removed.

"Quickly, search for the children, please!" he cried out. The others moved swiftly in their search, Tamlyn scanned the room. The walls appeared to be riddled with bullet holes, several dead Fachan and Shape-shifter's lay upon the floor. They too had put up quite a fight.

Tamlyn heard a slight gasp in a darkened corner of the room. He hastily moved to find Ahmed strapped to a chair. He was alive but only just. He had been stripped naked; most of his skin was removed. His hands and his testicles lay on the floor before him. These terrible wounds were savagely cauterized to prevent him from bleeding out. They had severed his Achilles tendons to prevent any means to escape.

"Ahmed!" Tamlyn shouted as he laid his hands upon the man's face, sending waves of energy through to block out the terrible pain.

"My friend, you live?" he said to Tamlyn for all the Elf could do was nod.

"They made me watch, as they tortured them....killed them," Ahmed mumbled through his tears.

Tamlyn could only shake his head. "I am so sorry Ahmed," he cried as he bent his forehead to Ahmed's gingerly touching. Tamlyn sent his mind in to share the horrific moment, forcing himself to endure the terror.

"I do not blame you my friend. I…I know what you did to them in their hives…the mines. If you had not done so… this, what they have done here…would be everywhere. My world plunged in darkness. No one…would be safe."

Ronan stepped gently to Tamlyn. "No one else did we find," he said quietly.

Ahmed smiled bravely. "Ali had the children at his home… I had a business meeting. They were not here," he said as he gasped for air. He knew was dying and fading fast.

"You will bring the wrath of God to these beasts… this I know. I can now leave this world... knowing that you…will avenge me. When I see God…I will ask him to help you… " Ahmed gasped as the light faded from his eyes.

"Be at peace my friend, you shall be avenged," Tamlyn said as he took to his feet once more. He moved to Morgan, who was finally getting shakily to his feet. He was terribly pale, the whites of his eyes shone in the dimness of the room. Tamlyn laid a comforting hand upon his shoulder, Morgan nodded he was ok.

"I am sorry Morgan that you had to see this. I wish with all my heart that it wasn't so." Tamlyn woefully said. Morgan could say nothing as Tamlyn went back to Ahmed, undid his bonds and gently laid his body down beside his wife.

"Come we must go," Tamlyn said to them as he led the way out of the home and into the street. A man confronted them, a machine gun pointed directly at them and he was not alone, as about twenty armed men took up positions all around. Tamlyn gently raised his hands in the air. His amber eyes instantly recognized the man confronting him.

"Ali, Ali, it is me Tamlyn," the Elf Lord stepped towards him. Ahmed's brother lowered his weapon.

"You saw what was done?" was all he could get out through his own red teary eyes.

"I have seen and shared your brother's last moments," Tamlyn replied, as Ali dropped his gaze to the ground.

"The children, are they safe?" Tamlyn asked and Ali nodded.

"They are at my home," he numbly said as he looked to the Ljosalfar assembled behind Tamlyn.

"You have others of your kind to fight the Djinn?"

Tamlyn looked to his comrades. "Yes we will eradicate them from your world. Of this you have my solemnest vow," Tamlyn promised, his eyes glowed with the passion of his words.

Ali smiled. "May God be with you! Go now, we shall take care of my brother, go before any more are touched by their evil," Ali said. Tamlyn bowed and created a gateway that opened to Morgan's backyard.

They all stepped through with Morgan right behind Tamlyn. As soon as he realized where he was, Morgan took off running up the stairs of his deck and in through the broken French doors of his home.

"Morgan NO!" Tamlyn shouted as Jeren hot on Morgan's heels entered in right after him. Tamlyn ran to get inside fearing that here too they were too late. As his foot entered the home he heard Morgan scream.

CHAPTER TWENTY THREE

Echoes of Memories Past

H IS HOME WAS a mess, it looked like it was ransacked–furniture was either overturned or destroyed. Of Marina, there was no sign. The front door was smashed in; it appeared they entered from both the front and back. The phone was ripped out of the wall and Marina's purse, its contents strewn all about. Up above the fireplace was Morgan's and Marina's wedding picture; Cailean's sword was driven through it, smashing the glass in the frame pinning it to the wall. Words were carved into the wall above it, Morgan knew instantly they were not the same as the others.

"What does it say?" he shouted in panic. Tamlyn knew the words crushing implications. He could not help but pale at their dark meaning. Morgan's eyes were wild with panic and Tamlyn worried that he would not be able to hold it together.

"It says, 'Need to feed,'" he answered, yet Morgan with tear stained cheeks looked desperately confused.

"What? What, '*Need to feed*'? What the fuck? Do they eat people?" Morgan shouted. Every nerve was frayed and supercharged in total fear for his wife. All he could think about was the gruesome killings that these creatures had just done. To have Marina and his unborn child go through that horror was a vision he could never live with and it flooded his mind. He could not shut it out. They had his wife and here he was totally helpless. His legs gave out as he fell to his knees.

Tamara stepped towards Tamlyn. "Is she pregnant Tamlyn?" Tamara asked forcefully. Morgan could not answer as his world was crashing down upon him.

"Tamlyn?" Tamara asked again, this time grabbing his arm in anger. Tamlyn broke off his saddened gaze at Morgan and looked into Tamara eyes.

"She is," was all he could get out, and Tamara shuddered as if she was struck. The Sharing she had done with Cameron and with Tamlyn all came flooding into her. The echoes of the past had come full circle. The Azael had once taken Kerry and now they had Marina. Both were pregnant and that bore deadly consequences. Tamara knew this far too well, as she had seen her sister die that horrible death through Tamlyn's eyes, the life being sucked out of both her and her unborn child as the Azael fed.

Tamlyn stared blankly upon the ceiling as the others tightened their grips on their weapons. He could feel the Blood-hunt oath pull him, adding to the already burning rage that festered deep inside. It drove him now to confront the enemy no matter the cost. Tamara could see it in his face enough to recognize its control, its demand to track down those responsible.

She knew the consequences of that ancient oath and the price he would eventually pay as one who was immortal. The Blood-hunt gave the oath taker incredible gifts, yet once done, it would exact its costly toll. Tamara hated her husband and brothers for taking it but the deed was done and it could not be undone. Tamlyn could feel rage boiling inside, burying all else. The visions of his past poured into his soul, reliving that nightmare on his home world as he too recalled that terrible memory of Jenna's last moments at the hands of the Azael. When her life force faded, he had been flooded with intense rage and hatred. He poured everything into that single moment, feeding it until he could think of nothing more than his vengeance.

The past echoed loudly in the present for Morgan as this nightmare played out once more. Cailean had to rescue Kerry from the enemy's cruel grasp and depraving hunger, now again for Morgan this dire circle would end forever.

"You can track her, as you did with Kerry?" Tamara asked, praying that they were not all too late. Morgan upon hearing that stood up, his eyes pleading to Tamlyn that he could find her.

"Yes, as I once did for Kerry, I can for Marina," he said quietly, yet to Morgan it was as a shout.

"Then what are we freaking waiting for?" Morgan growled.

"It will be a trap," Tamlyn stated but Morgan didn't care.

"Of course it is! I am not a complete idiot. But what they don't freaking know is that they think it is just you and me. Not them too!" he shouted as he pointed to the others. "That gives us a freaking edge!" Morgan added vehemently as he yanked out Cailean's sword from the wall and his wedding picture fell to the floor. His face painted in rage daring anyone to stop him.

Jeren and the others nodded in agreement with Morgan, this was the reason they all had come on this journey. This battle was no longer Tamlyn's alone. This was for them all; every one of them had suffered at the enemies hands. Here and now, retribution demanded their final eradication. Tamlyn knew it from the start, so long ago he led a legion of warriors against the enemy and he was the last of them. All friends and kin were gone and here he was about to do it again. Their faces showed the determination and sheer will to finish this; there would be no dissuasions here from any.

Tamlyn looked to them all, but to Tamara and Jeren he looked last and longest. "Morgan and I shall play this out. He is right; they are expecting just him and me. Put your tracers out on me. When I give the word, come in groups of two. Select your spacing carefully as

I will do my best to guide you." he shot a look to Morgan and looked to the sword in his hand.

"Do not think about it, let your subconscious be your guide, within it resides some of the best swordsmen that ever lived on your world," Tamlyn said fearing for his friend.

"Yeah, well they can all stand in freaking line," Morgan said angrily, anxiously waiting for Tamlyn to start this. If Marina was dead he would kill them all or die trying and he didn't care. She was everything to him and if she was still alive, he would move heaven and hell to save her.

He grabbed Tamlyn's arm. "If she is alive do everything to save her, do not worry about me. If she is not, do not stand in my way," he said harshly but he did not care. Tamlyn understood and he drew in his power, seeking that frequency, tuning in to locate Marina's soul. It took him some time to find it; he knew not whether it was still within Marina or reborn into a new body. The last thing he wanted was to come blazing in a room with a newly impregnated mother, it was doubtful that they would let him perform a Sharing to get a location on Marina's body.

He looked to Morgan and nodded. "Ready?" Tamlyn asked as Morgan tensed up, holding the sword in front while shielding his eyes from the gateway flare up.

"Where the hell are we?" Morgan asked as they landed in front of what appeared to be an old abandoned hospital. It looked creepy and the evening darkness did nothing but enhance that. The entire structure was completely overgrown with vegetation; there did not seem to be an unbroken window anywhere.

"We are well away from civilization this could have been an influenza treatment facility from the early nineteen hundreds. These were purposely kept away from the general population to avoid spreading the disease," Tamlyn replied.

"Are you sure Marina's in here? This place is huge," Morgan asked, looking around expecting an attack at any moment. "Do we just walk in the front door or should we sneak in somewhere else?" Morgan asked, hoping the Elf had a plan.

"The front door seems perhaps the riskiest choice, so I suggest we take it and spring their trap," Tamlyn replied.

"Then 'lead on MacDuff,' Morgan said nervously as they went up the stairs and into the vast complex. The front foyer was huge and once elegant in its day, now it was a deathtrap. Floors were broken in spots, debris everywhere, water dripped from several different places as Tamlyn took the lead. It was deathly silent within the building. No birds, no insects, no wildlife it seemed anywhere either inside or outside. The only sound was their footsteps echoing farther and farther into the building.

Morgan was lost, treading quietly through corridor after long corridor, up and down flights of stairs to get around areas too treacherous to walk on. He had lost all sense of direction.

"You sure you know where we are going?" Morgan asked yet Tamlyn was too focused on his environment to answer. Watching his path, following Marina's essence and sensing for the enemy took all of his attention. He knew they were being watched; they were being drawn deeper and deeper into their web. Perhaps it was to make sure they were alone, or to play on their anxieties and fears.

They were creeping along the blackened corridors when abruptly somewhere ahead a door slammed.

"Shit! Shit! Shit!" Morgan said through a clenched jaw, the hair on the back of his neck standing up in fear. "That scared the…." was all Morgan got out before three werewolves lunged out of doorways upon them, large terrible creatures with tremendous strength. One went after Morgan with a vicious backhand and sent him flying down the hall. Tamlyn's speed saved him as he ducked under a swipe of razor like claws and plunged his sword into its belly. Spinning around with his other sword, he buried it into the creature's skull just as the second beast plowed into him, sending them both crashing through the wall.

Morgan tried to move but could not, for he had the wind knocked of him. All he could do was watch the werewolf advance towards him. Cruel red eyes savoring in the impending kill. It launched itself upon Morgan, salivating jaws wanting nothing more than to tear out his throat. Without thinking, Morgan instinctively brought up his sword at the last possible second, impaling the black beast and killing it instantly.

"Morgan!" Tamlyn shouted in panic for he could see nothing but the terrible beast on top of his friend. Tamlyn hauled off the dead beast. "Are you alright?" he asked as he extended his hand to help him to his feet.

"I'm ok. That thing ran into my sword, so much for channeling my sub-consciousness," he said as he pulled out the sword from the creature's chest.

"You are alive, are you not?" Tamlyn replied with a forced grin.

"So this was their big trap?" Morgan asked as he looked upon the horrible creature.

"No this was a test. I think they wanted to see if we truly are alone," Tamlyn said his eyes still searching for hidden danger. He sensed something as they moved on, more of a smell at first, of death and decay, the farther down the hallway the stronger it got.

Wrinkling his nose Tamlyn cursed. "Reavers!"

Morgan looked to him as he too noticed the smell. "Those Zombie things?" he asked. They came to the end of the hallway that branched off left and right. Tamlyn was about to reply when the hallway behind them filled with Reavers. Men and women, all dead it seemed for at least a few days, all under the control of the Azael. Tamlyn was about to turn about but he stopped as the hallways to the left and the right filled up with more.

"We must charge through, it's our only chance. To stay between is death!" the Elf Lord dashed to the right, his swords flashed with eye twisting speeds, slashing and hacking into the heads of the Reavers, destroying the control the Azael had over them. Morgan covered Tamlyn's back as he put the Highland sword to proper use.

The Reavers bore no weapons other than teeth and hands. They tried to grasp their victims to bite, to rip apart or to strangle their prey. To Morgan they were far more spry than the Zombies from movies, nowhere near as fast as a Shape-shifter or a living person, yet the sheer numbers of them more than made up for it.

"Morgan come on!" Tamlyn shouted as he had dispatched the Reavers confronting them. They ran through an open set of doors. Tamlyn turned and grabbed a piece of a broken block of wood, he forced the doors closed and placed the wood through the handles on the door, effectively locking it.

"That should keep them off our backs for a while," Tamlyn said as they ran, skidding on dusty floors as he took a left turn grabbing Morgan's arm to turn in after him.

"Through there!" Tamlyn yelled as he pointed with his sword to a set of open doors. They were dimly lit from the inside, a sign hanging from the ceiling by a small rusty chain said 'gymnasium'. Once they charged through the doorway, they both skidded to a stop. The light coming from the moonlight shone through the line of windows skirting the gymnasium just below the ceiling. There were several steel drums with fires burning, casting off a dull orange glow, surrounding an operating table that they must have brought in from one of the surgical rooms. Around its base were bodies, discarded and in various stages of decomposition, the smell was overpowering. Tamlyn knew that they were once pregnant women and had been fed upon by the Azael to force their ghastly reproduction. Morgan looked to the table and the woman struggling with her bonds. She was stripped naked, gagged and tied securely to the operating table.

It was Marina. Six Azael stood behind her, decked out in their black scaled armor with scimitars unsheathed, orchestrating it all, firmly confident in this display of malicious terror.

Somehow, Tamlyn and Morgan both flashed with the same memory, to a dying world with Kerry upon the altar, almost fed upon by the same evil creatures. Suddenly all fear and doubt vanished within Morgan. All he saw was his wife, every ounce of fury and rage, of vengeance and retribution filled his soul for one purpose, to save his wife or die trying.

"NOOOOO!" He screamed as the room filled in front of them with Werewolves, Fachan, Furies, Fuaths, Ghouls, Sirens, and other Demons. Everything evil cast out of the darkest of nightmares from the blackest pits of Hell.

Tamlyn sent forth his mind, with a single command: *"NOW!"* smiling as he held his swords out before him. The host of enemies grew before them, growling and salivating in their anticipation, two against hundreds, a lone human and a hated Ljosalfar. The evil creatures suddenly silenced and parted opening a path all the way to the operating table that held Marina. One Azael stepped in front of her holding a familiar weapon. The spear, attached with a new shaft, the one that was stolen from his home–the black blade rippled in malice. The Dark Elemental within caused the rippling to move faster with anticipation and excitement. The Azael pounded the spear twice on the floor and then the opening in front closed off with the host of demons blocking the path to Marina.

Fury and rage built into a crushing crescendo within the Elf, fueled with the Blood-hunt oath, for here and now it would end this night. The gymnasium instantly flared with a magnificent brightness as five portals opened up, slicing through the demons that were unlucky enough to be standing in the way. Limbs and torsos flopped juicily upon the floor; all around the gateways screams of agony filled the air as the Ljosalfar went on the attack.

They were terribly outnumbered, yet the surprise and the portals put the creatures temporarily on the defensive. Tamlyn and Morgan fought together as the Elf's fantastic speed and deadly skill made up for any shortcomings from his human friend. Morgan channeled something deep inside; he did not think, he purely acted on instinct, never did he waiver as his sword carved his way closer and closer to Marina. Tamara and Jeren fought their way through the enemy to back them up. Jeren was devastating the enemy, for as good as Tamlyn was, Jeren indeed surpassed him. An Azael engaged him, its two twirling scimitars meeting Elfin forged steel with a resounding crash of sound and sparks. As quick and as skilled as the Azael was, it was no match for Jeren, only its ability of taking horrific wounds and still being able to fight kept it in the deadly struggle but only for a few moments.

Mikka and Ronan came in upon their left flank, battling their way through the enemy to support them all. Morgan was not even aware of them fighting towards his side; the only thing that he focused on was getting through the beasts to his wife.

A Fachan's short sword had slashed his shoulder, that and several other wounds he bore yet he buried the pain within. He could not let himself feel anything, as that would only slow him down. The shock of the supporting Elfish warriors quickly wore off as the demons' overwhelming numbers began to take their toll. Three of them fell to the steel, claws and teeth of the enemy. It was enough for Tamara as she opened her mind and within moments, dozens of portals opened around them, the Warrior's Guild of the Ljosalfar home world had answered her call. The tide of battle turned as the demons suddenly became doubtful and afraid. The Azael quickly realized that their advantage had shattered. Looking to preserve themselves and their cause, they tried to flee yet could not; the Ljosalfar wove a dampening field around the complex, sealing them all in. The Azael for the first time felt fear and from there it turned to desperation, making them even more dangerous. The Shape-shifters sought for ways to escape through the hallways and found their path blocked. Every exit was sealed off with Guild Warriors; in desperation they threw themselves into the deadly steel in hopes of getting through. These were the most deadly of battles as they tried to fight off their own extinction.

The cacophony of battle, the clash of steel, the screams of fury and pain, all seemed distant to Morgan as he closed the distance to Marina. All the Azael were now fully engaged as two charged at him and Tamlyn. Morgan was failing fast; the battle and his wounds were taking their toll. The Azael were deadly quick, it took everything he had to keep it at bay. Tamlyn, sensing Morgan's dilemma, parried his own attackers thrust with a powerful swipe of his sword, driving his opponent's scimitar into the body of the Azael fighting Morgan. The momentary distraction allowed Tamlyn to leap over his opponent and drive both his blades into its back then tossed it into its brother, knocking them both to the ground. They tried to get to their feet but were met by stabbing swords, as Tamlyn and Morgan repeatedly plunged their gory blades into the dying bodies.

"Tamlyn!" Ronan shouted in warning as the lead Azael with the spear sprang upon them. Tamlyn barely evaded a wicked thrust meant to pierce his heart. The evil point just passed under his left arm, as the Azael twirled the shaft of the spear, it twisted its stance then thrust the butt end, catching Morgan in the chest sending him crumbling to the floor. The Azael squared off against Tamlyn and he knew there was something different in this one's size and speed. He had seen it before, at the attack in the hospital, the Azael that tried to delve him. This Azael was their leader, the one whom the Lavender eyed Goddess contacted from Cameron's time to bring the photo and the tartan tie to Cameron in the past attached to the very spear that confronted him now.

The Goddess may have tampered with this Azael, made it stronger, faster and perhaps smarter than its demonic brothers. There was no doubt that this creature was the one who orchestrated the killings in China and Iraq that tortured and murdered his friends. That piece of knowledge fueled the fury within him as he danced the death duel with the Azael. They went back and forth in their deadly contest as Morgan rolled to his feet. Gasping for air, he could only watch as the two titans' traded steel lunges and thrusts, hacks and slashes. Morgan now up on one knee reaching for his sword saw a huge black shape lunge upon Tamlyn's back: a Werewolf's terrible jaws bit hard into his shoulder. The Azael took his opening and plunged the hungry spear into Tamlyn's chest. Tamlyn reacted out of instinct, driving his one sword into the head of the Werewolf gnawing his shoulder, while his other slashed the shaft of the spear sticking out of his chest.

In Tamlyn's eyes, everything moved in slow motion, the Azael drew forth its scimitars as Jeren suddenly jumped in front of him, engaging the Azael and Morgan diving towards him, screaming his name in horror. Tamlyn could feel the white-hot blade deep inside him, the poison of the Dark Elemental feeding upon his life force. He tried to pull it out but his hands lacked the strength. Morgan pulled out the bloodied pulsating blade. Tamara rushed to Tamlyn's side, crying in frustration, trying to stem the blood flow with her hands and sending her energy into healing the wound.

All around them individual battles were ending, save the one directly in front of Marina. She could do nothing but watch it all erupt around with her eyes glued to Morgan the entire time. She saw him knocked down by the headless demon, as Tom and the creature fought. This was all some terrible nightmare that she could not seem to escape. When they took her from her home, she somehow knew deep inside her that she would die horribly. All of this seemed strangely and uniquely familiar.

These beasts had abducted her just yesterday from her home. They had kept her here alone, and she had lost all hope of rescue. Surrounded by all these powerful and terrible creatures her death seemed inevitable. When Morgan and Tom first appeared, she knew there was no way they could overcome such odds. She wished that Morgan had stayed away. The bodies of dead women below her could not hide the fate that awaited her. Yet now with all the others joined in to save them her hope was renewed, until she saw Tom go down. Morgan in his rage pulled out the spear, lunged at the headless demon and plunged that terrible weapon into the creatures back, and out through its chest.

The Azael felt the searing heat of the spear pierce his frame–the shock paralyzed it as the Ljosalfar in front sliced off each arm then drove his searing blades into its chest again and again until it could feel no more. Morgan watched the creature fall in front of him then saw Marina staring back at him. He rushed to her side, freeing her from the table's restraints. She threw her arms around him as tears gushed out of her. She cried into his chest, sobbing through the idea that somehow they were safe, the nightmare was at its end.

Morgan cradled her in his arms, removing his cloak he wrapped it protectively around while telling her that everything would be all right. When she could finally stop her shaking, she looked into his eyes and he took her face in his hands gently.

"You're ok, I will let nothing happen to you, I promise. I love you with all my heart, in this life and in the next for as long as there are stars that shine. I will never let you go." As they kissed, Morgan could still hear crying. He saw Tamara still cradling Tamlyn's head with her bloodied hands.

"Marina!" Morgan said to get her attention as they scrambled to Tamlyn's side. Morgan looked to Tamara for any sign that he would pull through. She only shook her head and Morgan's world crashed around him.

"Tam… Tamlyn?" was all he could get out. It wrenched out his heart, for all Tamlyn had done for him; almost eight centuries of devotion and protection, he had deserved far better than this.

Tamlyn only smiled. "Do not shed a tear for me my friend… my time on this plane would not be long anyway. The oath of the Blood-hunt now that it is fulfilled… would have me fade away to nothing. To die here and now is a far better end. I go to the source, to be with my brothers and with Jenna, my soul mate. So you see… I too know of the way it pulls your heart. Fare you well my... true friend."

The light faded from those amber eyes as Morgan broke down–tears he thought he could shed no more would not stop. All those lives he had lived from Cailean all the way to now, the sorrow he felt from within was so incredibly deep.

"Good bye my friend….thank you…for saving…me," he said as he looked to the others. Tamara nodded to him through tear stained cheeks, and reached to take her son's hand. Jeren seemed numb as were the others. Ronan, Renn and Mikka, all bore nasty wounds yet lived, each one laid a gentle touch of their fingertips upon the head of Tamlyn, a token of remembrance of a stalwart hero and a legend upon their world. Tamara finally laid Tamlyn's head gently on the ground. She placed her hands upon his chest once more and summoned fire. The flames consumed him.

"Come, the flames shall overtake this entire structure, we must leave. Morgan, Marina, I will take you home," Tamara said as portals opened before them, and the Ljosalfar warriors returned to their home world. Tamara, Jeren, Renn, Ronan and Mikka, journeyed into the gateway that opened once again to Morgan's backyard. The Ljosalfar said their goodbyes to Morgan. Ronan, Renn, Mikka and then Jeren each in turn grasped Morgan by the arms and bowed their heads to his–a momentary tingle flashed in his head, a reflection of their eternal gratitude. The last of all was Tamara.

"I can never repay you for all that you have done," Morgan said as the lump in his throat grew raw at this parting.

"Oh Morgan, you need not repay anything. It is we who owe you our lives," she said as she laid her hand upon his chest. "For the past and the present, of the man you once were to the man you are now. The names of Cailean MacKenzie, Cameron MacLean and Morgan Hamilton shall be forever chronicled upon the ancient pillars of my world alongside the most valiant of the Warrior Cast. You will always be in our hearts as you were in his. Fare you well my friend," she said kissing him upon each cheek. Tears trailed down her beautiful face as the portal across to the stars opened and then they were gone.

Morgan turned to Marina, and hugged her tight. "After all we've been through, I could really use a case of beer and a few Big Macs right about now," he said with a smile.

"Shut up," she said and kissed him passionately.

Then she pulled away. "You're ok now, the seizures are gone?" she asked worriedly.

"Yep, gone, gone for good. Man, I could use a vacation."

"A vacation? Really…you? Well I say you deserve one, where should we go?"

Morgan smiled at his wife warmly. "How about Scotland?"

POSTSCRIPT

Scotland 1287

Lochcarron

T<small>AMLYN GLUMLY STARED</small> out over the tower wall upon the rolling waves of the loch. The gray skies mirrored his mood. He knew what was coming and still he could not truly prepare himself for it. He heard Tynan approach and by the old warrior's face, he knew this was the end.

"Tamlyn…he's askin fer ye." Tynan said and Tamlyn kindly nodded to him, saying nothing as they walked down the tower stairs. This always tore at his heart; it pained him greatly for all those he had loved on this world. Even more so today, this would be perhaps the hardest yet to endure.

Tamlyn entered Cailean's room and made his way to the bed. Cailean's children parted way to let them pass. Conner, Alexander and William, all were strong strapping lads that shared their father's looks and size. Matilda and the youngest girl Isabel were the spitting image of their late mother.

Cailean's eyes opened as the tall Elf approached. Tamlyn smiled and took his hand.

"My...friend...a...message..." Cailean tried to get out, he knew his death was near. The last few years after Kerry's passing had taken their toll upon him.

Tamlyn bent closer to his friend to hear his last words. "All gifts will carry a price...that only time...can reveal," Cailean said and Tamlyn looked to him questioningly. The light was fading fast from his eyes as Tamlyn placed his forehead gently upon Cailean's. The Highland Chief of MacKenzie then took his last breath in this world.

"Fare you well my true friend," he whispered. The girls began to cry, Tynan's eyes brimmed with tears.

"Is he gone?" he asked as Tamlyn nodded. "Is he...with her now?" Tynan choked out.

"Aye he is...he is with her," Tamlyn answered, catching just a glimpse of the hereafter before the veil once again closed. With tears in his eyes, he turned looking out the window, hearing the sea gulls calling outside the keep.

THE END

Every time I close my eyes all that I see is you.

It's been so long and now, I am lost, lost without you here.

I'm not gonna lie I need you by my side.

We were made for each other; I need you here with me forever.

Can you finish what you start, don't hold back just let it go.

I am here and I will always be.

And when you're gone I feel this emptiness inside of me.'

Lyrics from a song "The Truth" which my daughter wrote and one dear to my heart.

HISTORICAL FOOTNOTE: CAILEAN Fitzgerald MacKenzie was said to have saved King Alexander's life from a rogue stag while hunting. In fact, there is a painting commissioned in 1786 by the Clan Chief of MacKenzie, painted by Benjamin West depicting this historic event. It is called "The death of a Stag". The Painting resides in the National Gallery of Scotland in Edinburgh. Although history suggests this event took place in 1265, for my story I bumped it a few years to be just before the battle of Largs.

The Battle of Largs took place on October 2, 1263. Different chronicles state yet all agree Sir Pierce Curry was killed in the battle. Cailean Fitzgerald MacKenzie, Alexander Fitzalan, and Sir Alexander Steward of Dundonald the High Steward of Scotland were among some notables at that battle. From all accounts the battle was something like I described in my story, the weather played a crucial role in the outcome, Haakon it seemed underestimated the Scottish autumn storms instead of using it to his advantage it proved his downfall. He retreated northwards to winter in Orkney where he died only a few months later.

I am not sure if Sir Andrew Fraser Sherriff of Stirling or Cailean Mor Campbell were actually at the battle but they were real people living at the time and could have taken part.

Mark Douglas Holborn. 08/05/2013